The Collected Supernatural and Weird Fiction of Violet Hunt Volume 1

The Collected Supernatural and Weird Fiction of Violet Hunt Volume 1

One Novella 'Love's Last Leave', and Seven Short Stories of the Strange and Unusual Including 'The Night of No Weather', 'The Coach' and 'The Blue Bonnet'

Violet Hunt

LEONAUR

The Collected
Supernatural and Weird
Fiction of
Violet Hunt
Volume 1
One Novella 'Love's Last Leave', and Seven Short Stories of the Strange and Unusual
Including 'The Night of No Weather', 'The Coach' and 'The Blue Bonnet'
by Violet Hunt

FIRST EDITION

Leonaur is an imprint of Oakpast Ltd

Copyright in this form © 2020 Oakpast Ltd

ISBN: 978-1-78282-954-6 (hardcover)
ISBN: 978-1-78282-955-3 (softcover)

http://www.leonaur.com

Contents

Love's Last Leave

For furthermore, this very night one seemed to lie by my side in the likeness of my Lord as he was when he went with the host, and then was my heart glad, since methought it was no vain dream but a clear vision at the last. *Odyssey* XX. 85.III

In the fall of the year 1915 the war lay good and hard, so said Mrs Major Leclerc, on the women of the country; the men, at least, had the best of it; it was either kill or cure with them over there. But women, who had no vote, fought too, for they worked too and endured the beastliness of living in what were practically beleaguered cities. Food queues and tramping for lack of transit wore them out by day, while nights, punctuated by Zeppelins, put the finishing touch to the instability of their nerve centres and horrified their children so that they threatened to grow up idiots.

The men foregathered behind the line in comparative safety; even in the trenches, when the Boches were quiet, they enjoyed the concert parties that were sent out to them. But their women, used to the lights of theatres, the buzz of receptions, the flicker of sunlight on garden lawns, were now forced to live the lives of hermits. The only social function that survived was a sugarless and creamless Tea, where the socially idle, the invalids, and the war-workers met and rehearsed their plans for the enhancing of nourishment, bewailed the scantiness of female domestic labour, and attempted the location of absent male relations that was sedulously kept from them by a too careful censorship.

One afternoon in November the wife of Major Leclerc, only just home from her Food Committee, sat, surrounded by bored and unsatisfied children in the prescribed dimness of the high-pillared drawing-room that was a feature of the house of her husband's father, General Leclerc. Her clumsy tweeds, her serviceable hat pushed back, looked outrageous against the old-gold curtains, the rose-brocade sofa which she was sharing with Lady Maisry Scott, the Organiser-in-Chief of the branch of war work she herself affected.

Lady Maisry was both intimate and powerful enough to have no hesitation in reproaching the younger lady for the particular and only form of indolence she allowed herself to practise, that of letting herself go dowdy when she had plenty of money with which to keep up the standard of her rank and position as daughter-in-law to one of the great landowners in the south of England.

Lady Maisry herself, a duke's daughter, dressed beautifully. She was middle-aged, unmarried, and independent. She had published a little volume of poetry and a pamphlet recounting her pyscho-analysis experiences, but, in spite of this, was considered quite sensible and practical and had in her time served on many committees. She was what Mrs George Leclerc called a bit of a contrast. Her manners were old-fashioned, her conversation was modern. And though her soul was, according to the custom of her family, Catholic, her mind was open, receptive, and at least tolerant of all the modern forms of belief and unbelief.

She was tall and fairly good-looking, possessing the charm of complete parity with her surroundings whatever they might chance or she might prefer them to be, for the moment. She cultivated experiences and frankly loved to talk with strangers—in the gate—of the ducal mansion where she was born, to see what she could learn from them, while extending her intimacy to none who were not what in her aristocratic jargon, she called 'one of us.'

The Tremlett sisters, even the slovenly, rather plebeian Mrs George, she considered as emphatically belonging to the same caste as herself—good old country people, even before they married into the Ilvercote lot.

'What is the good?' Mrs George peevishly answered her. 'There aren't any social occasions now—not a party to go to not a man left in England to dress for. I just cover myself—and economise! Aggie is always at me. I quite realise that if George were suddenly to be invalided home and see me, he'd have a fit.'

Lady Maisry, looking at dear Gussy's neglected waistline, her too comfortable shoes, her hat which had lasted her two years, thought that the major certainly would—expire! Unless, knowing his wife, he realised that the will to be smart, or even very tidy, was not in her. She was handsome, but not handsome enough—and now she was older than when she had got George—to dispense with all the *toilette* adjuncts and the nurse-tending of a skilled maid, and her maid, Whitefoord, was *not* skilled and too faithful to be economised away by the decent soul that Gussy Leclerc was.

And even Whitefoord, using the privilege of the old retainer, complained that Mrs George had, since the major went away, started to let her figure go and to wear out all her old clothes, the unbecoming ones, the ones that the major had in Whitefoord's hearing forbidden his wife ever to let him see her in again.

Her lingerie was of the very plainest, so built that it would not tear in the terrible 'wash' that we had to put up with now that all the skilled hands were making and packing small, cylindrical copper vessels with portable death. She no longer had her hair waved or her nails manicured, which the major had heretofore insisted on her doing and she had sent all her jewellery to the bank.

'What's the use of tiaras when there are no parties, or cabs to go to them in, and I can't see my own way even round the corner to a friendly evening at the old Tremletst'?—those horrid white hems have painted on all the pavements confuse me so!'

And yet the major was not so very far away—at Poperinghe or somewhere near—he might get leave at any time.

It was well known that Miss Augusta Tremlett was not his first love. Both the sons of Major-General Sir William Leclerc had wanted the younger sister in the days when, as county *belles*, the Misses Tremlett had attended the Ilvercote balls. Everybody always proposed to Aggie first. It was a trick, men had. She had half accepted George Leclerc when Peter Leclerc, J.P., of Ilvercote, married but childless, killed himself out hunting and his cousin the general had succeeded to the property at the age of seventy-five. Willy, then, the elder, the less dashing, had become heir presumptive and Aggie took him though she had always declared that he bored her. He was tall, silent, a bit of a radical, and did not dance.

George—good stuff!—instead of going to the bad in the first rush of disappointment as he had promised his tutor he would do, proposed to the elder sister and married her. Both weddings took place on the same day, and Gussy, bursting with health and happiness, made a beautiful bride. She was indeed, so far as regularity of feature went, the handsomest. Aggie only came in as a beauty on the strength of there being a pair of them. Alone she would hardly have told. She was not really beautiful, only fascinating. Pale, frail, thin, looking as if the traditional breath of wind would blow her away, she was possessed of an allurement whose area of dominion was unlimited.

She had no artifice, no obvious method, yet the interest which she excited in the opposite sex was of so compelling and pervasive a nature that men went down before her like ninepins, lay about, and she did not stoop to pick them up. The open-air and above-board attractions of Gussy counted for nothing when her younger sister was at hand. When everything was going on all right with the elder, the younger sister had only to drift into the room to fetch a cushion or a book, and Gussy's little affair, such as it was, wilted and died.

And 'She who meant no mischief made it all.' In her bitter puzzlement the elder and handsomer sister found a phrase and used it. Aggie was 'psychic'.

Aggie's back was not supposed to be strong and she could not bear to wear stays. Her head often ached, and she slept ill, and often lay wake and read all night. But she succeeded in producing Peter and, after that performance, rested. Willy was so good and so devoted to her during that first year that she seemed to all her friends, so far as they knew Aggie, to have fallen very badly in love with him. Willy, of course, simply adored her. Gussy, quietly happy with her own George, bore her no malice for that little incident of heart transference long ago. And then the war came.

The major, who had been in the army since he was eighteen, went out in the first month with the Expeditionary Force. He was a thorough soldier. Willy, over age and supposed to be delicate, held out for a year, looking always unhappy. 'I simply can't stand seeing those young boys go—driven out, hounded on by those beastly insinuating songs. "We don't want to lose you, but—"' He mimicked the piteous ascending curve of the popular melody and relapsed into an uneasy quietude that boded ill for his womenkind.

For presently he sought and obtained a commission through his father's old friend, Sir Dugald Erskine, one of the literary generals, and after three months' training was sent overseas to the unhealthiest of spots, patient, absorbed, pathetic as ever.

Both their husbands swallowed in the war machine, the two young women took up their abode with their father-in-law. Mrs George Leclerc was housekeeper both in Eaton Place and Ilvercote Hall, while the general became more or less Aggie's charge. He was unable to walk except with the aid of crutches and lived mostly in his invalid chair. He had a capable valet.

Nobody expected Aggie to work or take any part in the war, but one dull day she came down to breakfast and said she had had a letter from Willy, and Willy seemed to desire that his wife should help a little, one way or another. . . . .make swabs say. . . .but then, her back! Stooping was a thing which she never could endure. . . .and all those women round! Munitions—filling shell cases—no, she could not bear to get all yellow and come out in spots like the girls at Putney, but she would find something.

She did, easily. In less than a week she got taken into a smart Government office on the strength of her rather remarkable knowledge of languages, Italian, French, and German, and for four months she went out every day all day. She and her chief became great friends. He was everything for the time. Gussy never was permitted to see The Chief—he was not 'quite—!' His speeches, plentifully reported by Aggie, made Gussy quite sure that he 'wasn't—!'

Of course, Aggie muddled them up, just gave you a word here and there, and forgot the point more often than not. Otherwise Gussy did not see how a man could talk so to a woman, and in an office too! The Chief's great subject—he seemed to have it regularly on his mind— was as far as Gussy could make out, a sort of Mormon idea! Men were just cannon-fodder. . . .Gussy had heard this disgusting phrase before, but she had never heard of women as fodder of drawing-rooms (so the chaste lady paraphrased it), existing entirely for the comfort and happiness and pleasure of the men who were putting up the fight for them and civilisation, doing the rough and painful work of the world, and dying for the sanctity of the hone.

So all that women could do, now that they were being guarded and preserved from death by men's efforts, was to hold themselves in readiness to repay the obligation in kind when the men came back and refuse them nothing. Every woman in England belonged individually and collectively to the men who had endured hell for her. As a matter of fact, all the good men of our race, would be killed off and it would be the bounden duty of women to see that of these some scion should be left to represent their virtues and carry on.

'And what about the promises they've made at the altar?' Gussy would exclaim, to be told that, as The Chief said, marriage was a Victorian chimaera and would entirely disappear in another ten years. . . Six women to one man as it was . . . .every woman only entitled to a fraction of a man. . . .and after the war, to less. . . .

War talk! War, Gussy supposed, had always upset people and made them immoral. Look what happened after the Napoleonic wars! *Di-*

rectoire costumes slit to the thigh, which showed through! It surely behoved women, decent women like her father's daughters, to keep their heads clear and their bodies pure and not to let themselves be led astray by selfish male reasoning.

Gussy was quite glad when Aggie broke down rather, and Willy, in a little private scrap to Gussy, begged her for goodness' sake 'to get Aggie out of it'. She had probably been writing some of The Chief's foolishness out to her husband, and though he worshipped the ground she trod on and called her his 'Christmas Rose', because she was so white, he was under no illusions or delusions as to Aggie's want of intellectuality. Just a slight pale thing that clung to you and never contradicted you or asked for anything more than a cushion and thanked you for that so prettily. Willy in his simplicity never thought of his wife as an enchantress of men and knew nothing of 'the offers she had had!' He didn't even know about George or, if he did, never spoke of it.

Aggie left the office the very day after Willy's letter arrived and, as far as Gussy knew, she never even saw or heard of The Chief again. He never attempted to carry on their friendship. He probably had his hands full of other female converts to his disgusting ideas. Aggie, thank God, was really in love with Willy or goodness knows what would have happened! She had no principles—in her petted, chaperoned, sheltered life she had never needed them, but now! These social upheavals seemed to be making fools of so many women!

Aggie did not seem in the least to resent her husband's care of her morals. Returning to the unheroic shades of domesticity, she just sat about the house that her sister governed, beautifully dressed, writing to Willy every day about nothing in particular and reading out portions of his letters to his father, with whom she spent a couple of hours every day. The old man seemed to like to see her dressed up and to finger the soft, pliable stuffs of which her gowns were composed.

Aggie fled from the tailor-mades and crackling taffetas as a cat avoids draughts. As a girl she had, of course, never been able to afford a maid. Old Whitefoord, who had been their nurse, 'did' for her and Gussy and proudly called herself their 'maid' now.

Aggie could have had a real maid—two if she had wished—for the general refused her nothing. But she preferred looking after her own clothes as she had done when she was a poor girl. Never having been used to it, she did not think she should get on with a proper maid who would want to dress her hair, which always looked so natural and

12

as if it was just coming down and never did though supported by a single hairpin, who would make her wear stays that would stiffen up her lovely yielding figure.

The Chief, who in private life was by way of being an author, let it be known in the office that Mrs Leclerc reminded him of a Flaxman nymph, her zone ready to be unloosed, her shoe latchet to come undone and be tied again by some amorous swain. Well, Gussy knew nothing of Flaxman nymphs and loosened zones, but she did think that Aggie—the way she dressed—if she were not so thin might have looked sometimes . . . .indecent.

Aggie spent a good deal of time over her clothes. The smart dresses she was not wearing just now were carefully hung in scented wardrobes or laid to long rests in box ottomans. Her linen, in shades of mauve, blue, and yellow, lay, tiny bouquets of exotic-looking flowers sewn on shoulder or hem, with sachets between their folds, in the drawers of Chippendale cabinets.

When she was in Wiltshire, cardboard boxes passed and repassed weekly between London and Hungerford. She would not trust country washerwomen, and a good thing too, Gussy said. Clothes like that would demoralise the village maidens who washed for the great house. Aggie never wore sports clothes, but during these autumn months in country and town a brown fur coat, high to the chin, to the collar of which she pinned some flower out of the hothouses which made a plaque of brightness that set off her pale hair and rebuked her dark, inward-set eyes that never glowed or glanced.

Whitefoord, who had so little to do for Mrs George Leclerc and her four tomboy daughters, was always trying to do something for Mrs Willy, who fascinated her. 'The desire of the maid for the star,' Willy used to say. He was too modest to realise that it was a case of love ricocheting. Whitefoord had known him as a boy and loved him as much as he loved Aggie and Aggie through him.

Whitefoord was always hanging about inventing messages, making opportunities to get into Mrs Willy's suite of apartments. When she could be sure Aggie was out, Whitefoord went right in—by the proper door on the corridor—she would not have ventured on any account to set foot in the haunted room which led into Aggie's bedroom, though it would have been a shortcut.

Once there she timorously opened drawers and fed her eyes on the minuscule articles of under-linen lying decorously there, like priestly robes in their awmries—Aggie's 'Holy Shirts', as Willy called them.

Or, towards evening, she would be passing try to get a glimpse of the lace *peignoir* thrown over the back of the carved state chair in front of the altar-like dressing-table, the satin slippers nestling near the valance of the bedside, or the lace nightcap ready to be placed at the last minute on the misty, wavy hair.

Tea had been brought and Mrs Gussy was stirring the pot. Aggie, who had been with the general, had drifted in, said 'How do you do?' to Lady Maisry, and took a chair not too far away to appear rude. She did not like people just now and wanted Lady Maisry to go. So did Mrs George, for Lady Maisry was still badgering her about her dowdiness and what she would do if the major came back suddenly.

'Do? Oh, just borrow some of Aggie's fallals for the occasion. You should just see some of Aggie's nightgowns! They're dreams! Slightly naughty dreams, too, I should say. I'm wearing some I had when I was a girl—plain, you know, just a little Swiss work—to finish them out!'

To the condemnation in her friend's eyes she rejoined: 'Oh, my dear, you'll just see, when the war's over, I'll launch out and make Whitefoord happy, and Aggie shall get the necklace and the tiara out of the bank.' Rattling her spoon in her cup she warmed to her subject: 'Oh, the joy to see our men in decent clothes again! I simply hate the sight of a British Warm! Willy looks completely swallowed up in his. Last time he was here, for a joke, he and Aggie got inside it and buttoned it up over them both. My George fill his out all right of himself. . . .Hullo, Aggie! Tired?'

For Aggie had left the room gently without any fuss, only her eyes as they caught the light were moistened with a faint sheen as of spun glass.

'So sad isn't it?' Gussy said, 'when they perfectly adore each other and haven't seen each other for over a year! It was only a strong sense of duty that made Willy go. He's a bit of a Conchy at heart. I respect him for going when he feels it's wrong. He never cared for golf or shooting, you know—spent all his time reading and painting—oh, and chemistry! Experiments! He used to say that he could make us quite a good ghost out of chemicals when we used to talk of Wild Darrell at Ilvercote.

'He's a bit of odd himself; his tutor at Oxford said that he used to slink about just like a ghost—no one ever knew if he was in the room or not, and once he gave a party in his rooms, good supper, wine, and all that sort of thing, but wasn't there himself, though afterwards he swore that he was and even repeated some of the things they had said on the night! It was when Agg came into his life that he woke up and got quite ordinary for her sake, dropped chemistry because it messed his hands and made them rough.'

How loyal poor Gussy was!

'So, you see, Lady Maisry, dear, how hard it was—how he must have felt it—going away from her. And yet, he did it of his own free will. He had all the job in the world to get passed; he hasn't a scrap of constitution. Agg cried and cried. I've never seen her cry since. It'd dried up. But he promised her then that he would be with her on Christmas Eve, if he died for it!'

Lady Maisry made the obvious rejoinder.

'Of course, he can't. The idea is absurd. Leave from there—and he's only been out three months! We don't know where he is exactly. But Aggie says that he'll win through—that she trusts him to keep his word. He *wrote* it to her once, but not since November, and we've heard in a roundabout way that his division was moved to Salonika on the tenth—the sickly! Willy is probably that, poor dear, by this time. And if he is coming, it's only three weeks off Christmas and he'd have had to be on his way now.'

'You'll be at Ilvercote?'

'Yes. No party. Just us and the Dad. Dad will go. He always thinks it will be the last Christmas he'll have there.'

'And my dear Peter?'

'Peter? Oh yes, your dear Peter will be down quite early. His housemaster isn't very satisfied with him this term. Says he mopes and doesn't take proper exercise. He's exactly like his father—always with a book in his hand. If you ask me, I think he is awfully worried about his father. There's such perfect sympathy between the two. And Aggie tells him he will see his Dad at Christmas, and the general too that he'll be sure to see his son. Willy's promised! Willy never breaks a promise. That's the way she goes on. To begin with, she's so ignorant, or pretends to be. She hasn't the slightest idea of the distance and she never looks it out on the map! She thinks that men just ask for leave, and get it if they want it enough to wrangle it. . . . They're all three living in a regular fool's Paradise. Goodness knows what will come of it! I give them up!'

'Too bad!' Lady Maisry Scott said vaguely. She had a lot of Christmas work herself, but would come again before they went to Ilvercote.

No. Mrs George really had no patience with her sister. She was deluding her father-in-law, brewing up a disappointment for him by

15

Christmas time. Mrs George grew perfectly sick of seeing the two heads close together, the white one and that which was neither light nor dark, gold nor brown, just the mysteriously coloured head of hair which was Aggie's, smoothing out the thin sheets scored with pale pencil characters in Willy's beautiful, scholarly writing.

When they had read the letters through they spent hours more trying to make out from the envelopes where Willy was. The one important letter holding the formal promise to be with her for Christmas, they had pasted into a sort of silver reliquary, and on this they both gazed, as if it were a rite, every day for whole minutes at a time. Gussy wanted very much to hold the letter in her hands and read it right through to see if there was 'anything practical'. It was no use asking the general.

When Aggie was in a fairly accommodating mood, she would ply her with questions. Aggie manipulated the postbag, but never in her presence, handing Gussy her letters and receiving her own, if she got any. Surely, Mrs George would hint, Willy mentioned dates, routes? Wouldn't he like to be met, say, in London, and then all come down together? First, a little dinner at the Berkeley to celebrate—that would be nice...the words died on her tongue.

Yes, very nice, Aggie said, but unfortunately quite unpracticable. How could she or even Willy tell the hour or even the day, coming from so far? That was in the hands of G.H.Q. Willy would wire, of course, if or as soon as he knew....that is, if he could wire. Everything was so topsy-turvy.

But when Gussy pointed out that, in order to arrive in England by the twenty-fourth or twenty-fifth, Willy must already have started and his letters, of which Aggie insisted she was still in receipt, have ceased automatically, Aggie got bewildered and then cross. Neither Willy nor she had made a point of dating their letters, consequently they proved nothing at all. The main thing to keep hold of was that Willy had promised to come—was coming—and as for the mere details, she was content, like the Dad, to leave the details to Willy. He knew where to come—the place where his father, his wife, and his child were!

About the first week in December the news from the Eastern Front was not particularly good, and Mrs George suddenly had the horrible fear that this *braggadocio* promise of Willy's—made quite a long time ago—was the result of some weird premonition of disaster, and that Willy, alive and well when he wrote that letter they had stuck in the reliquary, had been impelled to make the promise knowing that by the time its fulfilment was due he would be invalided home. That he had had no such luck but was now shut up in some filthy Turkish prison. . . or in some equally filthy and unsanitary Turkish hospital? Or left wounded on a field of battle, his name disc lost. . .Or killed outright, his body unrecognisable.

Ah, she was gong dotty with all the horrors she read in the papers! Leaving Aggie and the general to soothe themselves their own way, she flung herself into her job and forgot herself a little in it. She had to get them down into Wiltshire and established there in good time for Christmas—servants, cars, and all—and make arrangements for the children's party on Christmas Eve, which must not be forgone by reason of the elders' preoccupation. There would be no house party and very few grownups invited except those necessary for the care and conveyance of all the little children for miles round, who were to be brought for an hour or two to the old house to be as happy as coloured lights, pleasant noises, and sweet cakes could make them.

She did not see why the children—the poor little soldiers to come—should be penalised by the troubles of their elders, which one day would be theirs. War would always be war. And the children had suffered already. The raids, which could not in the nature of things be kept from them, had done some of them a lot of harm. The elders must see to it that in the return to healthy normality they might forget the sudden alarms, the barkings of the perambulating gun that was so close to Eaton Place. The raids, the doctor admitted, *had* affected Peter's nerves a good deal. He had contrived to be up from Eton, when the floods were out, on one of the very worst. They had all gone down into someone's cellar, and though the women hadn't turned a hair, it had made Peter silent for days.

And they were not over yet. At Ilvercote, however, in that old red-brick house, sheltered by the green trees of its park and set in the flat and humdrum fields of Wiltshire, it was very quiet if dull, and they could all go out into the garden without having to be rushed in at a moment's notice to 'take cover'.

There was a ghost at Ilvercote, true, and a famous one, but Peter was on familiar terms with it. He and his father loved Wild Darrell, the 'man in black velvet' who, at dead of night, had fetched the midwife of Newbury, carrying her pillion-wise on his horse and blindfolded to a lady who, some said, was Queen Elizabeth. The nurse had occupied her long session by the bedside in cutting a piece out of the valance and sewing it again while the Lord of Littlecote, standing by the stone-sculptured mantelpiece which had been prepared for royal visits, waited till the unwanted child was born and then put it on to the fire.

He was tried for murder and only saved his life by compounding with the very man who tried him, and surrendering his patrimony. The curse he had uttered, that none of the male kin of this estate-jobber, this peculating judge, should die in his bed, ought to have weighed heavy on the Leclerks, for they were his descendants. Willy and his young son did not, however, resent the curse; they were staunch believers in the Divine Right and, if anything, felt sympathy for the man who had abolished the danger to the royal prestige and saved the character of Queen Bess.

Though Aggie did not much like being at Ilvercote she was not in the least afraid of the ghost. Her suite of rooms comprised the so-called Haunted Room. As a boy her husband had had a fancy to sleep there and now it was called his studio. Some daubs of his hung there which Mrs George hated—so weird and unsuitable! There were forty bedrooms in Ilvercote House and no guest need be put there, so since Willy had been in the army Mrs George had had the door taken off its hinges and the room was 'shown'. That was Whitefoord's job—her 'perks'. It was the legend of the whole countryside and visitors used to insist on having a peep at the fateful bed and the fireplace on which the courtier had put the queen's bastard.

Without going in, the inmates of the house passing along the broad corridor with the high windows on the other side could see the foot of the old four-poster with its counterpane embroidered in coloured worsteds with lotus flowers, stags, and rabbits, and the identical chintz hanging from which the nurse had cut the incriminating patch. . . And if you went on your hands and knees and looked carefully low down by the foot, you could distinguish the darn. A door at the side led straight into Aggie's bedroom and was supposed to be kept locked. Aggie had some fine jewels. That did not matter. No one, either local lover or burglar, would care to enter her room in that way.

Mrs George was bored, not frightened by the sight of the coverlid with its coarse clumps of embroidery in strident ugly colours. She felt it sinister but did not say so, being unacquainted with any such meaningless adjective. She knew what she wanted though, and gave orders one day, on her own, that the door should be replaced. Aggie then insisted that it belonged to her set of rooms and she like it like that. There was nearly a quarrel.

Whitefoord suggested that no one knew exactly which was the haunted room. It might just as well be the square one over the porch which had such a splendid view over Ramsbury. It had been the bedroom where a maidservant had once been put to sleep, and she would have it that she had been lifted bodily out of bed in the middle of the night. Without accepting the hysterical maid's story, Mrs George had thought it would be as well to modernise the room and get rid of the glum old Spanish leather which covered the walls.

The general had agreed. Mr Willy protested but had been met with the stern answer: 'Your brother's wife, if she is good enough to accept the shelter of my roof, must have rooms which she considers suitable.' The leather took the workmen three days to strip off. It almost cried as it came away.

Some other rooms had been modernised. The general's apartments—on the ground floor for convenience of wheeling him in and out of the living-rooms—Mrs George, to cheer him up, had decorated by Maple. Opening out of the great hall with the portraits hung, in and out of the spears and lances and the buff jerkins and caps of Oliver's Roundheads hanging under the immense tall windows, so high up a giant could not see out of them, was the drawing-room, almost a replica of Eaton Place. Mrs George had begged the general to let her have one room with a ceiling less than thirty feet high and the general had given her her way. The sons had been too decent to protest.

By the middle of December, the general and his man, Mrs George and her four girls, Mrs Willy and Peter, and a troop of servants including Whitefoord and old Dawson the butler who matched each other in age and continuity of service, were settled down in the square rambling rooms with the uneven floors that sagged, shining with the unearthly white radiance of old wood that would have 'gone up' if so much as a match had been set to it and burned them all in their beds.

They feared that less than death by bombing, and like a stream in flush on to a deserted river bed, cheerfully flowed in and lapped round and up the walls with their dress nails and photographs and other belongings, occupying as many rooms as they could to make the place feel less big and lonely. There was perhaps some forced cheerfulness. The four girls were really encouraged to romp and whoop about the house and make a certain amount of noise.

Aggie did not help at this at all. She might as well not have been there. Except for her two hours a day with the general, and to that appointment she was not always true, she spent most of her time alone in her apartments, as Whitefoord called them. She did not lock her door. But so strong was the dominance of her serene selfishness which hurt nobody, that not even her sister dared open that door and go in or even knock more than once.

The children always said Aunt Aggie was 'moony'—a 'bit balmy'—quite off her head. They said what they liked. Their mother, scarcely reproving them, would send a footman to Aggie's door to knock once and told if he got no answer to come away. Sometimes Aggie received emissaries very nicely and sent messages by them to say she would be down to tea or dinner—and wasn't.

When she did appear, she was glancingly cheerful—perhaps a little sharp, like a newly-cut crystal. Then Mrs George would remark bitterly to nobody in particular that she supposed that when she did shut herself up like that it was because she wanted to be alone with Willy and her thoughts of him, which was all she'd get. She knew that she ought not to say such things, much less think them; it was just the war which was upsetting them all so—making Gussy at times almost dislike Aggie. George, just across the Channel, hardly ever wrote, while Willy, in the Dardanelles, wrote, so Aggie said, nearly every day.

Gussy tried to keep her head. Someone must be in a house like this. . . .but it was a fact that George was neglecting her. Of course, he wrote now and then, but his letters were scrappy and full of queer bursts of outspokenness and even coarseness that she did not understand. What she did understand was that he out-and-out despaired, that he was in a savage mood that she had never known him give way to, and was very tired of killing, for he wrote that even if the world or the English Government had to come to a end, he wanted to have done with what was practically murder!

He wasn't, of course, coming back for Christmas; he wouldn't even put in for leave; it was too beastly to have to come back and see them all and then have to go back into hell. Lately he had never sent his love to Aggie or given any messages for her. That was strange and a comfort.

Gussy was, God forgive her, growing a little to dislike Aggie. In view of George's refusal to ask for leave, Aggie's persistence in her delusion about Willy annoyed her sister. So did her new pose of wild devotion to Willy.

For Mrs George during those long nights when she lay awake in her bed at Ilvercote could not help remembering that Aggie—pretending that she had no heart and posing as horribly matter-of-fact in the old days—had demonstrably accepted Willy on a basis of quiet affection, whatever she may have got to feel about him since. Unkind people might have said, and did say at the time, that Miss Tremlett took Mr Willy because he suddenly became the heir. Never mind about that, but honestly, if Aggie had ever loved anybody but herself (which Gussy doubted), that man was certainly George.

George, although he had loved Aggie with all the violence of a great big nature, had now accepted her as a sister-in-law and, putting away the fact that she had once treated him so badly, had grown quite fond of her. That was always the way. The flirts of the world go about breaking men's hearts for better, simpler women, picking up the pieces, to mend with the rivets of tact and the glue of quiet and understanding affection. All this about Willy now was just fuss and take!

No—Gussy pulled herself up—you could not call Aggie's still, passionate intensity fuss, exactly, or deny that it was a genuine manifestation of her feelings. Aggie was too indifferent to the opinion of others to sham emotion that she did not feel.

Gussy put her thoughts away, latish, every night and valiantly without the aid of sleeping draughts, 'got off' about three o'clock in the morning. Three hours' sleep! She had a great deal to do, and about seven would throw open her window, a bold, brave woman ready for the day's work, and look out, serenely sucking in the softness of the scene.

The weather that December was very mild, quiet, and still. The dun dead leaves fell waveringly and tamely to the ground, as if they could not help it; doomed, unresisting legions going to their earthy bed. The silent, driving force of winter was behind them, but no rough winds bore them down or roared in the big, wide chimneys where the foolish starlings built their nests so that every year, when the time came for the fires to be lit the people of the house had the pain of knowing that these poor birds were to be burned out of house and home.

Peter could not bear that, any more than he could bear the sound of shots at dawn—which meant that the fawns were being thinned. Winter had not really come yet. Windowpanes in the morning were never streaked or laced with frost; and the old red bricks of Ilvercote House looked red and sodden as usual in the damp, dank air, as if the mortar that bound them was sweating blood.

Christmas! Peace on earth, goodwill to men! Though there was a war on the children lustily shouted the old refrain.

Through these last two weeks the 'things' kept coming, and by the twenty-fourth they had all arrived. The big fir tree smelling of mould like the upturned sods of a grave looked quite small when it was set up in the hall, with the six tall windows placed so high up that the hall was more like a church. Dancing was to be in the drawing-room, on the nice parquet floor put in by Waring. The furniture was shoved aside all except, in a corner, the little table that supported the telephone, the links that connected Ilvercote House with the battlefields of Europe.

Poor old Dawson was still inexpert at its manipulation and always would be. He could not, somehow, accommodate himself to this modern 'contraption' which, so far as he could see, never seemed to ring except to announce some trouble or other. He was afraid of it and ashamed of being afraid of it, and always protested that he could hear perfectly well.

The apparatus, placed just inside the drawing-room door, could be heard as far as the dining-room across the big hall, and the day of the party it had been ringing all the time, bewildering Dawson and making him very touchy because, though he swaggered, he made so little sense of the messages. They were all indulgent to him. The youngest of Mrs George's girls was cleverer at it then he. But they never insulted him by taking off the receiver themselves if he was there to do it.

The floor of the big hall was covered with rifled cartons which had contained the pretty, portable fairyland Mrs George had ordered from town. Out of them tumbled fruits of no earthly variety, apples and oranges opalescent like the pure hot waxen cheek of childhood; glittering jewels, blue, green, and red like sea anemones of enormous size slung on chains of red and gold; hectic pink and white candles like flowers on chestnut trees; cock-a-whoop dolls light enough to be balanced on the slender swaying boughs of the fir tree from the Baltic forest.

And once these tiny items posed and tied, the whole group must be linked together with ropes of tinsel, linking one bough to another like frosted sugar-candy, drooping here, gathered up there, as if the whole dark mass of the tree was festooned and garlanded in a glistening cage of icicles.

Mrs George, in one of Whitefoord's aprons and with the help of a little pair of steps, had been breaking her back over the job all day. Aggie, tall and slender, had been good enough to help her to tie the things on to the lower branches, and when all was finished to hand up to her where she stood shakily on the highest step, the Christ Child to be placed on the very top of all.

Then the white sheet that had been spread beneath to catch the shreds of tinsel and the fallen pine needles was taken up and screens brought in to hide the glory from the common eye for the moment, for the hall was the universal highway, and Mrs George sat down for the first time that day, apron and all.

The general, a long way off in his room, was saving himself for his half-hour's appearance that evening, just to open the tree. Mrs George had not seen him all day, but she had heard that he was well—rather better than usual. At six o'clock Mrs Willy came down again, dressed in the beautiful gown that she had had new just before the war broke out and which Willy had chosen. It looked rather out of place for a children's party, but after all Aggie obviously wasn't going to help to romp. She was going to wander about looking delightful, and Gussy, who was going to wear her 'old brown', forgave her for cutting a dash because she was contriving to be so sweet and even gay for the sake of the children.

Her eyes, with their long, intent lashes, shone with the radiance of those bright stars that you sometimes see low on the horizon and which seem to pulse and beat with a message to you as you stare at them in an effort to bring them nearer. Aggie always gave her sister the effect of being a long way off. Tonight her eyes seemed to jigger and dance. . . .even the children noticed it and said she looked sunny for once instead of moony. She glanced at her sister sitting there in the chair which William of Orange had sat on to sign the Peace, with her knees well apart and her hands on them, and then rather contemptuously turned away in the direction of the general's room.

Mrs George wished she would leave him alone. Although, of course, both of them would by now have abandoned their mad idea of seeing Willy that night, Aggie would be sure to talk about it—condole with the old man—try to make him think that his son's coming was only deferred. But one couldn't stop Aggie doing anything she had a mind, so her sister left it at that.

'Mrs Willy's been in to the general, ma'am,' Whitefoord, getting Mrs George into her old brown, whispered, just as the first car was heard to drive up to the porch. 'And I heard her telling him that she had put on the dress Mr Willy chose for him to see her in.'

'Tscha!' was all Mrs George could say, and later when her head was through the crackling of taffetas: 'Well, it can't be helped. I suppose she's determined to give Papa a bad night!'

She hurried down to receive the complacent mothers of the countryside, accompanied each by some bundle on two legs which when unpinned, revealed a fairy-like form dressed in the shining robes of innocence, agog and shy, as childhood should be. One after another the pleased elders, driving their broods before them, were ushered into the big hall, where the general, standing on his crutches beside his wheeled chair which he had left for a minute in honour of the occasion, received them.

He seemed perfectly calm, Mrs George thought, hardly excited at all. He was too old to be, or perhaps Aggie had been discreet? After he had got back to his chair, he looked at Aggie and she smiled back at him, a smile frank and hardy—sign of fellowship in a secret happiness.

At seven-thirty the general went back to his room. Aggie, too, disappeared, but she was back again for supper, when she helped, but not much. She was seen to hand a bun to a child, though she refused to pull a cracker with any of the older boys, several of whom begged her to do so. They were her slaves and adorers. But when Peter invited his mother to pull one with him—'Oh, Peter, no!' she exclaimed at first, but added patiently, 'Yes, I will.'

Gussy, presiding over the bran pie, knowing that she could not bear anything that even remotely suggested firearms, saw her blench and cower at the tiny report but recover herself bravely.

Then they were all led and hustled into the drawing-room for dancing, and Mrs George went back to see if Dawson had blown out all the candles. No, not all, and he had taken away the steps. She hunted for a chair in the hall which had now been allowed to relapse into its usual, Zeppelin-imposed darkness, lighted only by the logs lying in the vast stone fireplace that were never allowed to go out.

She found the chair and stood on it. From the open door of the drawing-room the noise of shuffling feet not on time, the harsh notes of the gramophone, came to her and, suddenly, another noise! . . . . her arms, outstretched to pinch a dying flame, shook the branch and tipped the little candle down to the floor, where it went out. The telephone in the corner of the drawing-room was ringing!

There was no reason why she should be agitated about it, for it had been ringing all day more or less. She called Dawson to attend to it.

She was still perched: she had found another candle smoking. She was slightly startled when Dawson's bald pate seemed to surge up and shine whitely close under her. Standing at attention he repeated a message he had received in an uninterested sort of way that, considering its nature, was not like him:

'Mr George and Mr Willy will be at Hungerford by the 10.12 and will you please send the car?'

Mrs George got down carefully and rubbed her fingers against each other because a little hot wax had got on to them and made them smart. She said: 'You must have made a mistake, Dawson.' She added kindly: 'The noise of that gramophone! And you're not very wonderful with messages, are you?'

'That was the message, ma'am, I assure you.'

He turned away and said over his shoulder in a low, determined voice as if answering an accusation: 'And what's more, ma'am, I'll lay my life it *was* Mr Willy's voice came over the telephone.'

She followed him to the fireplace where he was drifting senilely and put her arm on his bent old shoulder . . .

'Dawson, my poor dear man!'

He was sobbing, ye!

'Dawson, pull yourself together. Don't you see it *must* be a mistake? Don't tell anyone.'

She began to consider rather deeply, forgetting the sad old servant standing beside her with his head down, breathing heavily. Mr George and Mr Willy, he had said, the poor old man! No, not possible! George would never have been so thoughtless as to give her no warning!

And yet men got do put to it in the war—contradictory orders of G.H.Q.! Sudden alarms! There might be a raid in London and difficulty in getting through? Women had just to wait and see, nearly always. George, at any rate, might be coming? Unless the whole thing was a muddle of Dawson's?

Dawson spoke as if he had read her thought—and touchily, as if it had offended him.

'Muddle or not, I suppose I must send the car?' he said.

'Yes, of course. It can do no harm. Perhaps some of the children could—Nonsense I'm talking. . . .!'

She looked up at the tree where the little pinched-out candles were smoking and smelling and muttered, 'They're not all out even now.'

She really didn't know what she was doing or saying and was glad when she saw Dawson go away to give the order. But she quite decided not to tell Aggie, for certainly the Willy part of it must be Dawson's mistake.

She went back into the dancing-room and stumbled against Peter, who was leaning rather helplessly against the side of the door-jamb. She told him sharply that he had better go and lie down, for he looked ghastly. Then she kissed him as if he were a little child. She had no idea why she did that, and the angelic patience with which the lad took her raw, unsuitable gesture made her want to cry. But no time!

The party was breaking up and Aggie was actually making herself useful. She was helping a child on with its glove—a ticklish job which surely, she could not, would not have attended to if she was really expecting her husband to arrive.

Oh no! She could not—she must have given up the idea long ago. It showed how frivolous she was! She looked calm, happy, and beautiful—'just like the Queen of the Fairies', a poetical child remarked. Gussy herself was red and flustered. One mustn't let oneself get so excited, for it was all nonsense. . . . Dawson would really have to be pensioned off if he was going to lose his head like this!

He had disappeared. Probably, gone to have a pick-me-up. She had told him to. No, Aggie's confidence had not been fortified by any hint from Dawson. She had not had a chance of speaking to him. Her radiancy came from inside.

Mrs George kept repeating two sentences in her head: 'He said Willy's voice!' and 'Has he sent the car?'

In a dream she went on with her work, speeding the departure of her guests pleasantly, efficiently, as became the honourable *châtelaine* of a great house. Her own naughty spoilt girls had not her ideas. They were not attending to their departing friends at all, but had got up a fresh game all to themselves and were rushing about like mad in the empty ballroom.

Peter had gone, as she had told him, to bed, which proved that he knew nothing about his father being expected. All the better. So it all fell on her and Dawson, who, with red lips and a deathly white face as if he had dipped it in a sack of flour like a Pierrot, was manfully seconding her efforts, the marshalling and shepherding of the crowd of children gathered in the hall with their mothers and nurses, done up again in bundles as they came, unrecognisable except by the mothers who had so swaddled them for the longish drives home.

The courtyard was full of cars. Had Dawson sent the message to the stables? And in time? She could not get near him to ask.

Where was Aggie? Gone to bed too? Perhaps she was all the way down the drive waiting at the lodge gate—on the off chance? She could not know anything unless Dawson had broken faith and told her?

How awful it was! She did not know if she was standing on her head or her heels, though she appeared, she did hope, all right as usual, pronouncing goodbyes in the full spirit of kindliness and good-fellowship with the mothers who were thanking her for a delightful evening. Delightful evening, indeed! Never in her life had she been so worried!

She stood on the steps, half in, half out, once or twice turning right round to look across over the children's heads at the clock over the chimney in the hall. Ten-twelve! Ten-fifteen! . . . it was ten-forty-five now by the hall clock. No more cars were coming in—they all seemed to have gone off with their loads except the Warnford's big limousine. That was still drawn up in front of the porch taking up all the room, and there was Aggie, standing like a brittle spear on the doorstep among the goodbyes, the chivvying of lost and wandering children, cool as a cucumber.

Gussy felt unreasonably irritated. Aggie had a perfect right to stand in the porch—it wasn't cold and she wasn't particularly delicate—but Gussy ordered her—'Go in, Aggie, at once. You'll be catching a chill.'

The cold, cruel glare of the eyes that her sister laid on her was the first instance of actual misunderstanding that had ever been between the two women. Aggie seemed to resent her care as an impertinence, and more than an impertinence.

The Warnford children, who had sneaked back to join the game in the dancing-room, were reclaimed, wrapped up, and produced. The Warnford car—were they all in?—moved on, or did it drive away altogether? Gussy never quite knew, for another car wheeled with a knowing curve to compass the sweep of the drive. . . . and Aggie and she were alone on the steps, and their chauffeur, a man she had known for years, got down and opened the door for it.

Her husband in his British Warm, seeming very big, stepped out and she was enfolded in his embrace. Then someone jostled her—Aggie. . . .!

Aggie had pushed rudely past—there was no other word for it—and Gussy heard her crying out to someone—not George, for his head was turned away on Gussy's shoulder.

'I knew you'd come.'

George said as he linked his arm in his wife's and went back with her into the hall:

'Brilliant inspiration that of yours—sending the car! How goes it, Dawson?'

Dawson, turning what George had said about the car over in his

27

mind, presently said as if he couldn't help himself:

'Yes, sir—quite well, sir. Didn't you expect the car, sir? You 'phoned?'

But Major Leclerc took no more notice of him. 'Where's Agg?' he asked his wife. 'I just saw her for a minute.'

Then Gussy remembered the jostle in the porch which had seemed so unimportant at the time in comparison with George's first kiss for three months. Though Armentières was nearer than that mysterious place in the Dardanelles which they had never succeeded in locating. George had also made a point, without so much talk about it of being with his wife at Christmas. But why need he ask for Aggie first thing? Bother Aggie! Wilfully in her own mind she brushed Aggie aside rudely as Aggie in fact had jostled her on the step ten minutes before.

'Gone upstairs, I suppose. She was absolutely certain he'd come.'

'Come? Who? Willy? Oh, I remember your saying something about it in your letter. Aggie's mad. Always was. . . . I must go and see her. . .'

'No, wait!' Gussy said, in tones at once severe and appealing. She added: 'You'll only be in the way.'

Bless him, he had no tact—never had no time to have, just overflowing with general benevolence. Aggie was all right, for Aggie had got her man too, poor darling! Goodness knows how it had been managed! And she had got George, and his first hungry kiss had compensated her for his queer letters and the scarcity of them. She had no need to envy Aggie now. They were even. They would hear all about Willy and his adventures—and he must have had some to get here—in the morning over the family breakfast-table.

Not too early. Though they had to be down because of the children, who had been packed off to bed so tired with romping that they had gone willingly enough after a hearty kiss apiece from their father and a little package shoved into each hand that they were not to open till Christmas morning. Promise! George was sweet all round—nice to the old servants but not inclined for much chat with them. He said that tonight he was fearfully tired. He would not even see his father till tomorrow.

But he would not be too tired to let his wife talk and 'tell him all about it'—her troubles, her past fears, her little crimes and enormous penitences.

Gussy did not allow smoking in her bedroom and George had become such a furious smoker out there that he could not sleep without it. He was a little cross about her prohibition, saying she was a smart soldier's wife, not an old maid of Wiltshire, and should have got used to it by now. Aggie always let Willy—'I bet she's smoking herself over the fire in her bedroom. It's half the fun watching a woman—your wife, for choice—go to bed while you sit comfy in the armchair by the fire and she potters about over her little jobs of sorts. . . '

'Go and smoke with Aggie then,' Gussy had said, laughing. Nothing could make her cross now. The idea that Willy was watching Aggie go to bed at that very minute passed her mind, but she dismissed it in the excitement of having George all to herself! She promised to be quick getting to bed—said she wouldn't be longer than one pipe. It was a way of curtailing George's smoke—she had always heard that smoking was bad for George.

She dashed up to her room and found Whitefoord, not gone to bed as usual, standing there by the dressing-table all lighted up with three candles, one of which Gussy quickly extinguished.

'Oh, ma'am, I'm so sorry!'

Whitefoord was naturally quite as keen to avoid bringing down ill-luck on the family as anyone, but Whitefoord was upset and soon let her mistress know why. No, she hadn't seen Mr Willy nor no one hadn't, not even his father. Mrs Willy just seems to have whisked him off in the bustle without letting him have a word with anyone and shut him up in her part of the house. Dawson had taken a tray—sandwiches and some whisky to the door and knocked. Mrs Willy herself had opened it a very little way and taken the tray in without a word to the poor old man or letting him see his master whom he had known since he was a boy.

'How did you think Mr Willy looking, please, ma'am?'

Mrs George owned impatiently that she hadn't seen Mr Willy either. Whitefoord grunted. What had come to them all? To bed so early on a night like this! Of course, the general and the children would go, but she had imagined the four of them, the middle-aged ones, sitting up half the night in the big hall hearing of Mr Willy's adventures and the major's—Mr Willy's, of course, would be the most exciting, coming from such a long distance.

Dawson and she, as old retainers, would be spoken kindly to, wished a merry Christmas, and invited to drink the healths of the men who had come home. Ah, well! She couldn't understand modern people—so offhand, so forgetful of things everyone should remember, so disregarding of the old ways! When she was young!. . .

Mrs George said impatiently: 'Get me to bed, Whitefoord, as you're here,' keeping her there to do it, which also was quite unusual. She generally bolted into bed without much preamble, like a rabbit into its burrow, but tonight she actually wanted her hair brushed out.

Whitefoord obeyed, moving her brush gently to and fro. She was too good a servant to tweak and pull and show temper on the body of her mistress, but her determination to see 'her baby' that night, if only for a moment, was so strong that she was cudgelling her brains to find an excuse to get into Mrs Willy's rooms. She had been listening at a discreet distance from the threshold of the ghost room and she had distinctly heard their voices in there talking quietly. They were not afraid of ghosts it seemed. But perfect love casteth out fear!

She had been quite unable to make out anything they were saying except something rather like—'hold you in my arms once more', and that she could not be sure of! The phrase was rather repugnant to her old maidishness. How Mr Willy did adore Miss Aggie to be sure!

Presently, looking at the bed turned down and Mrs George's cast iron night gear lying unfolded ready on the turnover, she thought of a pretext and, while her mistress knelt down to say her prayers, slipped out of the room and proceeded along the dark passage to Mrs Willy's apartments. She traversed that part often enough in the daytime, but she had not been in the habit of going that way much at night. Servants were apt to give Aggie's domain a wide berth because of the gaping threshold.

The light of the full moon riding high, dappling the floor with cold, watery bars thrown from the blindless windows, did not help her to see, only confused her with a slight sense of unusualness. She came to the open doorway where more than half an hour ago she had heard the voices. She could get into Aggie's room that way, but her fear was so much with her that nothing, not even love, would induce her to enter it now. She would just have to go on to the proper door. But she stopped again and listened, hoping she might hear what was being said.

★★★★★★

Nay, but all was still and the moonlight lay across as much of the bed as she could see, bleaching the strong red and blue flowers of the counterpane to a dirty white.

She heard the stable clock booming out its thin, cracked strokes, like the weak voice of an old woman in a workhouse. Twelve!

The silence after the clock had done striking was more than she could bear. She started off for the proper door, feeling her way along the wall, knocked sharply, and almost afraid of the noise she was making in the deep silence of the night.

'Come in!' Mrs Willy's voice sounded soft and reassuring, and emboldened the maid turned the handle. Mrs Willy had changed out of her blue dress into a splendid *peignoir* that Whitefoord had never seen. She must have got it down in London within the last fortnight—or was it one of those in French nightgowns? It hung straight down from neck to hem and made her seem enormously, portentously tall. Her hair seemed springing from its roots as if alive.

She looked rosy and tear-stained, angry yet pacified, wild and complacent—there were no words that Whitefoord could have used to describe her air unless it was she that she had been getting out her makeup box again and brushing her hair till the little sparks ran all up and down it—as if she had just come out of a hot bath—pleased and proud, as she had looked on the day when she had held Master Peter at the font to be christened in Ramsbury Church.

'What do you want?' she asked Whitefoord, leaning up against the dressing-table with her head well up, like an actress.

Whitefoord kept her waiting. . . . The door of the ghost room was open and she stood there neglecting to answer, peering in quite vulgarly to see if she could espy Mr Willy. At last, reft of hope, she proffered the request that she had invented on Mrs George's behalf five minutes ago.

'Ma'am, could you lend me a nightdress for Mrs George? The major. . . . Her best ones haven't come back from the wash. . . . she would be so much obliged. . .'

Aggie, standing there quite still, pointed grandly to the wardrobe: 'Take anything you want, Whitefoord. . .'

★★★★★★

At Ilvercote, every morning but Sunday, everyone came down to breakfast except Aggie and, of course, the general, and at half-past nine, a little later than usual, for it was Christmas Day, Mrs George was in her usual place at the end of the table by the urn and the teapot and the coffeepot, attending to her sharp-set brood of girls who all sat around her. Yes, their father would be down in a minute—he had cut himself badly shaving and she had left him upstairs repairing the disaster with cotton wool.

'How funny he'll look with white blobs all over his chin,' the eldest girl, who had hoped to see blood.

The next excitement was Peter's pushing his plate away with a gesture polite as if the plate could feel, but one clearly significant of his refusal to eat breakfast. Gussy was annoyed but she dared not protest. He sometimes had these brainstorms and then it was no use interfering. In another moment or so he would get up and leave the room, and they would know that he was going to fight it out with himself in his own funny little house that his father had built for him on the banks of the lake a stone's throw from the house.

It was furnished, in a way, with lockers and a fixed table and some cane chairs and a bookshelf, where Peter kept his books—a row of classics—for Peter was already as great a reader as Willy. Mrs George would have much rather he did not go, for then she would lose sight of him until he chose to revisit them. No one was supposed to follow him to his *boudoir*, as the girls called it. Only, he didn't sulk, exactly, for they had often stolen a look at him through the hedge and he always looked gentle and good as usual.

He sat awhile looking on the tablecloth and Gussy hoped he would stay. . . But no, presently he rose slowly and, going out, passed his mother in the doorway. The two exchanged no salutation, as Gussy remembered afterwards, but for the moment she was quite taken up with Aggie's coming down to breakfast, and most improperly dressed for the morning in one of her smartest and thinnest tea-gowns.

'Hullo! You?' Gussy said sharply. 'Where's Willy?'

'He's gone,' Aggie said, speaking in little reports like the explosion of a toy pistol. She stared defiantly at the four girls, who had heard nothing of their Uncle Willy and so could grasp neither the significance of their mother's question nor their aunt's reply. They were not long piping up in a chorus of shrill questions. Aggie answered them stonily.

'Called away. Yes. Back to Suvla Bay.' She sat down in Peter's empty place and pulled a plate towards her. 'Give me something to drink.'

'Half milk?' Mrs George said, holding up the jug. 'It is so long since you have been down to breakfast that I forget how you like your coffee.'

She looked steadily at Aggie. There were some signs of disturbance about her that a sister could see although she spoke so quietly and had come down to breakfast this day of all for the first time since she had been in Munitions. To see Willy off, perhaps? But no one had heard a car. Could he have walked to Hungerford? It came across Gussy then, suddenly, that Willy had lain in this house that night and that she hadn't once set eyes on him, and now he was gone, so Aggie said, calmly, without a word of farewell, as he had come without greeting, to them all. It wasn't decent! It was shameful!

'But look here! How could he—' Gussy began and broke off sharply: 'What is it, Dawson?'

The old man's eyes were heading straight for Willy's place at the head of the table, where Gussy's youngest sat now. With an effort recalling his glance he found Mrs George at the end and near to him. He just got out:

'The general, ma'am!'

Mrs George it appeared must come quick. The general was taken very bad. Dawson took no notice of Mrs Willy sitting there, the wife of the eldest son. Perhaps he did not see her, Mrs George passed out, saying, 'sit still, children.' Without looking to see if Aggie followed her or not. As she got past Dawson in the passage on her way to the Dutch Room, she said to him quickly: 'have you the sense to fetch the major while I go straight to the general?' and without waiting for an answer passed on.

Old Dawson with his white face of fright, must have accomplished his errand expeditiously, and quite soon George Leclerc was standing by his father's bedside. Mrs George, while she listened bored and patient to the old man's faint babble, was noticing how fine and manly her husband looked, his thick, rather bull-neck encircled by the tight neckband of a collarless shirt, and in spite of those two blobs of cotton-wool patching his red, shocked face in which the eyes, not good at the best of times, looked small and retreating.

It seemed a long time waiting until Dr Porter got over from Hungerford, and some time before he did come the general, speaking suddenly quite clearly, said his dear son Willy had called him and that he had gone to him.

The general's man said that he had found his master at nine o'clock that morning lying on the floor near the door into the small enclosed yard in which the old monks of Ilvercote had grown their simples. The screen dawn in front of it had baffled him and he had fallen, but his valet had got him back to bed before he gave the alarm.

Porter was very late in arriving, and Aggie was fetched because they were not sure the general would last until he came. George and Gussy faced Aggie standing alone the other side of the bed in her beautiful an unsuitable morning robe. Gussy had hold of George's hand and he kept his head down and would not look at Aggie.

Peter was not present. He had been sick, the earliest symptom of

33

a serious attack of illness which obliged him to miss his term at Eton, for he was in bed for over six weeks, too ill even to be told that his grandfather had died and that he was master of Ilvercote.

2

Ay me, whilst these shores
And sounding seas
Wash far away where'er thy
Bones are hurled!

Young Peter Leclerc always reminded Lady Maisry Scott of a nephew of hers, also an Eton boy, who had died of a chill out rowing, and for Aggie's boy she had a peculiar affection. She took, moreover, a psychological interest in him, for he was, though charming, by no means normal and talked to her sometimes as if he were grownup and in a way which he never used to his own womenkind, regarding them as they regarded him, as something in the nature of amiable lunatics.

In the turn of that year she, in her flat in Mayfair, often wondered how the youth at Ilvercote was standing it—the war and family misfortunes combined? He had loved his father passionately—and his mother as an attentive elder brother might have done. He was just the kind of child that Willy the spiritualist and Aggie the materialist would have had. How was he taking his father's death? For 'missing' meant that, of course. It was worse than death because there was no grave to visit; the conclusion left *vistas* of horror for the contemplation of survivors.

She had seen nothing of the Leclerc women since the general's death at Christmas, but she knew that the house in Eaton Place was shut up and that they were down in Wiltshire. It ought to have been the other way. In London, there were distractions, lectures, concerts; that old, low, haunted house, set in the flat fields with no view from the windows excepting the dull winding rivers and cheerless downland, was bad for Peter and for the two widows. And she rather wondered why they, who professed to be fond of her, did not ask her to come to them in their hour of trial, as so many of her friends did.

She often thought of them, and one day in March, when her curtains were drawn and her breakfast tray set by her bedside, a letter from Mrs George Leclerc lay on it. She had been awakened by her maid as she was actually dreaming of that lady, and in that receptive trance a certain communication had been made to her. The details of the dream, as dreams will, was quickly fading out and before she opened the letter, she set herself to try to recapture some rags and tatters of what, a few seconds before, had been an unbroken web of memory's fabric. Dealing in psychoanalysis had made her somewhat adept at 'holding' spirit messages, and she was able to recall a threefold statement that had been made to her without words in the course of that dream.

George is dead of his wounds. Willy is missing, and Aggie is going to have a baby.

Lady Maisry Scott rememorized the sentences carefully. The two first phrases did not represent news to her, for she had, like the rest of the world, read them in the papers. George, in the Roll of Honor—

Major G. B. Leclerc of the 9th Yarrows. . . .on the thirteenth of February. . . at Hooge. . . .had died of his wounds before his wife could arrive to receive his last sigh and recommendations.

She had flown there, of course, Lady Maisry knew. There was a patch of French earth bought, wreaths—*immortelles*—a little garden round. . . She knew Gussy and her formal tenderness—poor Gussy, who adored him so who had not adored her! Lady Maisry has always been convinced that Aggie, who had gone back on him so horridly, held his heart. But he was a jovial, pleasure-loving, easy-going man and he made the best of it, while Gussy, the right sort too, had never exhibited a single sign of jealousy.

And Captain William Leclerc, reported missing on December the twenty-fourth! His death had been presumed and Peter had risen from a sick bed to find himself the owner of Ilvercote. She would not be surprised if he did not, should he live to grow up, marry Gussy's little Felicity and unite the two sisters more closely still.

The dream tendon connected her with the World not Realised had now broken definitely and given place to her recollections of actuality: Willy Leclerc's promise to his wife that he would be with her that Christmas, the truth of which George's wife, abundantly non-psychic, had violently scouted the day Lady Maisry had called on them in London.

She tried to remember the date of Willy's last leave before, drilled, trained, hating it, with a poetry book in his pocket, he had whisked into martial space. They had seen him off hardly expecting to see him again for six months at least. Yes, it must have been in the September of last year? Aggie's affair then. . .

But it could not be that Willy came back from there in less than three months! His promise simply represented a premonition the wrong way round. That sometimes happens, as there is no Time and hardly even Space in the records of the Soul's Wireless. Willy, who promised so confidently to be back by Christmas, must all the while have known subconsciously that he would be just about dying then, lying shot through the heart, in scrub or brush, out of sight of search-parties or exposed on the hot sand. . . .Nothing but his ghost could have won through to Aggie sitting at home at Ilvercote and thinking of him. . . .holding the thought. . . .

Aggie would, of course, be glad to have another child to remember Willy by and provide a spare heir for Ilvercote. Dear Peter had none too good a life and Gussy only had girls, and there was some uncultured fellow in Australia who would otherwise get it all.

Bless me, it was a rotten dream that she was still banking on! For she knew nothing of the happenings of either Aggie or Gussy; she had not heard from either of them since Christmas, just before they had established themselves at Ilvercote, and there was a letter lying on her plate that would tell her about it and impart surely such a momentous piece of news as that, if it was going to happen.

The letter was an invitation from Gussy—not Aggie, mistress of the house as Peter's mother—to come down to Ilvercote as soon as she could and for as long as she could. A veritable S.O.S. Gussy was profuse in her apologies for these three months of neglect. They had been, she said, unsuitably apportioning her adverbs, 'rather sad and very busy', but Peter wanted so much to talk to her about spiritualism, which he had taken up after his illness.

He was a queer boy and his illness had left him rather queerer, perhaps. He had actually said, speaking of his father, that he had far rather it had been 'dead' instead of 'missing'. Gussy thought it would be so nice for Peter if his dear Lady Maisry would come and allow him to get it, whatever it was, off his chest to her, for Lady Maisry knew all about it and wouldn't let him get fancying that his ideas were real, as some of 'your people perhaps would do.'

Gussy added vaguely:

'It isn't right to tamper with an heir. He has started an aviary—at least, not exactly an aviary because he doesn't think birds should be shut up at all. It is wild ones he likes and tames them and tells them things. Do you know, it has been most successful—with sparrows; as far as I can tell they are just sparrows—like London ones but much cleaner. He says it is the kind that live abroad in the winter and that's the sort he cares for. Swallows, perhaps?

'Anyway, he is very clever with the birds here and they come and eat out of his hand when he is down all alone in his lake house. Perhaps he will take you one day himself—none of us, not even his mother or Felicity, are privileged to go there. He says his mother is contra-indicative. He uses very long words since he lay and read in bed so much. Sometimes he doesn't come in to meals at all, and it is death to any of us to go and fetch him.'

Not a word about Aggie and her approaching trial. . . .quite soon.

The dream message that had taken such a strong hold of Lady Maisry's imagination was with her all the way to Hungerford. Before the train slid into the station, she saw the serious profile of Peter in the car on the Ilvercote road nearly on a level with the line. She loved Peter, but she had hoped that Gussy would come to meet her and give her the news.

Peter, who was fifteen and used to look eleven, had shot up during his illness and might now pass for fourteen. He was beautifully made—slim and graceful like his mother. He reminded Lady Maisry of a whippet. He had been trained in such boyish exercises as were suitable for him. The sports he did not care for he had not been by the authorities allowed to eschew altogether. Because of his 'beastly heart' he did not take up rowing, but he swam beautifully and Lady Maisry remembered seeing him quite naked in the lake at Ilvercote, lazily floating or with a quiet, precise stroke or two filing in and out among the weeds like a silver fish.

Like Shelley, he never seemed embarrassed by his humanity in any way. Lady Maisry thought he looked like the picture she had seen of the youthful poet in a frill. Peter did not wear a frill but a nice sensible Norfolk jacket, when at home, in which he contrived to look every inch the heir of this fine place.

He did not mention either his mother or his aunt beyond replying to Lady Maisry's question that these ladies were well. But he told her all about:

'What Aunt Gussy calls an aviary, that isn't made of wire or shut up but free to the air from Pole to Pole. There is nothing between my birds and Mespot, if they like to go there. . . I don't stop them. . . I tell them to.'

Lady Maisry thought it was wiser not to encourage him by asking him why. All this bird stuff was connected in some way with his father, and though she was an enthusiastic Freudian, she considered any form of psychology an ill equipment for the squirearchical, land-owning life which was to be Peter's if he lived.

The low, retired porch of Ilvercote, the yellow sweep of the gravel drive laving its steps as it were a tide, framed the two sisters standing to welcome Lady Maisry. Aggie at a first glance appeared less frail, perhaps a little more like a Christmas Rose than a Snowdrop. Peter, although it was just lunchtime, disappeared, and the presence and permitted babble of Gussy's girls—the youngest, Honor, was already ten years old—made conversation impossible.

Gussy behind the roast in the old-fashioned way; Aggie at the other end of the table, refusing to be bothered to cut the apple-tart—Lady Maisry, almost breathless with conjecture, surveyed them. Aggie's white camel's-hair robe was made loosely and flowingly, while Gussy's black silk jumper was cut carefully to obviate her slight inclination to stoutness.

Her face was less buxom than it used to be, her nice hair less abundant, her eyes sunken; she seemed far more changed by what she had gone through than Aggie. Lady Maisry remembered that Gussy had been supposed to adore the general, who as usual, adored Aggie. Though she was calm and self-possessed enough, her face had the effect of being nightly soused in tears and the red of her mouth had strayed beyond its natural limits. She had bitten her lips sore. In fine, she looked tragic; Aggie merely softly distressed.

Lady Maisry had hoped for a talk with Gussy some time after tea or dinner, but Aggie kept drifting in or out and gave her no opportunity. At dinner she asked after old Dr Porter and old Dawson, the butler, who had been rather a friend of hers.

Dawson was dead. 'Oh, when did he die?' was her exclamation, answered by Felicity, the eldest girl, before either of her elders had time to speak.

'Dawson died the very day we got the news of Uncle Willy's—' She stopped, tacitly reproved.

'And where's my friend Whitefoord?'

'Oh, you'll see her,' Gussy said. 'She's too old to maid us now; she gets the hooks always into the wrong eyes.'

'Mother doesn't approve of her telling us about the voices in the haunted room,' Felicity shouted on her raw young nestling's note.

Aggie, speaking like the mistress of the house that she was, said haughtily and languidly: 'Yes, I've had to depose Whitefoord—silly old useless woman. She had developed a stupid habit of prying. I was always finding her poking about the drawers in my room examining my underclothes—they are rather pretty. Willy always suspected her and told me to get rid of her the very last time he was here, but Gussy thwarted me.'

Gussy could not agree about Whitefoord. 'Of course, she is superstitious like all country people, but she does know what's what in a house and has been about us for years. She doesn't tell lies or pry and—what is there to find out?'

'Shall we go into the drawing-room?' Aggie said.

★★★★★★

Lady Maisry fancied Whitefoord would turn up at her *coucher*, in the old way, with something or other for her comfort. She was just getting into bed when there came the expected knock at the door. It was not a servant's knock. Mrs Gussy came in in her petticoat bodice with a Shetland shawl thrown over her shoulders, the old, usual Gussy. That was right. The two women without a word cling together for a time and Lady Maisry felt the salt tears of Gussy on her cheek.

'Get into bed and let me sit and talk to you,' the widow said. 'I couldn't manage before; Aggie sticks like a leech doesn't she?' And during the interview she looked continually towards the door and didn't seem to have much to say.

'How do you think Aggie is looking?' she asked, playing with the bed fringe.

'Beautiful, as usual.'

'And Peter?'

'Delicate, as usual.'

'He feels his father's death so acutely. He can't bear it spoken of. That's the reason he left the room when Felicity said that about Dawson. Dawson's mind went completely. He was crying out when he died and complaining of Mr Willy. He didn't know in the least what he was saying.'

'No, for surely Willy was always so nice to servants!'

Gussy hesitated, left off playing with the tassels and, staring full in Lady Maisry's face, spoke as if she wanted to impress a certain fact upon her mind.

'Dawson's complaint was that Mr Willy had come and gone without his even seeing him.'

'*When* in the Lord's name? When *did* he come? I keep hearing hints. Why do you all make mysteries?'

'We don't—not all of us,' Gussy said mysteriously. 'It was Christmas Eve!'

'But that was—'

'The day Willy was reported missing. . . .Hush!' She held up her finger.

'It's not Wild Darrell—only a knock at the door,' said Lady Maisry.

'Aggie, of course!' whispered Gussy. 'I knew she couldn't let us alone. Say "Come in." Not a word—I mean, don't ask her anything about Willy.'

Lady Maisry's 'Come in' was dilatory, but Aggie waited. Then she came in quite naturally, asking if Lady Maisry had forgotten her aspirin, offering to lend her some if she had.

'I never take it,' said Lady Maisry. 'Too dangerous.'

'Lucky you, then!' Aggie said, sweeping round to go out of the room again so quickly that the blue train of her undress twisted itself round her knees, encircling her slim figure like the cusp of a pillar and showed it up to the other two. Gussy's eyes were fixed on her sister' *negligée* with a little feminine envy; those of Lady Maisry beamed with a pure spirit of investigation.

'Well, goodnight,' Aggie said. 'Come along Gussy. Don't keep Lady Maisry from her pleasant dreams!'

Gussy murmuring a perfunctory 'Sleep well!' followed her sister out of the bedroom like an obedient sheep.

That London dream of a week ago would explain all Aggie's queerness, supposing it represented a message from her tormented *geist* to beg her old friend to come to her and stand by her. But it came from Gussy! Aggie, soft but utterly materialistic, would not be a *persona grata* in the spirit world. She was too thin, mentally and physically, to be able easily to communicate. Her sister, business-like and sentimental at the same time, full-bosomed, moist-eyed, and plastic, was much more likely to have got a message through.

Aggie had had, now Lady Maisry remembered to have heard, a very bad time with Peter. She seemed rather handy with aspirin! Perhaps the little fool was dosing herself to prevent a recurrence of the agonies of fifteen years ago? She knew, however, very little really about such matters. But remembering, and judging from the look of Aggie, standing on the threshold like a mermaid with her tail wrapped round her, there was no such thing and, according to dates, if it were, it would be imminent.

But then, women of Aggie's make. . .

Lady Maisry lay for a long time expecting the reappearance of one sister or another. But neither came—perhaps they policed each other too well.

★★★★★★

At breakfast the atmosphere was a little less depressing. Gussy's four gay girls with all their lives before them, as their mother often repeated, kept the house sweet, and it needed it, Lady Maisry Scott felt. Aggie, gentle, frail, and ineffably calm, was like a blister set continually. . . Poor Aggie! How did she manage to do it? She said nothing. . .interfered with nothing! . . . .Yet. . . . her state of mind, as it were, came through. . . .One had the sensation of a fellow-creature in deep emotional stress. . .agony almost. . . .But the four nice girls, even in their mourning, were each a living epitome of the spring, like tossing leaves, rustling clouds, early daffodils with round yellow soapy faces lighting up dark corners and sodden dells

They flashed in and out, interrupting untoward conversations, hindering bitternesses from coming to a head, clamouring for fun, for drives and picnics which was refused them, all in black as they were. Their mother, averse from the entire repression of young things and indulgent of their spirits, preferred that the signs of their juvenescence should not pass the limits—miles in extent—of Ilvercote Park. It would not be decent for any of the Leclercs to be seen about enjoying themselves—a widow and her four daughters and a boy whose father was missing, and by now accounted dead.

Peter, discreet beyond his years, seemed to be of his aunt's opinion. 'Certainly, we oughtn't to be seen in public or anything like that till we find out about Father,' he said, when appealed to suddenly by his mother to make common cause against these four children all in black and longing to go at least into grey.

Felicity was naughty.

'But everyone knows that Uncle Willy's dead and buried,' she said quite loudly before Peter. He corrected her.

'No, Felicity, not buried—that we know of.' He left the table.

'Oh, Felicity, you shouldn't! You've upset Peter, and now probably he'll not turn up again before night,' her mother said.

Peter did not come at all that evening. Mrs George said it didn't matter really, for he had a bed in his summerhouse and rugs and a gas stove that he could turn on, and it wasn't cold. But next morning, when there was no Peter at breakfast, Lady Maisry asked if she might not go and find him, but they said it was best to leave him alone. He

41

had things to eat down there—biscuits and ginger-beer.

At luncheon Felicity cried, 'There's Peter!' They all saw him from the low-silled window, standing on the lawn with his head bent down 'Watching a bird,' Felicity said.

''Tisn't a bird,' piped up little Honor. 'He's watching Davey laying a mole trap and—oh! Let's go and watch him too.'

Mrs George said to Lady Maisry: 'There's a mole-run under the grass and Peter would like to give orders that it is not to be interfered with, just as he hates shooting fawns, but we have to here, they get too numerous.'

'Peter says,' shouted Felicity on the sill as she got out, 'that moles are the mutes that sit on funeral carriages and make arrangements and keep all the underground cemeteries in order. That's why he's telling Davey to stop it.'

'Davey obeys me for the present,' Aggie said.

Little Honor came back.

'Peter's gone to his house. May we all go and take him some toffee we've made?'

'No, you may not!' Aggie said.

'May I?' said Lady Maisry.

Aggie smiled for the first time for weeks. 'Peter will be enchanted. Only, if he isn't—he is queer too, like his mother—you won't mind? He is so funny about his house, it will be sure to amuse you. Eates,' to the new butler; 'fetch Lady Maisry's hat and cloak.'

Peter was sitting outside his summerhouse overlooking the lake, on a mound carpeted with the greenest turf, and the black velvet body of a slain mole lay beside him.

'What are you going to do with that?' Lady Maisry said quietly, coming up behind Peter.

'Bury him. Raise him a hillock that shall keep him warm. It's what he does for others all the time. I always bury everything I find dead. It's the least I can do; but mother shan't have this one for her new winter coat that a battalion of moles has gone to make already.'

'You are a queer boy,' Lady Maisry said indulgently.

'And you're a queer lady—learned and rich—that's why I like you!' He looked at her wistfully—'You ought to be able to understand me.'

'My boy, what is there to understand?'

'Mother can't anyway. I don't know why I'm my father's son, and she has been my father's wife yet she can't make out why I bury things.' He sighed. 'I'm quite chummy with her—if only she was more like Antigone!'

'Antigone was the woman—correct me, you young schoolboy, if I am wrong—who insisted on a gentleman called Creon giving her brother a decent burial, wasn't she?'

'Yes! Capital! And wasn't Antigone right? Doesn't any unburied body cry aloud to Heaven?'

'Creon, of course, behaved as the conquering army has a right to do—treat his enemy's remains with contempt. They all do that. It was a matter of principle with him, wasn't it?'

'And with Antigone too?' Peter said slyly. 'She is my favourite heroine. She gave her life so that her brother should be buried. Good for her! Why can't I ....Look at that little fellow over there!'

He pointed towards the fence where something was hopping about which Lady Maisry, unlearned in ornithology, could only classify as a 'dear little bird'.

'He might happen to be the very one—

Call to the Robin Redbreast and the Wren,
Since over shady groves they hover,
And with leaves and flowers do cover
The friendless bodies of unburied men.

The 'friendless bodies . . . unburied men.' The singing voice in which he chanted this fragment of poetry he had got from God knows where made Lady Maisry Scott fancy herself in Eton Chapel. . . . The 'friendless bodies of unburied men' . . . .of unburied men. . . .and a boy saying it. . . .lying on his back on a green mound in a garden with blue eyes reflecting the blue sky.

Now she saw not green but red, the sandy desert, and a heap of bones. . . .the wind teasing and tumbling at them till there were none.
. . Raising her eyes to shake off the intolerable vision, there was the same hedge. . . of barbed wire with dark, tanned strips hanging on to the spikes of it, flesh maybe, or clothes rotting bit by bit, fluttering in the air like a signal that there is no one to take up. . .

Peter chanted:

Call for the ant, the field-mouse and the mole
To raise him hillocks that shall keep him warm;
But keep the wolf from thence, that's foe to man.
For with his nails he'll dig them up again.

'Or, jackals, eh? Can't you see why I look after moles and feed the

43

birds, especially the migratory ones, for they are the ones that might go over there—or have come from there. . .'

'Ghastly boy!'—she wanted at any price to stop him—'On this beautiful spring morning, talking about jackals and vultures! I don't wonder your Aunt Gussy is anxious about you. You have far too strong an imagination, dear. That's what's the matter with you. You must try to control it.'

'Why?' he asked dreamily, stroking the mole. 'Why mayn't I be like Antigone? There's the bell for your tea.'

'Won't you come too?' she said. The bell from the house was pealing maddeningly, as if a spiteful hand was pulling it.

He looked at her; his eyes were full of tears which he did not, boy-like, try to hide. He was not a boy. His constant agony had aged him and given him the horrid aplomb of woe.

'No, I won't come, thank you. They don't understand. Won't you say you do?'

'Yes, dear, I do understand. . . . and I believe somehow, though your Aunt Gussy is not poetical but practical, she would. Why don't you ever talk to her?'

'I do appreciate her. But then she hasn't had to bear what we have. It's all right for Uncle George with a wife to go across to France at once and see to a nice green grave and a headstone and *immortelles*. . . . . No jackals about. Aunt Gussy's a fearful brick, but she'd only say I was silly and have a nice cup of tea. No, I'm not coming in. . . . Tell them, please, will you dear?'

He rose, threw his thin, stick-like arms round Lady Maisry, and dismissed her. He certainly had a way with him. Lady Maisry hoped so much he would live to forget all this. She wanted a talk with White-foord about him. Whitefoord, if anyone, must hold a clue to it all, the old body who had nursed Peter's father as well as Peter.

After tea she gave the ladies of Ilvercote the slip and asked the new butler which was Whitefoord's room—she was sure to have a nice one of her own as the old family servant—and was directed to the room which had been the general's, with the door into the yard with the stone-bordered beds filled with clumps of herbs of which no one knew the use.

Whitefoord welcomed her. She was all there. Not at all superannuated-looking. . . Why had Aggie taken such a dislike to Whitefoord, calling her silly and useless?

Before entering into any set conversation Lady Maisry must needs appreciate and comment upon the gallery of family portraits with which the old servant had covered the walls and mantelpiece of her room. There was the general and the general's wife, the beautiful daughter of the Earl of Norhamshire, and his two sons, Willy and George, as like as two peas in boyhood at any rate.

They were both fair. They had both good noses. Only George's mouth was fuller and his cheeks. She remembered that George, after the outbreak of the war, had grown much thinner in the face while stouter in figure. On another table were the likenesses of Aggie and her son, who resembled George rather than Willy, and Mrs George and her four daughters, Felicity, Maud, Mary, and Honor. On a table, all by himself, was a photograph of young Peter, enlarged.

'You haven't left yourself room to move,' Lady Maisry said.

'I'd rather have them there than knickknacks,' said Whitefoord. 'They're all I live for and pray for, though I am a silly, useless, old woman.'

'Mrs Willy—' hazarded Lady Maisry, wondering if Whitefoord would seize the opportunity to abuse the mistress who had spoken of her in those terms.

'Well, she's not like the others,' Whitefoord admitted. 'And I never see her now.'

'But you were about her when Mr Peter was born?'

'Yes . . . but after that, she . . . . It's as good as lose your place if you go into her room without being invited. And there's only one way in now. She that was all for having the door into the ghost room taken off once has had it walled up. Won't have it shown. Says it isn't decent and frightens the younger servants. This new lot, perhaps? I don't mind ghosts, I don't, no more since that night. . . . You wouldn't believe it but, nowadays, any night when the moon is at the full, as it was then, I walk along the passage and stop where the door used to be and bend down and put my ear to it, and I can assure you, my lady, I hear voices as I did on the night the two boys came home.

'There's no hindering of ghosts. Come they will if they've promised. Stone walls don't stop them nor the waves of the sea, and their feet can carry them to a waft anywhere. It's imagination they come on. And as a matter of fact, they've laid Wild Darrell. You've heard of him? The murderer who was the master of Ilvercote House once and had to give it up to the very judge what tried him in exchange for his poor life. Well, the ladies talked to him on Planchette and he said on it that he was in the pains of Purgatory—they call it—and begged their prayers. So Miss Aggie—Mrs Willy—wrote to friends of hers in Belgium, where she was at school—Spa—I believe it was, and they got a priest to say masses for his soul.

'The Leclercs, you know, were always Catholic. The general was a good one. The younger ones don't bother. But I say it is of no use cockering Wild Darrell up in Purgatory without getting him to take off his curse. You know he said that no one of the family who turned him out should ever die in his bed.'

'Well, but,' Lady Maisry said, 'I suppose he did take it off? The general died in his bed all right.'

'Never you believe it. The general died in that little yard out there, with his head in a clump of sailor's flannel. They had got him back into bed all right after his seizure, but he was out of it again when his man wasn't looking. He kept saying his son was calling him, all the day before. He was ready to go. Why did they keep him? He was hardly sensible then, my lady! They will be saying that this room is haunted next, but, as Miss Felicity says, "Let 'em all come".'

The old maid's slang seemed pathetically discrepant. She sat in her rocking-chair opposite Lady Maisry, swaying to and fro with her hands on her knees, too tired to be careful.

'There's queer things goings-on in Ilvercote. . . . It's not nice here now. Have you noticed, my lady, that neither of them two sisters ever say a word to each other except through you or maybe the children? Eates, he notices it. He speaks against Miss Aggie and we shut him up but don't tell the ladies. Miss Aggies suspects, I think. She's going to dismiss him. We're always having changes now. I'm the last of the old lot and Miss Aggie wouldn't much mind getting rid of me. . .'

'What's the trouble between them, Whitefoord?'

'It's Mr Willy's visit—if there was a visit. . ? Miss Aggie says he did come and Mrs George says he didn't. There you are! Mrs George can't forgive Miss Aggie being so positive, and Miss Aggie, she can't abear even to have it hinted that Mr Willy didn't come—and then there's all this unpleasantness. Mrs George says to her patiently, as if she was a baby—which she is, spoilt all her life—that it was Mr Willy's ghost come to tell her that he was thinking of her but would never see her again—at the moment of death.

'So, ghosts do. But she doesn't seem to care about letting it be thought it was a ghost came on Christmas Eve. She wants it real honest flesh and blood. I shouldn't like Miss Aggie to hear what they're saying about her now in the servant's hall.'

'No, of course not. It's the best thing to say, about it all—what Mrs George says. He's dead now whether he came then or not. Of course, she must expect to miss him—he was such a dear!'

'Being dead isn't what Miss Aggie minds, I tell you. Neither she nor Mr Peter. They'd both rather he was dead and done with for different reasons may be. Of course, Mr Peter doesn't like to think of his father not being properly buried. That's vey respectable of him and I wish it could have been, but—war is war, my lady, and we're all out to suffer, women too, I'm not the same since the raids. I can't think clearly or put one date and another together.'

There was a pause—significant, painful. . . .Lady Maisry knew of what the old woman was thinking.'

'Sometimes I think the curse is on me too, for, on my word, if I were to die tomorrow, I swear I heard those two speaking together in the ghost room three months ago! Mr Willy—my baby! I wish to God it had been—different.'

She wept, the painful tears of the old.

'You poor old dear! You would have preferred that your baby should have deserted from the army so as to keep his promise to his wife and then gone back like a man and got shot for it, and his colonel cover it up for the sake of the boy by saying he was missing.'

'And could you bring yourself to believe that, my lady?'

'I do believe it,' said Lady Maisry firmly.

★★★★★★

Aggie was not there at luncheon. Gussy said she had been doing a faint and had gone to her room.

'You won't see Aunt Agg for a week, I bet, Lady Maisry,' Felicity said. 'It always lasts as long as that. She is an old cheat. Mother's been up to her and says she looks A1.'

Gussy indeed appeared to take the view of her eldest daughter. She owned that she had actually said to Felicity that she as fed up with her aunt, which she knew was wrong of her. She had been up to see Mrs Willy, yes, and had satisfied herself that there was nothing particular the matter with her; there could not be, she looked so awfully well, and gave a description of the spectacle Aggie presented—took care to present—lying like a white flower on her sheets trimmed with lace and all sorts of pretty, fluffy bits, Shetland shawls and silk camisoles, peeping up all round her.

'She wasn't cross with me for coming up,' Gussy said. 'Aggie still cares to impress me! She just said that her back ached and if she might go on lying still for a bit it would be all right. Aggie always did know how to take care of herself. She is not really delicate. All she wants is to be fussed over when she is well and left alone when she isn't. Always must be a picture, and in the very middle of it too! And the men have always played up to her and given her what she wanted.

'It's the only way to live with her. Willy knew it. He was always— what do you call it?—*aux petits soins* with her, and George too. The first thing that George said to me after he had kissed me that night, he came home was, "Where's Aggie?" He knew he'd got to pay his respects to her pretty quick or she'd sulk for the rest of his leave.'

'Where was Aggie?'

'Gone up with Willy, I suppose.'

'I don't know what Aggie may have wanted, but I don't suppose Willy would be particularly keen on George bursting in when he hadn't seen his wife for months? Do you mean to say that you let George go and dig her out, first thing, like that?'

Gussy had grown sullen, her lips red and her eyes full of retrospective anger—'I don't know if he went there, but I know I wouldn't have been the one to stop him going. It was for her to turn him out. George was awfully funny that night. . .'

'Sh-h!' Lady Maisry breathed involuntarily.

'Yes, afterwards at bedtime he kept me up waiting for him till after twelve—even Whitefoord noticed how slack he was and how careless of my feelings.'

'What excuse—?'

'Oh, they say all my fault,' Gussy said humbly. 'I never did let him smoke in my bedroom—it is do disrespectful in one's husband, and the smell hangs about for weeks. But still I wish I had. That night of all nights I ought to have been indulgent. That's Aggie's pull over men. And another thing—that ass Whitefoord had got three candles blazing away in my room. It brought down all the ill-luck she says—wise after the event, for next day, as you know, the general died and then George and then Willy. No, Willy must have died *first* because we got the message "Missing" in Christmas week.'

******

And it was full May and Lady Maisry was still at Ilvercote, except for a short run up to town to put her affairs in order. When she came back to the big, dull, waiting house in the green fields after the absence of a week she found things had taken a turn for the worse.

No one met her and a new butler who came to the door did not know her. She heard voices in the drawing-room, and saying, 'I suppose the ladies are in there?' she walked into the room just as she was, holding her umbrella and her bag. It was teatime but there was no sign of tea. The sisters were both sitting on opposite chairs. Aggie looking like a snow leopard at bay and Gussy, the good homely brown bear, protesting peevishly.

They were both so absorbed that though they took in their guest's embarrassed entry they accepted her at once as part of the scheme of things. Gussy spoke, shamefaced:

'Look here, Lady Maisry, we are at it like two fighting cocks. It's a shame when you've only just got into the house! You ought to have some tea. Have you had tea?' She made no further progress towards hospitality but continued: 'Aggie says she intends to go to Salonica to see if she—to find out definitely about Willy. That's her idea. But look here, I ask you, is she well enough to go dashing off alone to the Continent? She is only just out of bed this morning and she has fainted twice since. Gave us all a horrid fright—the girls all saw it—and yet she won't let me send for Porter. I ought to have disobeyed her, that's what I ought to have done.'

Aggie said nothing.

'And she's written to Cook's, yes, she *has* actually, to know about fares. Why, I tell her, they won't let her go messing about, even in France, now—a woman—and to the East is worse. She won't believe that dear Willy is dead and still keeps harping on his being here at Christmas. There's only her word for it. Nobody saw him but her and nobody believes it. It's her delusion.

'She hasn't been very well and this house is haunted, everybody knows it is. People hear people talking . . . . Aggie say something! You make me seem such a beast before Lady Maisry. I hate saying it, but, Lady Maisry, isn't it practically impossible that Willy could be here without anybody but her seeing him?'

'Willy made me a promise—' Aggie began.

'Dead men can't keep promises! Don't be absurd.'

'The live Willy,' Aggie said sturdily, 'would keep a promise to me at the cost of his dishonour, if he couldn't come without. And if he deserted so as to be here, of course, he wouldn't let himself be seen.'

'Well then, if he did come like that, he'd still be dead now, for he'd be shot as soon as he got back, and if he was a man of honour he'd go back and give himself up. You daren't say that Willy wasn't a man of honour!'

She stuttered. . . .repeated the last phrase. . . .

Lady Maisry spoke:

'Gussy, dear, let up a little! Don't you see you're going too far? You're talking in the clouds. All this sentimental talk about honour! To come down to realities, how could he desert from there? Too far.'

'I don't know but I mean to find out,' Aggie said.

'Then go and find out—all sorts of beastly things. Make yourself and me more miserable than we are,' Gussy shouted. 'Only I insist on your having Porter to see if you are fit to go, even as far as London.'

'Nothing would induce me to have Porter,' said Aggie very coldly, rising and backing towards the low French window, where the soft, clear close of the spring afternoon seemed to invite her away from this hot lair of viperous family passions let loose. The room seemed as close and foetid as after a children's party. Lady Maisry fanned herself with a magazine, but put it down gravely when Aggie, with her hand on the window fastening, appealed to her:

'I'll only say this, Lady Maisry. Aren't you being rather unnecessarily cruel to me? As for my sister, she has her reasons for the attitude she is taking up and I have mine—for not seeing Porter—the ass that killed the general by his stupid muddling—not getting there in time.'

'I never heard you abuse Porter before,' Gussy said. She seemed to be thinking. . .

If only Gussy would not shriek, Lady Maisry thought. It gave such a dreadful tone to what was, after all, only a discussion of ways and means. And Aggie, after all, had a right to see or not to see the local doctor whom she mistrusted. She might be intending to see a specialist? But Gussy's voice rose after she had done her thinking, and she made one lumbering step towards Aggie, who cringed.

'No, that's not it,' she shouted. 'That's not why you won't have Porter. You *daren't*.'

She had said something awful—unforgiveable. Ashamed and humiliated at this tremendous fall below her standards, she bowed her head and waited for a reproof and a lead from one whose sense of decency and justice was not, like hers, obscured by family rancour and long-pent-up local passion.

Lady Maisry recognised the obligation. She loved the sisters and she had known their mother. To her it fell to adjudicate between the two young women and bring them together again. But she must first convince herself with no assistance from either of them. Gussy would never help to elucidate the problem—too muddly-minded! Not Aggie—too deep!

How then? There was no sign. . .

Ah, but trust her dream, now become part of her mentality! It was rushing in upon her with the force of a spring spate, flooding the banks wreathed with futile conjecture, washing away this and that paltering supposition and, woe's me!—Pity! Pity for Aggie! Aggie, the lax! Aggie who never said No, and never really wanted to! Aggie, primed with the ferocious war maxims of The Chief, and hard upon the soppy state of free-thinking in which these had left her, the exhausting, long-drawn-out expectation of Willy's coming so suddenly withdrawn!

And most conclusive of all to Lady Maisry, the fact of her early engagement to George and George's death. Since Lady Maisry had been made acquainted by Gussy with some of the immediate circumstances of this sad event and had talked to a man in the War Office while she was in London, she was convinced, one way and another, that George's death had been self-sought. George, desperate, distracted, thinking of his wife and children, had volunteered for a forlorn hope.

She said to Gussy slowly, adopting ever so little her old pacificatory Committee manner—Ladies, Ladies!. . . .For it would be as well to say something vague but clinching; something to warn one sister that the game was up and the other to be merciful:

'Perhaps, Gussy, it is becoming important for Aggie to get you to believe—'

And when she had spoken, she felt she had been what she would have called a cat. How could she have brought herself to sneer at this helpless, bereaved creature who just looked at you and went down? Aggie's eyes did not flash or plead or defy; they simply seemed to go out, to rush down swiftly like a binnacle light on a boat that founders in a storm. There was simply no more Aggie. The fond sister ran up to her, stumbling and knocking over tables. . . .

'Darling, darling, don't mind what she says! I ought not to have asked her. We are sisters. . . we must stick together through all, and we will. Lady Maisry only meant it for your good, and as for me. . . I'm just abominably jealous, that's all!'

She flung herself on the floor and mimicked the support of Aggie, holding her by the knees. Aggie stood quite pale and still while her sister, her face buried in white folds pleaded with her and Lady Maisry.

'Don't go away, dear Lady Maisry, you know us. Stop and get Agg to forgive me and say that she will be nice and go away after all!

You might be an angel and take her. There are such nice places to go to—quiet, where nobody knows one—and I'll stop on here and take care of everything and tell people what we want them to know and look after Peter. Peter mustn't know anything. We'll tell him it was the ghost that wretched Whitefoord heard—Wild Darrell. Everybody believes that he haunts this house.

Aggie said—contained: 'Let me go, please.'

Gussy began: 'If you and George—'

Aggie, with a glance at Lady Maisry, fallen silent now, began with a cold determination to unwind her sister's hands from their grasp of her dress. She spoke, employing all the force of which her hands were capable to get rid of Gussy's embrace:

'Look here, that's enough, you women. You are killing me, I tell you. Gussy'll drive me to my death—she and her George. . .'

Gussy, relinquishing her hold and rising, said: 'Not *my* George. Nobody could say that he was ever my George. He was yours through and through. You—you ought to have stuck to George and you didn't. We shouldn't have had this if you had. It was wrong of you to marry Willy. You married Willy because of his money and the position, and George—poor old George—married me out of pique. He loved you. . . and now he is dead and can't speak for himself! But I am so hardened I'm not even jealous now. It's too bad for jealousy. And I knew it all along. . .'

To their mutual friend, who stood waiting to come in when at last she might be useful, she said piteously: 'Lady Maisry, help me to persuade her that I'm not jealous of her and George. I am not really. I do understand. . . . .'

'You devil, you don't.' Aggie from the window shouted, 'with you Wild Darrells and quiet places! . . .Pouah! I tell you once and for all George was nothing to me nor I to him. I'm going to Peter—to my son.'

With a quiet sob she pushed the long window open! The way down to the lake and Peter's sympathy lay clear before her and she started forward. She then appeared to waver and, coming back a little way into the room, spoke more caressingly:

'You two numbskulls! Don't you know anything about these sorts of things? Lady Maisry, you! Understand please, I made Willy come to me. I just wrapped him all round in my thoughts like a cloud or a cocoon and brought him to me, safe and sound—all there was of him—all that mattered. Try to get that into your heads. You people all trouble so much about the body and its doings. The body's nothing. It's only the window-dressing of the soul—what one cares for, really!'

She paused and looked round at them both. Lady Maisry, who, for the life of her, could never count Aggie quite sincere, now imagined that she was desirous of ascertaining what effect her tirade had had upon them. . . . was watching for her effect, even now. But her voice had gained a sort of shaking, piercing, penetrating timbre, as if the inside of some delicate machine, stripped, taken to pieces, was speaking.

'Gussy! Lady Maisry! Perhaps some day you'll come to believe it. . . . I swear Willy's soul came to me. And now, if you don't take care, mine shall go to him.'

She went out of the window quietly and down the box-bordered path set with little plots of smiling, low primroses towards Peter's summerhouse. She looked perfectly virginal. . . .her demure and chaste walking impressed the two heavily-made, matronly women she had left sitting on corners of the same sofa looking at each other.

'I'm sure that she's got all that rigmarole about the soul from The Chief,' Gussy said. 'Aggie never could have invented it for herself.'

'I don't know,' Lady Maisry said. She was thinking thoughts, pursuing indeterminate trails of psychology that was far beyond simple Gussy Leclerc's comprehension, and rather resented the abandonment of them in order to answer after the mode of the other's thinking. 'She's put it over us at any rate, hasn't she? I still can't think her quite sincere. . . .posing, going off with a Virgin Mary air like that! But then I must say that I never considered *that* person altogether—' She arrested her profanity with a jerk. 'At any rate, Aggie's cleverer than I thought. That last was masterly.'

Gussy said innocently: 'What a funny word to use about old Agg! We never thought she had an idea in her head except to make herself look pretty.'

'Are you sure Peter is down at his house?' Lady Maisry asked roughly.

The butler was rung for and catechised as to the whereabouts of everybody. Yes, Eates knew for a fact that Mr Peter was down there; he had just been up to the house to get some maize for a wounded pigeon or woodpecker he had found. The young ladies were not back from their drive in the car. They had all four gone to see their grandmother Tremlett at Newbury.

'That's all right,' Lady Maisry said. 'Peter will be good for her. She won't have to pose before him. Then, in about half an hour, we'll go and look her up, and mind you don't say another word about it for the present.'

'About what?' said Mrs George, though she knew. Then—'You mean about her going away? Can she? Will she?'

'She must,' Lady Maisry said. 'Did you see that man's face? Aggie has given him notice, you say, but there's still Whitefoord left, who'll take care to tell the next butler. All the house knows, and consequently the whole neighbourhood, about the voices in the haunted room on Christmas Eve. People will put their heads and dates together. Yes, I'll take her somewhere. It's only May. . .'

'Then you do think . . . .' Gussy shuddered.

'My dear, you have been very brave and forgiving. Go on being both and . . . shall we leave it at Wild Darrell? He was a bad man and must serve our turn now.'

She rose; Mrs George was crying slowly, softly, like rain.

'Don't you worry, old girl! You've been a thorough brick.'

'Even if I've been a brick,' Mrs George whimpered, 'I've not been a lady. Fancy telling her to her face that she funked seeing a doctor, as if she had been a servant in trouble.'

'It's pretty much the same thing. . . .My dear, forgive me, but I do hope that your brother-in-law is really dead. Dead as a doornail. Dead men tell no tales and don't cause any to be told. Just imagine if he were to come back now on top of all this! He would die all over again.'

'Ah, but he won't. He is,' Gussy said. 'I feel it is as stupid, unpsychical people like me do feel things—in their bones. Unpsychical—that's not the right word—' She laughed, without mirth. 'But I have, God forgive me for saying so, cause to be thankful that George is gone too!'

They went to their rooms. Women always after scenes of this kind, go to their rooms, if they have any. Lady Maisry thought it over while Gussy lay on her sofa in a mush of tears. Lady Maisry was older, stronger, and did not lie down. She threw open her window and looked out towards the lake. It was quite warm. Aggie would not hurt, even sitting by its banks in her thin dress. It would cool hot blood a little. . . .if it was hot? Women who have done what Aggie had done were always supposed to have hot blood. Appearances were deceptive in her case, for, to look at aggie, one would not use the word sensual or even sensuous.

Lady Maisry, exhausted, through the sweet spring evening whose air was like a benediction sat and thought or let thoughts run through her—an art she cultivated. And, slowly, some conception of Aggie Leclerc's impossible position came to her, also notions, rude and abominably unorthodox, that, shared, might have made plainer perhaps to one sister the sharp short trial of the other that Christmas eve and justified in some sort Aggie's breakdown—in the region of dreams, as she pathetically would have it.

For now, taken on another plan, the behaviour of Aggie Leclerc last Christmas was beginning to seem more comprehensible to Lady Maisry Scott, whose education was still going forward on all sorts of lines. Poor Gussy Leclerc, the average English woman whose training, one might say, stopped at her first baby, would never be able to follow her friend's gropings into matters that religion had settled once for all. Gussy would have been terribly shocked at the new modes of crime-assessment that her friend was commencing, would find her anti-moral accommodations improper, impious even.

Lady Maisry had come to think of the equally uneducated Aggie quite dispassionately, as one of those simpletons who have been through the ages selected as subjects for the revelation and illustration of a law one day to be more fully understood.

As of poor, patient Penelope, the wife of Odysseus, while the wooers caroused at his expense in the hall below, dreaming of one who lay by her side all night in the likeness of her lord.

As the Maiden of Bethlehem for whom, as cynics say, her friends invented the dove.

And there was the Stigmata, the fixed idea of Francis of Assisi, which by and by, the result of strongly focussed contemplation, called the blood to the surface and procured the red splashes on the hand of the Saint.

Perhaps Aggie's intense concentration on the performance of the promise Willy had made her might have something of the same effect? Her obstination combined with his; their mutual desire which had enabled his passion to clothe itself with the simulacra of unessential matter and his spirit to assume the likeness she knew him by, even to induce the thin Cloud of Witness that supported his appearance, the voices of Whitefoord and the telephone message of Dawson.

The unconscious medium repudiated the ghost theory. She had been naturally convinced at the time that it was Willy in flesh and blood who had come to her. That was because she had desired his company so deeply and held the thought of him so tightly for several months that the mould of her impressions could receive no other; the frame of her mind was so terribly ready for him that, on the spur of the moment, it would have been impossible for her to adjust it differently and see clear.

But exaltation of all kinds, spiritual and sensuous, dies down—cannot last. Advantage had been taken—there was no better expression for it than the vulgar one....and later, immediately perhaps, had come the revulsion, the bitterness of realised self-deception and the piteous attempts to make a good job of it! Injured vanity, self-sought loneliness, the brooding, the dreary seeking for excuses and ways out, had turned Aggie into a savage, a mad dog, under her silken soft exterior that had taken them all in.

She ought to have been treated quite differently, the insulation she had practised broken down for her. She had willed that it should be broken down, witness her dream message to Lady Maisry, and Lady Maisry should have accepted the office and taxed her with her difficulties and helped her to solve them the moment she got down to Ilvercote, instead of leaving the poor girl to fend for herself.

Did Mary get the people of Bethlehem to believe in her story?

And, supposed she failed, what sort of a mentality had the woman who stood at the foot of the Cross with her friends, who knew? Were they kind and patient to her?

Willy's beauty of character, his self-abnegation, his dreadful fate ought to have made his womenfolk kinder to his wife.

It was not too late. She went out of her room and found Gussy.

'Let us go down to the lake and see if we cannot get Aggie to come in now.'

★★★★★★

It was necessary to drag the lake for them. They found Aggie first. Her long hair was held fast in Peter's hand.

And the kind but uncultured fellow from Australia possesses Ilvercote, and the haunted room is still shown, for he does not care to sleep or live there, but spends most of his time on his yacht, racing, and taking risks...

The Night of No Weather

She had got herself there, she did not know how, for she did everything nowadays like a person in a dream. And beautifully attired in half-mourning, she felt ill at ease and nervous; she had nearly lost the habit of putting on a quite, quite low-necked dress, of telling her maid to call a cab, and of being driven half across London to spend a few hours in someone else's house. But a little more than a year ago she had done this night; before the death of her mother and the subsequent exasperating and revolting will case that was now settled, so much to her disadvantage that she hardly knew yet whether she would again be able to turn round, let alone go out.

As she had been *persona grata*, one for whom hostesses scrambled, because of her looks, some little wit inherited from her mother, and the prestige of her father's name—he had been rather a prominent figure in his day—she had had the *entrée* to all sorts of good houses. She still had that, thank God. The law *tracasseries* had not in the least reflected on her morals, though slightly, perhaps, on her discretion.

But it was a little difficult to face them all, to take up that kind of life again, to begin the indigestible lunches in the middle of the day, the crowded teas, the set dinners; and after her severe illness, the late hours, so that often, at midnight, she would be careering round and round the misty masses of shrubs called squares, along the echoing empty streets of sightless unlit houses where all the sensible people were lying asleep, till at last her conveyance would draw up at one great lighted portal or another, floored with red baize and studded with flunkeys, past whose majestic figures the solemn dance music rolled out towards her and invited her to the amusement proper to her age and station.

And now, because 'all that' was over and she was only thirty, her friends had forced her to begin again. It had to be done some time.

57

She had ordered a suitable dress, white with some black about it or, rather black with some white, and had accepted Lady Bellair's invitation to her ball in Belgrave Square. Or was it the Dorimers'? She felt a bit confused as one does in the season when, because there are two or three things a night, one simply does not at times know where one is.

She had come there, wherever it was. She was sitting in the marble hall; through the festoons of real green leaves and real roses that hung straight down from the ceiling she watched the maze of dancers pass and repass, and laughed to think that, for a moment, she had had a doubt. Of course, it was Lord and Lady Bellair, her great friends, who had insisted that Miss Ethne Aragon should, at their ball, break her long social fast. She had come on condition that she should not be worried to dance or talk, but just loaf about and take it easy. She was to be a voluntary wallflower; she was handsome enough for people to admit her validity of the plea of freewill.

Maisie Bellair, a pretty young hostess, yearning to have plenty of time in which herself to dance, had taken her friend at her word. Miss Aragon had made her quiet, unnoticed entry and, having shaken hands with Lord Bellair and Lady Bellair's mother, Lady Masboro', had backed out of the circle of potential introductions and sat now in the midst of this whirlpool of slowly gyrating bodies—there was no 'Kitchen Lancers' at the Bellairs'—as alone as if she had been on her native moors of Northumberland. It was a regular system of heart-beats—systole and diastole—the way she used to hear her own heart going on at times, when she had been worried beyond bearing.

The flux and reflux of the dancers entering in and passing out of bliss, the music—now ceasing, the hot special air of the ballroom seeming to stand still, the rustling, conscious dresses swirling round her, submerging her—then the wailing, grovelling notes of introduction summoning them back, the low thudding of the first bar of 'The Choristers'—taken from a hymn—sliding along the polished parquet floor like the ground-swell of heavy, significant, advancing waves or, translated into colours, like the smoke of a nascent heather fire that would soon have its way, as the music gained, increased: all-pervading and enduring. . . .

She was alone again, staring down, at her feet, along the empty floor that rayed out to the wide hall, to the outer door where the flunkeys in their red coats and white stockings were silhouetted, stamped upon the night. . . .

During the periodic human flushings she saw, now swallowed up in the crowd, now resurgent, the faces of persons of her acquaintance. There were friends even; but none of either category seemed to be aware of Ethne Aragon, sitting there in her beautiful new dress. That great man, the new attorney-general, though she saw him seldom now since his rise to extreme eminence, had always been pleased to have a chat with Miss Aragon whenever he happened to meet her, and he had made a point of calling on her two or three times during her mother's long illness.

Yet now he stood for moment between two dances, alone, and never raised his keen eyes to hers; it was as if she was an empty chair. Now and again good dancers, to whom she, Ethne Aragon, in virtue of their proficiency, had been accustomed to give three or four dances a night, came and stood quite close to her, knitting their brows, consulting their shirt-cuffs, making up their tale of partners. Girls like herself, came and stood shamefacedly alone for an agonised space; but, unlike her, the whole forces of their being seemed concentrated on an effort to seem careless whether they were asked to dance or no. Some of them were acquaintances of hers, but their non-recognition of her did not seem so very odd; women have no time to waste on other women in that deadly game which a ball is.

The reason she supposed, that no man asked her to dance was that she looked weak and disinclined to adventure herself in the crowd, and as the business of a dance is dancing, none was Good Samaritan enough to care to sit down and have a chat with an invalid who ought not to have been there. So, to avoid catching the eye of a socially useless person, they just looked through her.

It was a horrible sensation. She felt as if she were a dead person watching the ways of the humanity she had recently cast off. She ought not to have been persuaded to come. Why did she not now go? She had no inducement to stay, nothing to keep her.... She stayed on, she supposed, because it would have been so easy to go. She was like a man who has purchased a lethal weapon with which he can commit suicide the moment he finds life unbearable, and only delays because he has now the means of departure so ready to his hand.

Life was just like a party—in her case a very dull party. Everyone considers that he has a perfect right to leave any such gathering and go home the moment it ceases to interest him, supposing that no one else's pleasure is dependant upon his remaining. It was the same with life! She herself had always maintained the right of every person born to settle the date of his own death. That was what it came to, the liberty of the subject. She had seen to it, as far as she was concerned. She had a little sachet in the drawer at home which she had managed to get, while she was in training at The Bevan, from a fellow-nurse, who drugged. . . . and who succeeded in finishing herself neatly. . .

Suicide was not a crime. . .

******

The music had stopped without her noticing it. She had been occupied. . . . They would all be back again in a moment! It was rather disagreeable to be so constantly overlooked but she was getting used to it. Besides, she was just going to take her leave of the world as represented by social occasions like this. She would never go to a dance again. She would just watch the nonsensical pageant through again and see if any more friends chose to ignore her!

Yes, here was Laura La Primaudie, the rich little American widow, her brother-in-law's great friend, who, according to his advice and after old Mrs Aragon's death, had taken the long lease of Westerly Lodge off Miss Aragon's hands, to her supposed benefit. And Florence, Mrs La Primaudie's sister-in-law.

And with them, sure enough, was Edward! He had to go out just now alone; Maud was having another baby. Ethne's sister was one of the sensible ones who drove her husband forth as much as possible on these occasions; she liked the La Primaudie women to be the ones to amuse Edward; they were safe, decent sort of women and rich enough to give him a good time.

How was it that Edward had managed to get into the house without her seeing him? How could he be there so long without coming into her view? How had he got there at all?

He dawdled. He was showing something—some bit of decoration—to Mrs La Primaudie. Ethne watched him. He was bound to pass her sooner or later. She had not set eyes on him since her mother's death. He was really rather good-looking—a touch of Jewish blood that ran to nice curly hair and quite a good figure, except that a love of good dinners was beginning to produce the usual results.

He was a University man and did not look like a shopman—as he practically was, though he claimed the right to call himself an architect—at any rate a high-class designer and vendor of decorations. That must have been how he had got to know Maisie Bellair—decorating her house. And of course, Maud was a social asset and Maud's money, of which that practical person had known how to secure such a liberal share. . . . .It must have been some such way as that, for Ethne had always considered the great London hostess to be her special friend and, although there had been no open quarrel, so to speak, for Edward and his sharp solicitor had managed to get the matter settled out of court as soon as they had worried her into her long illness, Maisie Bellair was certainly aware that there had been unpleasantness.

Perhaps it was Maisie's policy for her? Possibly? Maisie was very sensible, and, having so much money, did not quite know the value of it, and how a few hundreds, more or less, make a prodigious difference. Had she ever wondered in her purse-fed security how her young friend, if she recovered, was going to live?

Well, if Edward came and spoke to her, she would speak to him. She was his relation, after all. She had never really taken to Edward, but she had been quite nice to him on the day when Maud brought him triumphantly home to Westerly Lodge as the captive of her bow and spear. Her mother had, however, frankly loathed and distrusted him. She had repeated very often:

'Ethne, you are the only one left. Do see if you can't present me with a son-in-law that I can like.'

And to that eye-opening phrase on Edward's dealings with her as son-in-law and executor the shrewd old lady had added:

'But I am afraid you won't marry at all. You are too fond of pets.'

★★★★★★

Ethne could not see very far into this psychological distinction between pets of one kind and pets of another, but she was ready to admit that had more dependent animals, considering the size of her London garden, than anyone she had ever heard of. This was what the old lady meant. Her daughter had not inherited her sense of humour. Pets certainly monopolised a good deal of Ethne's attention and thoughts, but hardly, she imagined, to the extent of rendering her impervious to the attentions of the various suitable young men who had *not* asked her to marry them.

Maud, her younger sister, had had heaps of offers, and Maud certainly hated her. It was Maud's respectable rule to speak of all dogs as 'he' and all cats as 'she'. Ethne, on the other hand, allowed cats to sleep on her bed and in it, her owl to sit on her nose and scratch it, and her bulldog to bite her. She had nursed her cats and dogs through illnesses and had sat up for whole nights with them, and when, at last, her efforts had proved unavailing, she had herself borne them weeping, to the lethal chamber.

Even the early senility of pedigree animals had been taken seriously by her. When Freddy and Wuff Wuff had become tottery, their backbones all knobbly and ridgy and their eyes sunken, she had spared them the irreparable outrage of Time and had herself carried them to their expensive and painless deaths. She had received, standing tense like a mourner, the last pathetic, almost grateful glance upwards of the doomed one as the box lid closed upon it.

She knew that animals do not dread death, although they resist it until their instinct bids them to accept it in lieu of a dreary and diseased length of days. This meekness of theirs surely corresponds to the zest for suicide, regarded as a solution and a refuge by overwrought human beings.

******

She was very weak. Tears came into her eyes when she thought of all these deaths.

Roy, the great white bulldog, of whom she had been almost afraid, had died in the fullness of life and the prime of his ugliness—poisoned. The tradesmen had not liked him and pilferers had feared him. The semi-detached house where they lived—her mother and she—had been considered very liable to the attacks of burglars, and the old lady, timid in the house at night while her daughter led the life that kept her abroad sometimes until the small hours, had insisted on the dog being made to sleep out of doors.

His kennel had stood in the back of the garden of Westerly Lodge, at the end of a long passage leading from the gate to the back premises. Ethne coming home alone from this or that gathering, had always counted on seeing the white form of the dog glimmering at the end of the long, flagged path bordered by shrubs that ended in the kennel. She would look for his slow, deliberate uprising, as he heard the click of the handle and the thud of the closing gate, and for his frantic, fulsome welcome when he recognised her.

He would stand there, spreading his legs out to back and front, stiff with some hours of sleep. He did not hurry, for he knew that, rain or shine, she would come to pat him, and hold his muzzle and say goodnight. . .

She had had something else to notice on her way to the kennel—something quite unique and charming in the way of pets. In a large roomy enclosure of wire, in which a man could stand upright, lived a little brown owl with very bright eyes. Ann Veronica in her abode must have noticed on Miss Aragon's way back from Roy's kennel, and before she started to go up the five steps to the front door. There was a couple of wooden bars stretched across the cage for Ann Veronica to sidle along, and sometimes, on dark nights, it was not possible to make her out.

She was not white, like Roy; in the daytime her russet feathers alone shone like gold. But when she had not been able to see the little owl, Ethne only had to put her finger through the wire wall and to make a friendly noise. Then Ann Veronica would immediately rustle up and answer, hooting a little piteously and hoarsely—a faint cry like a complaint. Then, if Ethne repeated her remark, Ann Veronica would repeat hers and grow very excited and, finally, shriek out so madly that her mistress had to leave her lest all the neighbours were disturbed and complained next day.

But one morning she found Ann Veronica cold and stiff in the aviary.

Roy—Ann Veronica—Freddy—Wuff Wuff! And others with other ridiculous names, whose demise, accidental or providential, was each a separate wrench! . . . Why should she sit in a ballroom and remember them all with such terrible distinctness, this night of all nights? Surely there was comfort in the thought that all these loved creatures had died before Mrs Aragon had passed away, while Ethne was still mistress of the house and possessed old, devoted servants who helped her to look after them.

The animals that were still alive and well when the crash came had had to be pensioned off with those very old servants, unpensioned, who also were lost to Ethne in the upheaval. She had only the horrid, neutral, uninterested, service-flat maids now.

Edward had managed it all. He had come in like a hungry lion as soon as the breath was out of Mrs Aragon's body, roaring for the will, for stocks and bonds, plates and furniture, jewellery and pictures, as the Law—more or less—allowed him to do. He had rectified abuses, deleted the old ways, the old servants: sold the house that he had hardly ever entered except for a meal. He had secured the lion's share for his wife and, having made everything shipshape, left his sister-in-law thoroughly lonely, uncomfortable, and wretched.

It had been old Mrs Aragon's instinct to dread the selfish iconoclast. During her lifetime she had managed to keep him out of her affairs, but, five minutes after death, her desire was a dead letter. A clean sweep the good Edward had made, carried out at the expense of all but himself, his wife, and his child, and with a merciless precision that daunted and silenced his simple sister-in-law. He treated her like an idiot, if not as something of a rogue; he had fiercely disregarded any single wish of hers that was not bolstered up with all the forces of the law.

In her lifetime Mrs Aragon had tried, rather futilely, to safeguard her one unmarried daughter and make life comfortable and pleasant for her. But everything she did had turned out worse for Ethne instead of better, and better for Edward and Maud instead of worse. She had come in for so very much less than her mother had intended. A friend of hers—the attorney-general—who had so lately failed to notice her, on hearing of the result of the compromise to avoid publicity that Edward had worked for, had remarked that Edward Arnold was considered in his profession to be a very 'keen' man of business. She had often wondered if he meant by that Edward was a little inclined to be dishonest.

✶✶✶✶✶✶

Well, anyway, Edward and Maud had come off a great deal better than her mother had desired. But then, as the same right honourable gentleman had also said, unless a will is very wisely made it is so easy to misinterpret it, and Edward had employed another very keen gentleman, a solicitor, to work the matter for him. . . . The women of the family in these days, before the granting of the vote, are apt, the great man said, to go to the wall, especially when they are unmarried and have no one to look after them.

He seemed, indeed, to think that it was more decent that an unmarried woman *should* go to the wall—preferable to law-suits and unpleasantness before the public; better, as it were, for public morality. Because, officially, families are supposed to be united and it was better that an unmarried woman should go a little short than that the spectacle of a litigious family should be presented to the public. . . .

✶✶✶✶✶✶

However, this might be, it had been borne in upon Ethne, less than an hour after the death, in a few well-chosen words from Maud, that she would not have enough money to keep up Westerly Lodge now. Yet Ethne had given the dying woman a clear promise to go on living in the house that her father had died in, and her mother assured her, almost with her last breath, that she had made that feasible by testamentary disposition. That promise had been brushed aside. Edward, without much discussion, had set about disposing of the lease for the benefit of the estate and, whilst she had been in the Nursing Home, he had taken a flat for her—a flat where they would not allow animals

64

to be kept.

★★★★★★

On came the dancers again in a wide stream temporarily circumscribed by the arches that led out of the ballroom, then flowing out free again, spreading into the corridors, the hall and the lobbies, settling in two by two into the lodges of flowers, the cosy cornets screened by leaves. The white-draperied girls of her own period—her own year—she really knew them all and their flirts too!—floated by her beaming with satisfaction, carrying on just as if Ethne did not exist. She felt absurdly out of it. . . .

Edward passed her again. He was heated and put his handkerchief to his brows furtively. A mature business man of forty-five, he kept up his dancing. On his arm was Mrs La Primaudie, his tenant—her tenant. Ethne had to get her share of the rent of Westerly—Edward doled it out to her.

Now, here she was, brooding, going over again in thought those unpleasant matters that had made her ill. She would be bringing on one of her headaches. She really must not; the doctor had warned her that she could not afford another breakdown. . .

Better go home. Why did she not go home? What kept her here? Not pleasure, certainly! She was not enjoying herself in the very least. And, as for duty, she had done her duty by Society all these years, and now Society neglected her, gave her the cold shoulder—no shoulder at all!

She was fully justified in leaving. She ought to leave out of pride. And out of boredom. She felt a wild longing to hear Ann Veronica's shriek, to see the white bulldog shimmering through the dark, to feel Freddy softly brush his body against her thinly covered ankles. Ten to one he was already crouching up to the front door, waiting to be let in, pining for his warm niche beside her pillow. . . .

She would, she must, walk out, get into a hansom, and go. She would not trouble her hostess, dancing herself now and difficult to find, with goodbyes, nor yet Edward. He had seen her, that was certain. How nasty of him! He ought really to have known better and tried to keep up appearances before the world. It would have been quite easy, for she had not talked in her Nursing Home, and even if she had been going about, she would not have—she was a lady. Nobody beside herself and the attorney-general—though that was a serious item—knew how badly he and Maud had behaved.

Edward might easily have given himself the trouble of crossing the floor and shaking hands with his sister-in-law and just telling her how Maud was. Mrs La Primaudie would have released him for a moment or two; she and the Aragons had been on calling terms in the old, gay days at Westerly, where she lived now and entertained quite a different set of people—all except Edward, who was there every other day on an average And Ethne herself, though she had not cared to call, was on friendly terms; she owed Mrs La Primaudie no grudge for having taken Westerly Lodge if it had to go, and Mrs La Primaudie was always nice to her when they met.

It was growing intolerable. She must make a move. She could see, from where she sat, the wide-open door of this great palace of a house, belching light and music out into the quiet June night. The tall electric standard lamp opposite glared into the porch, filled by splendid footmen standing easily about...till their employers should have had enough of it.

People were beginning to leave. She noticed one pair who, to her knowledge, had a standing intrigue that had lasted over a year, the man clapping on his hat with a slight reverberation, the woman, lightly veiled, pulling the flap of her cloak together. They hastened forward, deprecatingly, and breaking up the group of servants as little as might be, and passed out into the open....lovers escaping to their bliss....

They were right. Outside was freedom—freedom from the oppression of this foetid ballroom air that was nearly choking her. She put her hand to her throat and rose, feeling a difficulty in drawing her legs together. She was numb—quite numb—yet conscious of a wild straining to be free. For, outside, once across that wide porch, down those three majestic steps of a throne, lay deliverance, the end of oppression and the quiet airs of Home. Yes, over there, beyond some streets and squares and the main road and a hill to go up, she had a nest to fly to as well as the guilty two who had flown. Love too....her mother sitting up for her... the hearty wag of a dog's tail...

Her limbs were heavy and ached, her disinclination to move amounted to positive pain. She saw a taxi-cab waiting, a little on one side, at the end of the strip of red carpet, and made for it. Oddly enough the group of footmen did not move to let her pass. There was room enough however.

★★★★★★

Presently she found herself walking up the steep hill that led to Westerly Lodge. She had always been used to dismiss her cab at the foot and walk up the hill to spare the poor horse. She did so now; the habit had remained.

It was fine; at least it was not raining. There may have been stars. There was no wind, for not a leaf moved. Neither cold nor warm: a night in Fairy Land where, as everyone knows there are no seasons: a London night of no weather. Like all Londoners, she did not trouble to look up at the sky; the pavements and the sudden queer varieties of the flagstones were her barometer. They were all dry tonight and struck very cold to her slippered feet. The tarred roadway, where the three roads meet on the very hub of the hill, gleamed dully. The branches of the black trees in Blundell House garden leaned over the palings on the other side of the road where there was no pavement, only a narrow path.

It was lightish, but it was still night, for everyone was still asleep—the way they are when you come back from balls—and the blinds of the houses were drawn like heavy lids over closed eye. . . .Not a bird cheeped, nor the owls in Holland Park that were wont to visit Ann Veronica and hoot at her. All conscious life was withdrawn and retired within its borders—within itself. She was alone in the world, picking her way, trading delicately on the hard pavements, a slight, stooping figure, yet conscious of an almost unearthly independence.

She was not light-headed, yet her feet seemed to her hardly to rest upon the ground. She was buoyant at the thought of what was going to happen to her, and her sense of detachment was so intense that she felt as if she might rise indefinitely into space—that she was merely held down by her moiety of mortality. The heaviness that had overcome her in the ballroom an hour ago was gone. . .

She breasted the hill and stood where the three streets meet under the tall lamp-post. Just as she ceased for a moment to place one foot before the other it struck the hour from the steeple of Kensington Church, a chill, metallic sound, beating faintly on dead, indifferent ears. Time did not matter anymore.

She saw the two policemen standing as usual where the alley between hose big, seignorial houses in vast groves of tall trees, forks off. She knew it must be two o'clock in the morning, or thereabouts, for it was at that hour that those two met on the changing of their beat.

They did not as usual acknowledge her salutation. It caused her no surprise tonight. Everything was different. She minded nothing now anymore—not even Edward's behaviour at the ball or the attorney-general's. She was out of it all—done. All she wanted now was to get in and lie down; this mortal weariness was coming on again. . . .

She turned the rounded corner of Westerly Villa—there was Westerly House between her and Westerly Lodge, her own place, with the name plate on the plaster pillar of the gate and the prickly holly bush hanging over it, like a stone pine of the South beside a Roman temple. It came forward over the pavement and formed a natural roof for the wayfarer, the bill-sticker, the loafer, and the beggar in rainy weather.

Out of a sense of altruism she had cultivated the shape and growth of this particular tree to be, precisely, a refuge. She had persuaded her mother, as far as it was possible, to withstand the importunity of the Inspector of Nuisances, who pressed her continuously to have it clipped. Edward, naturally, had backed up that pertinacious official. He declared that the bush broke the line of the street and helped to muffle up the approach to the front door in a way that made it unsafe and unseemly for his giddy sister-in-law to come home night after night, as she was in the habit of doing. She stood, he said, the chance of being set upon by any burglar, whose presence would be masked by the shrubs and that bush. No policeman could possibly flash his bull's-eye properly up the flagged walk and to the steps and door beyond.

Ethne had stood out against him, but certainly his representations, made so constantly, ended by making her nervous. The negligent stillness of the night awed her. She longed for a breath of wind to lift the swathe of her hair or to stir the boughs that hung over the walls of her garden. She stood outside the gate, peering, like a burglar contemplating a new hunting ground, through the interstices of the iron lacework of the garden gate, trying to pierce the darkness and fathom the new secretiveness of the Early Victorian villa that she imagined herself to have left only a few hours before and that was going, she felt, once she should lay her hand on the brass knob of the gate and entered in, to strike her as tremendously altered.

Dense, impenetrable, smothered in a faint, dusty mist, unpierced as yet by the rays of the imminent dawn, the little suburban garden lay. She saw the guelder rose-bush with its heavy white bullets of flowers sagging across the path; the acacia tree that straggled down and shut in all the smaller boughs and their leafage. Somewhere beyond those shadows lay the broad steps, carefully hearthstoned by faithful maids, that she would have to ascend and stand, exposed to the eyes of lurking thieves shrouded in the bushes, waiting for the moment to rush forward and force her key from her hand, and thus gain an entrance into the house. That was what Edward was always telling her. . . .

She thought over all these contingencies like one living in a dream that bears no consequences. Her fingers closed on the handle of the gate, and it rattled slightly as usual as she turned it in the socket to enter. The tangibility of the first object she seemed to herself to have touched since she left the Bellairs' gave her firmness. She entered and looked up the walk towards the steps and the ugly, *stucco* house, clumsily bossed and ornamented, its Victorian decorations now submerged under successive coats of paint.

It looked tonight as if it had been freshly done; she had no idea that this white rough-cast would look so well and stay clean so long. And there was a little dreamy globe for electric light above the porch, showing so faintly on the strange blue door that she could hardly be sure of it. Changes! Why? Who had made them since she had been out? No matter; she must go along to the back and say goodnight to Roy.

She turned aside to the narrow passage running along the side of the house which tradesmen used and at the end of which the bulldog's kennel stood. A low, brick wall was all that separated Westerly Lodge from Westerly House next door. The cats were fond of sitting on it. They found they could so easily drop off into the other garden when disinclined for the society of dogs or other curious and disagreeable persons.

They were all of them there now. . . .a greyish row of quiet, scarcely discernible shapes, their thick, smoke-coloured fur showing faint against the damp brickwork in this London false dawn. And beyond—beyond, there was Roy waiting for her!. . .

The great bulldog's form loomed whitely in the deep shadow of the privet bush that had sown the ground round him with white stars. With his short legs firmly planted, pulling a little on his chain, he stood waiting much as usual, but more patiently, for his chain did not rattle. He was as quiet as he had been that awful week when the poison of the burglars was beginning to tell upon him and had nearly done its work corroding his vitals, eating into them with the deadly red lead from which, when it is once introduced into the system, there is no escape.

She dragged her heavy feet towards him. What a long time it took her to get there!

And all along the wall sat the grey breed of cats—Freddy and Teuf-Teuf, Wuffy and the others. Those that had sickened and gone into the lethal boxes and those two last survivors that had found a home with her old nurse! That little squat motherly one, at the end, with the green eyes glimmering that were quite wrong, must be Teuf-Teuf. A chauffeur in Paris had named her long ago when cars were new. They all sat stretched along the wall, their paws tidily disposed in front of them to suit the narrowness of the space. Their haunch-bones stood out sharply; they looked as if they had been mummified, or turned to stone like the grey pillars at Carnac.

She laid her hand upon the back of one after another as she walked past them. Perhaps because her hand was gloved, she felt no thrill of a living body under it. They did not respond at all. That upset her a little. Normally Teuf-Teuf would have bowed slightly, while Wuffy would have stood right up and arched his back with pleasure.

But she was in haste to get to Roy, who stood there stiffly, not barking, waiting proudly till she could leave these others whom in his strength he disdained. She must make haste. But on her left hand was the great cage of Ann Veronica. In the darkness she could not see the little owl, but she knew that if she spoke Ann Veronica would answer as usual. Generally, when there was no moon, she had to address the owl first, but tonight she experienced some difficulty in using her voice. She had not spoken for so long. She stopped at the side of the cage, making up her mind to speak. . .

Strange! She could not hear either. She could not hear Ann veronica fidget on her long perch that ran across the cage and ended, fixed, if Ethne stood close up against it, within an inch of her cheek.

Ah. . . .she must have managed to make some sound, for the little owl answered faintly, as it were from a great distance. Again! But it seemed more like a human sound and to come from even father off.

Ethne gave it up. The unreasoning depression—for of course she had just been to a party and had enjoyed herself so much—the craven lassitude that was coming over her, submerging her, drowning her as surely as if she were sinking to the bottom of some sea, was too overpowering to be fought against. She made no step farther, though indeed she had not forgotten the bulldog. He was still standing there waiting. But he would excuse her, for she was so tired. He would just wait a little longer and then turn round and round and lie down in the kennel again as he had done every night for nearly a week after he was poisoned and had died, so that they had not suspected foul play.

She turned back. The moon had risen and was shining in her eyes. The grey, quiescent shapes were still there, easy to distinguish, flattened out on to the plateau of the low, brick wall, indifferent, not even watching her. Well, they were all of them getting older, and for her part it seemed as if she could not be troubled so much as to raise her hand and touch them again. . . .Her feet, scraping the gravel, bore her slowly along round the pillar at the corner of the steps of the door. There was a handrail on the right side, but she did not need to use it, the return of every step was perfectly clear in the now outrageous moonlight. She avoided brushing the jasmine fronds that were trained with immense care to the wall on the left.

She could not see quite plain, but it was by an immense effort of will that she inserted the tiny key that hung from her wrist and pushed it home firmly; she knew that, otherwise, the door did not yield at once Edward had not changed the latch for Mrs La Primaudie or asked her, Ethne, for the key which she held! How then did Mrs La Primaudie get in?

The blue door opened easily enough now, however, and with a last conscious effort she flung the door wide and entered.

The hall was dark as usual. She felt her way to the spot over the tall chair where the switch was.

She could not, however, find that. No matter, there was a light under the dining-room door. She could almost see through the door. Someone had left the light burning! Her mother could not, surely, be sitting there still? Long hours after midnight.

She must be sure to put the light out before she got to bed—by moonlight, if not daylight. . . .For it would soon be day. Events were moving quickly now. It was near the end. The silver cord was loosed. Time and Space were not. All this was written and she had now no fear, no doubts, no self-consciousness. . .

The dining-room door had opened swiftly, she had merely willed it to open . . . .Yes, there sat her poor old mother by the right-hand corner of the dining-table, where she always sat now for her meals, for her card-play, to talk and listen to her few friends. Her cards lay in front of her now, but she was not looking at them. She was looking up at her daughter with the bleared, kind, ancient look of patience and love with which she always greeted that dear prodigal who was so dissipated and went out every other night.

Ethne Aragon did not know whether she said it or whether she only thought it—that she had come home. . . .and that it was not so very late.

★★★★★★

Laura La Primaudie's sister-in-law ran up the steps of Westerly Lodge from the taxi-cab in which she had come to take her sister on to the Hirschs' dance. Mrs La Primaudie opened the blue door herself, came right out, and stood on the step under the little electric globe, buttoning her glove.

'Edward not with you?' Florence said.

'Been. I say, that Miss Aragon Committed suicide last night,' Mrs la Primaudie said. 'In her flat. She was dressing for Lady Bellair's party, which she declared she was quite well enough to go to. Her dress was laid out on the bed. She seems to have died quite alone, on the sofa under the window, with that great electric standard lamp opposite the flats shining right in her face. The maid who found her thought she had been murdered. Poor thing!'

Florence who was older than Laura said:

'Ah!' as if it had been something she had remotely expected. 'Murdered!' Then she added: 'It isn't the sort of thing that's likely to make Edward very popular. If I were you. . . .'

Mrs La Primaudie shivered a little, though it was June.

'Lise has given notice,' she said. 'she says there is something wrong with this house. . . . .And Florence, before the Bellair's ball, they think it happened! And yet, you know—all last night—while I was supposed to be enjoying myself—I could have sworn that Ethne Aragon was there, and it took away all my pleasure. I didn't see her. But she seemed to be in one of those flower alcoves—you know—in the big hall. And when I got back here, the light in the dining-room was not out. And I had the oddest feeling. . . . .I almost called to Edward to come in for a second and cheer me up. She may have been dying just then. They say she could have taken the poison about nine in the evening and it acted slowly. . . .All alone she was. . . .not even a cat or dog for company! She was to have rung for one of the flat servants to do her up. But she never did. They thought she had managed it herself and gone. Of course, she wasn't fit. It was not till this morning that they found her on the sofa, with her hand on the sill. By two, the doctor said, she was certainly dead. It's rather horrid for Edward.'

'It was rather horrid of Edward,' the sister answered, and when they were both in the cab, she completed the sentence that she had begun and not finished before.

'If I were you, Laura, I don't think I would have much more to do with Edward, he's no good to you to flirt with, really! Can't. And he will certainly be under a cloud for it.'

'I don't think,' Mrs La Primaudie said determinedly, 'that I would have anything more to do with him if he were in sunshine for the rest of his days, with no wife and pots of money—blood money! I should always be seeing the eyes of that poor thing looking over his shoulder!'

The Telegram

Her mother was dead. Her life stood altered.

She would be no poorer, it was not that. She was an orphan, and all her mother had had came to her. That meant seventy thousand pounds, plate, linen and the freehold of a fine old house in Lower Seymour Street, that they had moved into a year before the old lady died.

Things were no more altered socially than they were altered pecuniarily, for the Damers' set naturally corresponded, as sets do, with their postal district, and Miss Alice Damer could therefore continue to command an entrance into the best circles. Only she realised that she must henceforth enjoy all these good things to the tune of a paid companion, having no poor and amenable relations handy whom she could draft into the household economy, and afterwards snub into a colourless, bare existence.

She was thirty-five, and her years did not weigh on her, except mentally. The first faint physical signs of the debacle were, so far, evident to herself alone, and then only in moods of unusual depression. She was still young enough to need a companion. Her pretty red-gold hair was as red as gold, as pretty as ever, her visits to her dentist as few, her eyes as deep, and her step as elastic, although she had given up dancing. She had made this sacrifice more from a sense of fitness, as a concession to the needs of the young girls coming up all round her, and who deserved their turn on the floor, than of social necessity.

As a matter of fact, she had never been really fond of that over-energetic, disordering form of amusement. She loved the world and going up and down in it immensely, and her way of enjoying parties was to sit out if it was a dance, away from the music if it was a concert, and in the back of the box if it was a play. She was a flirt.

Not an outrageous, noisy, ill-bred flirt, but what is known as a quiet flirt, with many strong and efficient strings to her bow. Did one of them, being after all only catgut or mere man, snap occasionally—that is to say, get married out of the circle of her charm—Alice, in her quiet way, promptly renewed the string, and supplied herself with a new admirer, as good at fetching and carrying as the old. In her mind that was the chief use of admirers—to prevent one's *looking* neglected—of course one never really was!

She was a woman of many "affairs"; she liked living, not exactly in hot water, but in water at least warm, and was seldom seen talking to women, though she was quite nice to them, as intrusive but law-permitted aliens in the *pays du coeur*. None of her friends would have dared to ask her to a ladies' lunch, or any over-womaned party; a man had always to be "got for Alice," else she would have been hurt, and quite unable to play her part properly. She was unused to, unversed in her own sex.

On the other hand, she played fair and never took other women's men, or encouraged their husbands to play the pretty game with her. People said that for her, that she never made women unhappy, only men. She was never very sorry for a man's love-troubles, for she had a theory that a hopeless passion or two did a man no harm and that the more he proposed the merrier—for him. She never told anyone how many offers she had refused. Men often did propose to her, and she refused them all, and boasted that she had never been engaged for even an hour, and that no man had ever kissed her. The bloom was not off Alice, unless so much mental coming and going in her courts had produced some such subtle effect.

"Why should I marry?" she used to say to Everard Jenkyns (good old Welsh family), when he importuned her to relax her rule in his favour, and even go so far as making the vast experiment of marriage with him as her partner. "There is no earthly hurry."

"No, but perhaps a heavenly one," he had inanely replied.

"I may never marry at all. Girls, economically, don't need to marry as they used to, and at any rate I am independent so far as money goes."

"So, the way is clear for you to marry for love."

"I don't think I shall ever fall in love."

"Then take a man you like—and you like me?" Everard was not at that time sufficiently far gone in love to make him inattentive to, and unappreciative of the use and value of "cheek," in discussing such matters with his princess.

"Yes, I like you; but, as you know, I don't love you. And I'm so made that I must be quite sure in my own mind that I am absolutely, positively incapable of loving madly before I let myself go with anyone, even you. Don't you see, in the interests of morality, one must be sure of oneself, or there might be catastrophe, with a strong nature like mine?"

"No," said Everard patiently and earnestly. "There would, I am sure, be no danger of that with you. Your husband might feel perfectly safe in your hands."

"Thanks. Why do you say that?"

"Because the power to flirt never implies the power to love, I am afraid."

"Well, Everard, you can't say that I flirt with you!" she exclaimed noisily.

"Oh, no. Your knowing that I am desperately, dully serious about you protects me a little, and you do pay me the doubtful compliment of taking no trouble to attract me. You honestly never put your best foot foremost with me, or pose like a heroine to your most humble valet."

"Yes," Alice agreed, laughing a little bitterly. "I promise you never to encourage you in any way. I would let you see me with my hair in curlers, if I wore them! Anything to convince you of the purity of my intentions. I simply will not have you say that I lead you on or encourage you."

"My God, Alice! I don't say it! I know well enough I am a d——d fool and have nothing whatever to go on."

"A fool to love me?"

"A fool because I am a lonely man and don't like being a lonely man, and yet this feeling of mine towards you will keep me so, so far as I can see. I don't suppose I shall ever marry. I know I shan't. That's what you've done, Alice, and I may just as well go away and make my will in your favour, for I shall never have any wife or child to leave my money to. I feel that it will be so."

"Really, my poor Everard "—she tried very hard not to look flattered—"this is most sad. I couldn't have believed there was such fidelity left in this wicked world, and to tell you the truth I don't believe it possible, even now. I'm really not vain enough—if I *am* cruel."

"Not so very vain, and not a bit cruel. I honestly believe if you thought you could get up any sort of feeling for me, you'd say so. You never will say it to me—but to someone else, I suppose. You are human like everyone else. It's all rot about not being capable of loving;

every woman is or is able to think she is, and that's enough in a great many cases. Oh, you'll find the man sooner or later, and I—well, I shall wish you every happiness and be godfather to the kids. Nice little flirt's kids, with pretty hair like yours. Now, I'd better go away to the Temple and make that will, as I've quite made up my mind to die a bachelor."

"Nonsense," said Alice sharply, more touched than she liked to own; "I won't even be friends with you if you go on like that. Leave things open. Not for me, of course. It must be quite understood that I don't accept any such sacrifice of your life as waiting for me would entail. Believe me, I know myself, and I know, somehow, deep down, that I shall never fall in love with you. That being the case, don't you think I should be really behaving rather badly if I allowed you to think that you could ever melt me by faithful service, and little things like that?"

"All right. Beggars don't choose. You shall have the faithful service all the same, and it shall not hope to melt you. Will that suit you?"

"We'll leave it at that, then," said Alice, permitting the young and promising barrister to kiss her hand, and devote his wits and energies and the rest of his life to her use. She could always find work for him.

He did it all as he had said. He was thus able to be "about the house." That was his retaining fee. Whether it was painful to him or not in his present state of mind to see so much of Alice Damer, it was a fact that he did have to meet her continually. She sent little business-like notes round to his chambers nearly every day—short, sensible, not encouraging notes. He made all the arrangements for their journeys and their parties and their entertaining of their friends. He saw her mother and herself off to the Continent every year when they went to do their cure, was attentive at the carriage door, bought the railway literature, and pumped up the air cushions.

He could always be counted upon to be odd man at a dinner party, and if it was humanly possible, and sometimes when it was inhumanly impossible, threw over any other important engagement that he might have had—important to himself, be it understood. His clerk thought he led a "dog's life." What Everard thought was never recorded. What Alice thought was simply this, that Everard liked doing little things for her and was by temperament a born bachelor, although he still cultivated that touching delusion that he was lonely and wanted a companion. It was only that he wanted her, and seeing her this way, every day off and on, was really the pabulum his soul cried for; other and more full-blooded men would not have been content with so merely spiritual a sustenance.

At any rate, he never showed any tendency to stray from the portal and outer courts of this austere temple of respectful worship. Alice had no cause for jealousy. Her victim never twisted or wriggled on the hook of her attraction, his ready smile on seeing her flourished as ever, only there was more "drawing" in it, as expressed by the hatchet lines of his mouth. In short, Everard grew thin. His chest was rather narrow. He coughed often and tiresomely. Lung symptoms seemed to be developing themselves there. Alice, out of gracious regard for him, had suggested his accompanying her mother and herself to the Riviera one winter, instead of seeing them off and falling back into the fog of Charing Cross as usual. He had refused on the score of his pressing work, promising, however, to wear a respirator on the very bad days.

It was a pity he had not gone with them that time. For all that she was a flirt, and men were her material; Alice didn't know them at all. She met a man out at Cap Martin, a man Everard would have seen through at a glance. This common adventurer made love to her; he managed to engage the poor flirt's affections. There was nothing in it, no magnetism. He was a better flirt than she was, that was all, and while Alice had money, he had none.

She returned, and confided her woes. Everard had his work cut out for him. He interviewed this handsome predatory person, and succeeded in retrieving Alice's letters for her. It was a supreme bit of service, and Alice was truly grateful to him. The wretch went out of her life, leaving her in a rather deplorable condition of nerves and mind.

And Everard threw himself into the situation as no man who is not deeply attached to a woman unpicturesquely lovesick for another could have done. He visited her every day, and comforted and consoled her by allowing her to talk about it all. Alice's grief furnished the theme for many a dreary summer's afternoon, when Everard used to take her up the river to distract her mind. It was a trip she had always firmly refused to take with him in the old days on the score of propriety, an excuse that masked dread of boredom. Boredom was not in it now—it was acute tragedy. Poor Alice forgot all propriety when once she was towed well out into midstream. There she gave way and allowed the echoes of Datchet and Laleham to echo with her sobs. For she had been awfully hard hit.

Once, indeed, Everard remembered, but with no pleasurable sense of a lover's guerdon gained, she had leaned forward in the boat with the abandon of despair and kissed her patient confidant. It was the only woman's kiss Everard had ever received in his life, and it had tasted of salt tears! Still, it was a love symbol, the nearest Alice could do in the line he wished, or had wished, for perhaps he did not now desire her quite so urgently as he had done.

Everard had never been handsome at the best of times, but that summer season rang the final knell of his good looks. His crow's feet and his cheek and jaw lines were awful—Alice herself noticed them.

"I believe it is you, Everard, who are going to break down now!" she said to him once when it was all over, her misbegotten love buried fathoms deep, and she cared to look round her a little and notice what other people were doing.

The very violence of her passion had perhaps caused the flame to burn itself out in this young lady of the world, this parlour warrior, this heroine of a hundred ballroom fights. At any rate, her emotional crisis passed away, leaving her who was already hard a little harder than before to Everard's business precautions and his adroit playing of animated safety-valve to the deserted one. Alice, luckily for her, had not needed to confide in a member of her own sex.

Her zest for "the noble game" of flirtation had died down, too. She was less interested in men, and rather more interested in herself than she had been, and condescended to enjoy a party, even if she came away from it without the tendrils of a heart of sorts reaching after her. Her superficial bloom returned; she had never lost, only temporarily mislaid it. She was a fundamentally good-looking woman, with neat, regular features, a good figure and perfect constitution to fall back on. To Everard's satisfaction she now proved the validity of these fine assets of beauty.

But she had spoken a true word in jest. Everard Jenkyns went and had a bout of brain fever. He was popularly supposed to have broken down from overwork.

Alice Damer and her mother were most kind and solicitous, and as fussy about him as they could be without setting the public tongue a-wagging. Alice now worshipped on the altar of convention again, and would not have been seen up the river with Everard or near his rooms in Paper Buildings for anything. Her mother was old and unwieldy. So, they "wrote." They were quite careful—but as it was, old friends opined that Miss Damer was going to settle down and take up with her old and tried suitor. When taxed with this by the ill-bred privileged she maintained boldly that there was nothing in it, that she and

Mr. Jenkyns thoroughly understood each other. So, they did. Everard was grateful without any expectation of favours to come, and thanked her prettily for grapes and books and things.

He recovered, and went about his own business as usual. Alice's business was not pressing just now, so the two rather lost sight of each other, Alice holding him in reserve for future extremity. She supposed, sometimes aloud, that he was "busy getting on" and making up for the time lost in his illness. There could be no woman in it?

"Rather a wreck—poor old Jenks!" his friends observed with affection, for he was a general favourite with men, and most unfairly persisted in attributing his state, not to the illness he had undergone, but to Alice Damer's fast-and-loose playing. She heard this, but tossed her head, confident in the good understanding that subsisted between her and her slave.

"I have never encouraged Everard. He knows I haven't," she declared to her mother.

"He says so. I think you have been quite horrid to him, Alice!" was the old lady's single solitary pronouncement on the situation. She said this lying on her bed during what was to prove her last illness. Alice was gentle and kind, but repressed all sentimental leanings on the part of the invalid, who had a mother's natural wish to see a vagrant-hearted daughter settled in love and marriage before she died.

"Mother, how often must I tell you that Everard—Mr. Jenkyns—and I understand each other?" she repeated coldly. She had never chosen to call Everard by his Christian name, though her mother, who was fond of him, always insisted on doing so, and Everard obviously liked it, and clung to this side entry into the intimacy of Alice's family. It did not matter. Alice and he, as before said, understood each other, and old ladies, everyone knows, have a way of attaching themselves to young men, and selecting their daughters' suitors for them by the light of their own predilections.

★★★★★★

And now, her dear, silly old mother was dead and buried, and the proud, sensible daughter sat all alone in the big Seymour Street drawing-room, with the three large windows that needed so much stuff for their curtains, and the beautiful Adams mantelpiece whose shelf Alice could hardly see over. The Damers had only been in the house a year; it was freehold, and Alice's. It was rather a large and dreary abode for one young woman to inhabit permanently, yet the young woman thought she meant to do so!

A companion, she sadly supposed, in that case must be procured sooner or later—later, preferably; if she could have her way, not at all!

Alice was nearly forty, though she looked younger. Why should she not use her age for all it was worth and establish herself on the easy footing of years of discretion? Nay, there would be complications there; her womanly instincts rebelled against the aspersion of "discretion" and the constant assertion of her maturity which would be involved in her adoption of that attitude. She would be asked to play chaperon herself, she would have to "dress old." No, she looked so young for her age, it would be ridiculous, when she could as easily carry the other theory through and pose as a breakable, compromisable commodity.

She must make up her mind to accept the *duenna*—she must get in a woman to quarrel with! It came very hard! She had been used to going about alone and receiving guests by herself in this house; for the last year Mrs. Damer had been unable to dine down or preside at her own table. She appeared beautifully capped and lappeted, to set the seal of chaperonage for a few minutes before dinner, and then prettily said goodnight to her young guests when dinner was announced. Alice was quite equal to it, and always invited another woman, preferably married, to her charming dinners.

A companion would, by the conditions of her office, take part in every function, "quiet" dinners as well as noisy ones. It would be far worse than a husband, for a husband would at least leave the tea-hour free. All Alice's serious *tête-à-têtes* had been used to come off then, in the little room off the stairs, that was really part of the hall and in no way shut off, but so delightfully private. Little, soft, rosy cosy late teas had been Alice's great social weapon; all the more fetching were these free and easy interviews in that she wasn't in the least like an American, though she did see young men alone, with a mother stowed away somewhere in the upper fastnesses of the house.

This problem of the companion was associated with the first glimmering in Alice Damer's mind, of the possibility of a husband's suiting at this juncture. The notion of a companion precipitated him. He came in by the door of convenience.

A husband! Well, who was it wanted to marry her at that moment?

Men's names, long shelved, came into her mind, but not Everard's. Like the poor, she had him always with her. He was always available, but the others, unaccountably enough, did not rush into the arena of her requirements at once.

She must be growing old! Did people think her old? She had not noticed that they did, she could see no sign of "the coming of the crows' feet," of which this "backward turn of *beaus'* feet" was supposed to be ominous. For surely, a year ago, plenty of potential husbands lay ready to her hand? . . .

The signs of age, if there were any signs, were on the outside. Alice, internally, felt as fit as ever. She was still game for anything in the way of social folly, she could sit up as late as any one and dozed off happily the moment she got home and her head touched the pillow. She did not have to read in bed or play "patiences" to induce sleep. Her figure showed no fatal early inclination to "spread," she didn't know what it was to "sit over a fire," and she proudly refused to avoid lobster salad or anything else indigestible at supper. . . .

Unless, indeed, the craving for marriage itself was a sign of age, a subtle token of the need for support, the birth of an instinct for clinging?

She rose and looked at herself in the old, unbecoming Empire mirror that Everard had got for her at a sale at Christie's once, for he was a connoisseur. No, very few lines, no look of fatigue, even in a bad glass! And as much colour in her hair, that poor Everard admired so, as ever there was!

Poor dear Everard! . . . No, not poor dear Everard. He had been growing rather slack lately, and forgot her flowers and fish and game now and then. He had been kind, of course, and considerate over her mother's death, had continually called to inquire, though the presence of authorized relations in the house had rendered his visits nugatory as far as she was concerned. Alice was formal about death. She had seen much of it. Still, she had liked to see his card in the hall, though unable to ask him to come in because of Aunts Polly and Gertrude.

It had been an awful, unmentionable time, the sort of life that everybody must lead at times, when Death is in the house; but now it was over and the aunts had gone home, making her promise to give them a month at Taunton next week, when she had got things a little straight and done seeing lawyers. And that was over, too. Her nerves, that had been a little upset, though she had expected her mother's death, had righted themselves, too. She cried about her mother every day, but only once in the day, and she began to think she should like to see someone who wasn't "family." Why should she not begin with Everard? When the companion had come, or the husband, she would have very little opportunity for *tête-à-têtes* with him. Unless he was that husband? Well, we should see! . . .

She settled that it was to be tomorrow, a quite impromptu invitation. If it were ceremonious, she could not have him alone, and she wanted him alone. She set about ordering a nice little dinner for him, consonant with his tastes, which unluckily she did not know. Everard had dined in Seymour Street before, but only on big formal occasions, never alone, so far as she remembered.

Everard replied in fairly good time. He did not say he was previously engaged—for he knew that she would never forgive him for not throwing the other people for her—but ill. At least, not ill, but with a Very bad cold. As the dinner, she had said, was quite informal, might he ask her to postpone it a day or two until he had a little got the better of his cough, which would make him a rather tiresome guest, apart from the danger of chill, to which he found himself more liable than formerly. He would like to suggest Saturday night—his birthday? . . .

"What a funny old-maidish letter," was Alice's comment; "all about his cold and that! I never knew Everard notice a cold before? I suppose a man gets finnicky, living so much alone. He's no exception to the rule. I'll have to wake him up a little."

His cool deferring of her invitation afforded him just that touch of masterful self-assertiveness Everard had always lacked in his dealings with this young woman. She now firmly made up her mind to marry him, that is, if he continued to carry things off so well. He would be better than a companion, and—there seemed to be nobody else!

At a quarter to eight on Saturday evening she was all ready, dressed in black and looking very handsome, on one side of the brightly burning fire, for there was a slight touch of frost in the air. Her senses were alert, she found herself actually listening for the sound of his hansom driving up to the door. Quite loverlike, she thought, with a little laugh, to herself! She remembered the last sentence in Everard's old-maidish letter, which she passed over on first reading. He had informed her that this was his birthday. She welcomed this as a touch of sentiment—the sentiment she had not in the old days been solicitous to cultivate in him, but had carelessly let die. She wished she could remember exactly how old he was today? If she had been able to allude to it it would have pleased him. . . .

No use, she could not recapture the knowledge. She supposed he might be somewhere about forty? And he was late! How dared he be late, for her? Was there a fog perhaps?

She went to the window, parted the heavy curtains, and looked out. Rather misty—but not enough to prevent Everard from keeping time, if he had started early enough to dress! How rude if he hadn't? She remained drumming on the pane with her long, slender fingers, looking down into the empty roadway.

She had not heard the door of the drawing-room open, but suddenly, before she had time to turn away from the window, Everard stood beside her with his handkerchief held up to his face, a familiar gesture of his for which she had often reproved him.

"How are you?" she asked him, rather frigidly. "What a draught you seem to have brought in with you!"

"May I shut the door?" Everard said, suiting his action to the words.

"Come to the fire, won't you? You are cold."

She spoke more cordially, but, in spite of her definite intention to propose herself to Everard that evening, the curious sense of physical alienation which she knew now had held them apart all these years, returned to her with tenfold vigour. Her instinct had been right. Physical leanings counted for something, and there was no real affinity between them. Alice shivered a little, for she was a sensible, business-like woman, and she firmly meant to over-ride the absurd and awkward shrinking, and marry him. Her mind once made up, she never went back.

He was holding his thin, blue-veined hands to the blaze. His eyes seemed to avoid hers.

"Yes, that's right," she said. "I hope you have got a good appetite? I have ordered such a nice little dinner for you."

"How kind of you! But really, I eat very little except fish. My doctor has cut me down remorselessly."

"And do you attend to him? You never used."

"I have to attend to his orders. I am in rather a bad way, Alice. The base of one lung is quite solid . . . and the other is gone."

"Nonsense! I believe you're as right as I am, barring this little bit of a cold, that you'll soon get rid of. You haven't coughed once since you were in the room, do you know? I fancy that living alone as you do, you go and get ideas about yourself, and then rush out and call in a doctor who frightens you."

"May be," he said slowly. "Loneliness certainly doesn't improve one's perspective. And I haven't been inside anyone else's house for a month."

"There now, what did I say? And what do you do, when you are at home? Sit over the fire and grizzle, "and think of your sins—and mine, eh?"

"Not yours—much!" said he, with a chilling effect of partial for-giveness which benumbed Alice, whose fighting spirit was up in arms to bring him to her feet again.

The maid announced dinner, and Alice took his recalcitrant arm, which gave her the sense of being glued to his side. On the way downstairs she thought, "Poor dear, he will want civilizing all over again!"

"You'll drink champagne?" she suggested, when they were both seated.

"No, water, please." He added, speaking to the maid, "Thanks, no soup!"

He allowed a helping of fish to be placed on his plate, but he did not eat a mouthful, that Alice could see.

The dreary dinner progressed. Alice Damer ate for two, and every now and then looked furtively at the man she had made.

It was her fault; she saw it now. This man had been her slave; she had been his inhuman master. She had laid him on the rack, she had starved his heart, for bread she had given him a stone. This was what their fa-mous understanding had amounted to; the ruin of a man, a pale, thin, hectic mask, sitting opposite her, pretending to eat—the play of his thin wrists that manipulated his knife and fork drove her frantic—his sullen eyes refusing to meet hers, as in tones that only faintly represented the rich, soft, legal, measured voice she used to know, he responded gently but dully to all her conventional openings, and allowed the subjects she started so painstakingly to drop one by one.

What would the servants think? Little pearly drops of dismay and effort broke out on her own white forehead; the effort she was mak-ing was too much for even her social fortitude. Yes, she knew she had behaved badly to him, but he might let her down more easily! Vexing of him! For what she had to do, must be done, in spite of difficulties.

The last course had been removed, two punctilious, slightly shocked maids had disappeared, and the couple were left alone over the walnuts and the wine.

She spoke to him quite crossly, in a voice she could hardly com-mand. "Aren't you interested in anything, Everard?"

"Yes, dear, in some things—for instance in your calling me by my Christian name—for the first time," he replied quietly.

Alice felt uncomfortable. Such a direct thrust from this petrifaction suggested that he had seen through her, who hardly realised herself, and what she was doing.

"Oughtn't I?—I forgot."

"Oh, don't apologise, it doesn't matter. . . . I wanted you to badly, once, do you remember? Strange, when it does come—one is more or less past caring—"

"Coffee?" she asked. "I make it myself now, as you see!"

"Yes, please."

She made it. She handed it. She even let her fingers graze his as she passed him the cup. It was literally the first time she had ever practised her own special art of flirtation in Everard's connection.

Then there fell a silence between them. The patent coffee machine ceased to bubble. Its duties were sped. . . . Alice, sipping a restorative draught of the tonic liquid, broke the silence bravely. She felt that she owed it to him to take the initiative.

"I am feeling very lonely—now," she said softly.

"Poor child, you must be," he answered gravely.

"And I think I—I understand a little better how you must have felt all these years."

He lifted his fishy eyes for the first time to hers. "Yes, but I am used to it, now."

"But, Everard, it hasn't done you any good?"

"No, I daresay not."

"Everard, do you think—now—do you believe we—you and I, I mean, would have got on together?"

"How do you mean? In what relation?"

"I mean—in the usual relation—if I had wanted what you wanted?"

"Well, you know, I thought so, then."

"Not now?"

"No, not now. Did I not tell you that I had grown philosophical? Whatever is, is good."

"Oh, dear! Then you tell me that you think it is good, your living alone, with not a soul to talk to, or exchange an idea with, no one to look after you when you are ill, as you are now, but just to sit mooning over a dying fires—"

The ghost of a shrug was vouchsafed her. "Oh, I keep my fire up, and I mix my own grog and drink it, and warm my own slippers. It isn't so bad."

"Everard!" She rose to her feet and he imitated her, supposing that a move to the drawing-room was contemplated. "No, I am not going up yet, not till we have had this out. You do make it very difficult for me. It is as if you had lost the key—you will not understand *à demi-mot!*"

"Why should it be *à demi-mot?*" he repeated after her, catching, however, none of her fire. He sat down again and motioned her to do the same. Then he spoke, dully, but very clearly,

"Let us talk quietly, and not get excited over it. A man in my condition has no time for vagueness. I do understand, quite well, and I will show you that I do. You are willing to marry me now?"

"Yes," she cried breathlessly. "Yes, poor Everard! And you—you don't want me to anymore?"

"I want nothing! Don't think of me. Let us consider only you. Now tell me, would this marriage be of any use to you?"

"Use to me to be married to you, Everard?" She started.

"Sorry, but I can only put it from the point of view of utility. My personal desires are dead."

"Ah, I killed them."

"Yes, my dear, you killed them. I can't pretend to any extravagant feelings of joy at what I suppose we must call your capitulation. You know, they give better terms to beleaguered fortresses the sooner they surrender? You, Alice, in your pride and impregnability left it too long. The wine got musty in the bottle, the cord got frayed and rotten. I am no good to you or anybody. My life is done. I thought all this out as I lay there—wrote some of it down even. I never thought I should get a chance of telling it all to you in person. I could not rest. In my delirium—"

"Delirium! Oh, Everard, what nonsense!"

He put her exclamations aside. "Well, I have told it you now, and I shall rest in peace."

"If it's any consolation to you, you have had a good scold—a good go at me!" Alice cried angrily, adding with bitterness, "And plus the satisfaction of refusing me!"

"But not at all!" he said, turning surprised, lacklustre eyes on her. "If you think a marriage with me would do you any earthly good, you shall have it. I ought to have made that clear—"

"I wanted to do good to you!" she wailed.

"Too late for that. I won't pretend, even to salve your conscience, Alice, that I care anything at all about it. Besides, your conscience has no need of salving. You were perfectly right not to marry me, in your heyday and mine, if you could not love me; you are very kind and perfectly in order to suggest it now, as a way of making me useful to you, as you have done in the past. I am at your service now, as ever. I am reserved to your use, as good as married to you already, though not you to me, and quite ready to go to church with you tomorrow, if you decide that we shall do so. I am your property.... Only, my dear, it is a pity you tied me up in brown paper and left me on the shelf so long. Fatal delay! Unused, I deteriorated! You have had me warehoused so many years that now, when you choose to untie me and take me down, you find that you have to make allowance for depreciation of stock. I think I wrote that to you—or said it! ... How it did amuse Mrs. Clarkson!"

"Who's Mrs. Clarkson?" she asked through her tears.

He did not answer, but rose, and took her in his arms. Pale flickers of posthumous triumph lighted up his kind, lined face. Weakly victorious, he enfolded her, and she shrunk and shivered out of his embrace.

"What is it, dear?"

"Nothing, oh, nothing! Only, I don't believe I can marry you, Everard, after all I—"

He did not ask her why, and she could hardly have told him that the momentary contact had affirmed the sense of physical aversion she had always thought she felt for him. Now she was sure. Oh, what was she to do? ...

She stood timorously away from him, as it were freed from the clasp of a corpse. How could she tell him that? And then she reflected consolingly that according to his own words marriage meant so little to him now, that she need perhaps never kiss him when they were married.

Her colour returned a little as she formulated this evasion. . . . Many a conscientious woman has forced herself before now to marry a wreck, to pay conscience money.

There was a good fire burning, she motioned him to one of two leather-covered chairs drawn up on opposite sides of the fireplace. "It's warm here. We won't go upstairs. I am really getting rather frightened about you, Everard. I was incredulous at first, but I do believe now, that you have been ill."

"Yes, I have been very ill."

"But why come out? Why didn't you send an excuse—ask me to come to you?"

"Would you have come? Well, as a matter of fact, a telegram was sent you. Mrs. Clarkson *said* she had sent it."

"Mrs. Clarkson—your landlady—your bedmaker? Oh, dear, how unkind you must have thought me!"

"No, I don't know that I thought anything about it. I said she might send it, and then it passed out of my mind entirely. Everything did go clean out all at once, somehow . . . it's a most unusual sensation—very like death, I should think."

"Everard, I believe you ought to be in bed now, you ought not to be here—pleasant as it is. Go home, and I'll come and nurse you to-morrow. I can safely do that. I am—engaged to you!" She spoke with mouth awry, putting the greatest constraint upon herself.

He smiled. "Awfully kind of you, dear, but I've got a nurse already. Mrs. Clarkson is a nurse."

"Everard! you're dreaming! Do you mean a whitecapped creature, with starched cuffs? How could you be here if that were so?"

"I don't know, but I am here, you see. Mrs. Clarkson certainly did send you a wire to say I couldn't come. She asked you to come to me, I believe, though I forbade her. As I told you"—he sighed—"I forgot it all. . . ."

"But then why have you come, and why haven't I got the wire?"

"Wrongly addressed, I fancy. I was too ill to speak much. She looked the address up in my book and I have only your old one there."

"It shows how I've neglected you."

"But it's as well you didn't come. The nurse is excellent. These hired people do best because they have no feelings, whether it's merely putting on a poultice, or finally laying you out. . . ."

"Oh, don't, Everard!"

He rose. He looked preoccupied.

"It's after midnight. Do you realise how late we have been talking, right into the night? The daylight will surprise us in a minute! . . . Oh, dear me! I must be off." He rose, and stood, wavering like a wind-blown taper. "Goodnight, dear Alice, I shan't forget you have kissed me—once in your life. Oh, no, twice; once on the river—that day, the twelfth of July. I loved you—I wish you had loved me too!"

"I; did—I do," she averred, her lips chattering.

"Too late!" said he, taking a woollen comforter out of his pocket.

"Everard, I don't think you are fit to go home alone. Let me send someone with you. Or stay here, the servants are not gone to bed, and there's a spare room, slept in only last night. Aunt Polly—"

"And your reputation?"

"I'll risk that," she said. "I've behaved too badly to you not to make you some amends."

"But it's all nonsense. I am all right. Strength has been given me—"

"How funnily you talk! Well, since you will be foolhardy and go back to your nurse—is she pretty? You know I don't believe in her. You are thinking of your landlady, who's been mothering you a little, as she should." She put out her hand and rang the bell. "A hansom, please, for Mr. Jenkyns."

"You shouldn't have done that," he said. "I meant to walk."

"Well, you aren't going to be allowed to walk! You must take no risk. Have a good night's rest, and be well enough to marry me tomorrow—by special licence." She looked up in his face with terror-stricken audacity. How could she do it!

"Would you really?" He was out in the hall by now, and the maid was whistling for a cab. "Well, we'll see!"

"I'll come to you at eleven in Paper Buildings. I know the way. I've been there once."

"Dear Alice, how unmaidenly you are grown all of a sudden! I like it, though. It is some compensation—"

"But will you really marry me if I come?"

"If I can," he answered gravely.

The hansom had come rattling up. She gave a twist to the comforter. "Keep it well over your mouth. . . ."

"I will kiss your hand first."

She controlled herself. His touch was pain to her. She wailed, as the hall door closed—

"Oh, I don't love him! He is dead. I have killed him! I'll marry him, that is my vow!"

★★★★★★

The strayed telegram was brought her next morning on the tray with her tea. It had been as Everard had surmised, wrongly addressed to the old house. It ran—

Mr. Jenkyns unable to go to you tonight. Ill. Come if prefer.

"She must have been in a rare fright when she wrote that, whoever she is!" thought Alice, who could not bring herself to believe in the presence of a nurse in 82 Paper Buildings.

Her exaltation of last night had left her. Everard was such a wreck, poor dear! Every bit of charm, and he never had much, had departed and left him sear, dry, stupid and unsympathetic. But she meant to marry him, and repair her sins, and be able to live without a companion. Even an invalid husband was better than a hired *solacium*. She would go and see him this morning, but of course they could not really be married at once, out of hand, like that.

In a week or so, after a few preparations had been made and when he had been nursed up and made to look a little less ghastly. She could not allow a ghost to lead her to the altar. Then they would go off somewhere warm for the honeymoon, to the Riviera or Egypt, and Everard would revive under the combined influences of sun and agreeable society, and love—that is, if he was still capable of feeling the kindly glow of a delayed, but at last gratified passion.

Perhaps he was not quite so dead after all; perhaps in time she would find herself able to submit to his kisses without a politely suppressed shudder? Though she could easily account for that symptom of hers. Starved physically and mentally, as he seemed to be, what wonder that all the magnetism had gone from him? Alice, none other, would nurse him back to life, make a charming, attentive, affectionate husband of him, one whose kisses she would get not to mind so much.

She drove down to the Temple and dismissed her carriage at the gate on the Embankment, and walked up, quite unnecessarily, for Everard's rooms in Paper Buildings had a road in front where a carriage might stand. But she did not mind walking. It was a lovely morning. The famous fountain in the court was playing merrily, and suggested springing hopes of all sorts—and possibilities of revival. She walked along to Everard's rooms with a light step, laughing a little to herself at the thought that she was going to earn for him the reputation of being "a dog." She did not suppose many young ladies sought out the dry student lawyer in his rooms! His landlady, or laundress, whichever it was, would be shocked, and a good thing too. His character was altogether too immaculate, and a picturesque smudge or so would improve it in the eyes of men.

Alice had all the sweet, headlong depravity of mind of the excessively innocent. Using her tortoiseshell *pince-nez*, she read the name of Everard Jenkyns printed on the wall on the right hand side of the open door of number eighty-two, and plunging into the dimness, began to ascend. She met a man on the first landing who looked like a doctor. He seemed in a hurry to get to his hansom, which she had observed standing there. He merely peered in her face and passed on before she could ask him if he was the doctor, and if so, how Mr. Jenkyns was?

She went on ascending till she found the right door, knocked, and stood there, breathless. . . .

A foolish fear assailed her as she waited. She found herself dreading the first sight of Everard as he would appear on opening the door to her; she remembered with annoyance the poor, lank, gawky face, which always made her think, as she used to tell her mother, of a boy's compendious clasp-knife, with all the blades open! He would smile, of course, and look pleased to see her; it was a strong step for haughty Alice Damer, whom he had sighed for so long, to visit a man in his rooms at half-past eleven and ask him to marry her!

He was a long time coming! . . . She rang again, more firmly. . . .

The door was opened, by a nurse. Everard had not been raving, then! He was probably in bed? . . . She formally muttered his name.

The nurse seemed to have been expecting her. Murmuring, "You would like to see him, Ma'am?" she led the way into the sitting-room, out of which the bedroom obviously opened. The door was ajar. The nurse did not stop. . . .

"But not in there!" Alice stammered.

A strong note of disapprobation pierced in the woman's voice as she turned round sharply—

"Why not? He's dead. You're not going to faint?"

"Oh, no," said the poor girl, striving to adjust herself to these new and unexpected circumstances. Like a proud, plucky automaton she entered the bedroom, and looked on the form that was faintly outlined under the sheet, so thin Everard had grown. She had good nerves, and could always bear shocks well. But an immense, searching pity, a world of value for the dead man, combined with self-depreciation, filled her, and she wept silently. Her noble calmness and self-restraint won the admiration of the nurse, who had been condemning the heartless creature wholesale for having left her sweetheart to die alone as she had done.

"What was it, Nurse?" she asked.

"Double pneumonia. Collapse. I telegraphed to you, Miss—you are Miss Damer, I believe? He objected, but when once he became unable to speak, I took it upon myself. I thought you would want to be here."

"Of course. But I have only just got it."

The nurse accepted the *amende*. She could not realise that Alice was struggling to form a comment on the apparent inconsistency of a man sick unto death being able to dine with her, hoping at the same time that dates would be proved not to fit and all be normally explained. She stammered something vague as the nurse laid down the covering sheet, and disclosed the still face, looking, however, no more emaciated than Alice had seen it in life and no longer ago than last night.

Alice was painfully aware of the tacit suggestion on the woman's part that she should bend down and kiss that waxen mask, and re-coiled, though the nurse had said no word.

"Oh, I can't kiss anybody dead. . . . It's awful of me, Nurse, but I can't!"

"Some can't!" said the nurse resignedly. And this girl was the poor gentleman's *fiancée*, so she had understood? . . .

She was a little pacified when Alice unfastened the bunch of lilies of the valley that she was wearing, and laid them on the dead man's breast. Then she turned away and dried her eyes. She was a beautiful creature, the nurse thought, and was conscious that the faulty young lady was slowly acquiring her sympathies.

"When did he die? When was it?"

"We don't know exactly, Miss. In these cases

But he last spoke about seven."

"What made you think of sending to me?"

"Because, Miss, for days before, when he was wandering worst, he talked about you. We gathered, the doctor and I, that he was more or less engaged to you, Miss, but that you was rather too fond of putting him off. Said it had been going on for years, and that he was fairly worn out. So he was, poor man; he hadn't an ounce of flesh on his bones to spare—"

"Yes, but—" the girl exclaimed impatiently, "I want to get at the facts. He died, you say, this morning at seven o'clock?"

"Spoke last at seven o'clock last night, Miss, I said. Died sometime in the night, or, may be, directly after he did speak. At least, part of him may have died, as ignorant people seem to think. He was hardly breathing at a little before eight, but the last spark may have held on longer."

"I suppose you know, Nurse, that he dined with me last night, at a quarter-past eight," said the girl stonily, looking away from the nurse's apathetic face, which changed at once, sympathetically;—

"Miss, you're upset! You took it so calm at first. Have some brandy. You have had a shock. One understands—"

"He dined with me," Alice repeated obstinately.

The nurse stared at her, and shrugged her shoulders. Poor girl!

She was evidently one of the outwardly quiet ones, who smother the symptoms of disturbance, only to feel the shock more keenly. People take these things in such a variety of ways. The idea of the dinner party had got fixed in her mind by the shock; she was unable now to let go the idea of Everard's keeping his engagement with her. She had received the telegram all right, of course, there could be no doubt of it, and some domestic reason had prevented her from responding to the summons. Or, possibly, that same backwardness and want of interest which had affected the smooth course of the engagement had been at work. She hadn't cared for him much, though she had been persuaded into giving her word. . . .

In an even tone, calculated to restore the shattered nerves of the shaken girl, the nurse remarked—

"Mr. Jenkyns' sister-in-law, the one that lives in France, will be here presently, to see about the funeral arrangements. He wanted you to have all his old china and books, Miss, he used to say so, and doubtless that will be done. . . ."

But Alice Damer had gone resolutely across to the bed from which the two, in the course of conversation, had unconsciously deviated.

She dexterously turned down the sheet, and stooping, performed the rite of love, the little act of devotion which she had refused him just before. What was she saying? Mrs. Clarkson observed closely what she considered one of the curiosities of mental stress.

"I kissed him last night, when he came to me. . . . So you see, whether I liked it or not, I did kiss a dead man! And it's no use minding now, is it?"

She kissed him repeatedly, with a pale semblance of passion.

The nurse took her arm gently and led her away from the bed, and she submitted to be placed in a chair.

"Miss, now you've done that, you'll feel better. I should go home if I were you. Take that hansom outside. It's the one you came in, perhaps—and you haven't paid him?"

Alice signified a negative to this, helplessly, but allowed the nurse to pin her veil on for her. It hid her tear-stained face a little. Then the good woman led her downstairs and out on to the pavement. Sure enough, there was a hansom waiting there, and the nurse hailed the driver.

Gruffly, he turned round, and stared at them.

"And I say," he appeared to be remarking, "and I say, who's going to pay me my fare?"

"Why, the lady will, of course. Get in, Miss, I'll hold your dress away from the wheel."

But the cabman was not satisfied, nor did he address himself to the task of resuming his drooping reins. He seemed to have had a shock too.

"No, I didn't mean her. Who's going to pay me three bob for last night and for waiting 'ere? . . ."

"That's no affair of ours," replied the nurse cheerfully. "You must take the lady—where to, shall I say, Miss?"

Alice, crouching inside, mumbled the address of her home.

The cabman swore.

"No, I'm damned! You get out. I ain't a-going near that blasted house again for nobody I took a fare from there last night, I did, and drove him here, and here I may stop till Domesday, I suppose, before I sees a shilling of his money! 'Tain't right! . . ."

He was obviously drunk, but not dangerous, so the nurse thought.

"Come, come!" she expostulated.

Alice, frightened, prepared to get out.

"Oh, what's the matter?" she moaned.

"Matter! Matter's this. I drove him here right enough, and pulls up where he told me—and my gentleman doesn't get out, seems as if he was a-going to make a night of it in my cab. Drunk, I says to myself, and I opens the trap, meaning to take my fare and clear him out, but Lord bless me—why, there wasn't no one there!"

"He'd got out, of course," said Mrs. Clarkson, "while you weren't looking."

"'Bilked,' says I. And, thinks I, I'll just come and wait here till I sees my gentleman come down those stairs again."

"You'll never see him come downstairs again," said the nurse, with a flash of inspiration, "except in his coffin! Come, get on! Take the lady where she wants to go."

She thought of it all—afterwards . . . but then nurses see such queer things! She had taken the cabman's number.

The Operation

"Yes, I think that might hang a day longer. I can finish up the mince for my lunch, and you must do something with the turkey legs for dinner. Let me see—and there's fish today. And then—well, suppose you make a savoury?"

"Master don't care for savouries, Ma'am!"

"A sweet, then. I don't care. And that's all, I think?"

Mrs. Joe Mardell, in her neat morning shirt, *coquettishly* finished with a man-like tie, and the severity of her attire much modified by the bows and loops of waved hair that crowned her head, turned and was about to leave the dark basement of the little house in Kirriemuir Street, West Kensington, when a door in the upper regions banged.

"There, he's off, and I wanted a cheque!" Mrs. Mardell observed with mild irritation. She glanced at the kitchen clock with a degree of confidence she did not place in the elegant time-keeper, cased in jewels, that hung on the front of her shirt. "Why, it's only half-past ten?"

"Master's early gone this morning," said the cook. "Gladys took his breakfast up only ten minutes ago." She paused, then summoning her courage, she asked—

"Ma'am, are people usually buried on Christmas Day?"

"Why, you silly woman, it depends on what day they die. Who's been dying?"

"I'll swear," said the woman eagerly, "that I saw a corpse being carried down the steps of number thirteen just over the street opposite nearly a week ago, and I reckon it back Christmas Day! . . . It's been worrying me ever since. Yes, I saw the mourners and hearse and feathers and all—done quite proper. I was looking out of the front staircase window—"

"Neglecting your work, Vance? Serves you right. You saw Whiteley's sale cart, perhaps? You were looking sideways through the red panes, and glass, you know, refracts oddly. . . . Who lives at number thirteen?"

"Oddly enough, Ma'am, I don't know, though I mostly could tell you the names of everybody in the street. I might ask one of the tradespeople—should I?"

"Yes, do if you like. Brr!" She shivered affectedly, strong in the pride of her health and good looks. "It seems a cold time to choose to be put into the ground! One would sooner be cremated, this weather!"

Holding up her crisp befrilled skirts, the second wife of Joseph Mardell, the popular comic actor, who was just now drawing crowds to his Christmas extravaganza at the "Quality," made her way up from the dark basement to the abodes of light above. Noiselessly, she let fall behind her that swing door at the top of the staircase which effectively divided the world of society from its service, and exchanged stone and oil-cloth for soft carpets and silken curtains. It was a very pretty little house—*her* house. She admitted Joe into it. Her husband-lover, Joe. She had managed to keep him her lover. All wives should.

She glanced, as she passed by, at the hat-stand in the hall. Joe had stupidly gone without his fur coat, though it was freezing. Or was it that it needed a stitch? How careless of Gladys! He had left his big umbrella too, for there it bulged in the rack, beside her own delicate silver-topped one. Careless Joe, willing enough to ignore the mere physical claims of the self he morally bowed to! Moreover, he forced everyone else to do so likewise. He must have his own way, and brooked no check where his mental desires were concerned. It was perhaps the secret of his sway over men—and women.

She thought of him, Joseph Mardell, the greatly-sought-after, and hers, with complacent affection, glancing up consciously at the branch of mistletoe which was entwined with the square glass lamp that hung over the front door. Joe had passionately kissed her under the mystic bough, a week ago, for luck, on the first night of the successful piece. And luck had come, and seemingly remained with them. The booking was splendid. And they were rehearsing a more serious play that was to follow the Christmas jollity. Joe was so busy he didn't know where to turn for a spare five minutes. She did not complain, for if things went on like this, they would be able to move out of West Kensington, where you couldn't get a smart parlour-maid to stop with you. Gladys and her finger-nails was a sore trial.

She entered the dining-room, and her eyes sought the sideboard. Ah, Joe had had some sense after all, and had remembered to refresh the inner man before leaving, as the violated Tantalus betokened. He lay in bed late. He rarely breakfasted, and never with her. She rose at eight—on principle; she could not afford to keep actors' hours and ruin her complexion.

She stood pensively by the small piece of Sheraton furniture before she opened a drawer and took out of it what she had come to seek. Last night's oranges and apples beamed there on a pretty dish. Joe's cigarette boxes, flung about, needed tidying up. The presentation silver bowl given to Joe by his fellow-actors on the occasion of his first marriage, shone in the centre with dignified lustre. They had chosen something quite different to present to him as a memento of his second venture. That was in her room now. The bowl had a dwarf fern in it now, but sometimes it ran over with punch, or was packed with roses. Another use was contemplated for it; if Joe and she were to have a baby, which, sadly enough, did not seem likely, the bowl would be used for the christening.

Mrs. Mardell took a pretty little checked duster out of a drawer, and went upstairs to her drawing-room on the first floor. She carefully picked up an iridescent bead off the carpet, the spoil of the dress she had worn last night, and placed it on an ash-tray. She then proceeded to rub up the several minute objects on her silver-table, wishing heartily that she could afford to have them lacquered, and thus dispense with her daily task. So occupied, she looked wholly pretty and half domestic, a little soubrettish, like those neat-aproned maids who flutter early about a stage-scene and usher in and lay the tables for tragedy.

There was no harm in Florence Mardell. She was a smart, novel-reading, Sandown and Ranelagh going woman, easily dressed, easily amused, a little detached, perhaps, in her interests, and careless of the more serious issues of life, but quite willing to simulate and assume social crazes as they came up. She played a good game of Bridge. She glanced at the deep Reviews as well as the *Windsor* and *Pearson's*, and improved her mind on the slightest opportunity. You could always get her for a subscription lecture of sorts, and she quite approved of Female Suffrage, without, however, actively concerning herself in its propaganda. She never "fagged." She was always beautifully dressed in a severish, strapped, mock-manly style, and could wear successfully the very largest hats when they came in.

She had been the widow of an officer, and had lived at Wimbledon in a big dull house standing in its own grounds. She had first set eyes on Joe Mardell playing a strong "Macheath" in *The Beggar's Opera*, to the most ineffective "Polly Peachum" of Julia Fitzgerald. Miss Fitzgerald was his wife; had she but known it, it might have made a difference, but very likely it would not have.

Then and there she had fallen in love with the actor across the footlights, impulsively, violently, madly, and she had not rested, being of an acquisitive, pugnacious, predatory habit of mind, until she had persuaded a journalistic friend of hers and his to bring about an introduction. With her effective crown of real golden hair, waved and curled *in extremis*, her clean, fresh suburbanity, she had fascinated "Macheath." He was known to be weak, *volage*, and full of moods. Florence was, on the contrary, strong and pertinacious, she had taken him in a mood, and let her love profit by it. With fond remorselessness she had driven him to drive his wife to divorce him.

All this she had compassed in her own calm detached way, as if unconscious of the larger issues she was stirring—another woman's happiness, a man's honour, and an actor's art, for Joe was a genius, and recognised to be one, in spite of, some people said because of, his strange limitations. A little man, almost a dwarf, he could play the burly Falstaff and the courtly Biron; he could write articles in the Reviews; he could hold supper-tables in a roar. Julia Mardell's happiness had been sacrificed, for she adored, and was known to adore, her husband. To oblige him she had condescended to make use of some of the more complicated and recondite cogs of the machinery of the English law of divorce, and had tamely surrendered, without humiliating him, one of the most fascinating men of the day to another woman.

Yet Julia was quite as good-looking as Florence, if in a different style. She was the full-souled, full-breasted, large-eyed Junoesque female type, and only undertook the playing of a minx like Polly Peachum to suit Joe. Such a majestic walk as hers, such dark swimming eyes were of no avail to the actress who aspired to play one of the wayward mistresses of the highwayman. It was the measure of Julia's love and her power of self-abnegation. Joe was prepared to take the whole play on his own shoulders, only he must have a sympathetic woman to act with.

He did find Julia sympathetic in those days when he loved her, and before the pretty widow from Wimbledon had leaned out of her box and shaken her golden locks at him. Then one day the two women met. Matters were arranged. Joe, susceptible, weak, hustled and busy, succumbed. . . . Lawyers acted for him. Julia was compliant: Florence "keen." Joe worked on and was divorced while rehearsing a new play.

He himself never knew how it all happened!

There was a large signed photograph of Julia in Joe's study now, standing unframed, concave and dusty on the mantelpiece; Joe had not dared, or cared, to give it a more polite or permanent abiding-place. Indeed, Florence had had some thoughts of removing it from its even so humble position; her friends wondered how she could possibly bear to have it there for Joe to see every day! But she was capricious. One never knew how she would take things. It was their expressed opinion which perhaps induced her to let it stay, curled up and drooping slavishly as time went on, and the dust and heat of the fire brought its proud head low.

Florence bore Julia no grudge, she should think not, indeed! Julia had been very good about it, had made no difficulties, but on the contrary, had smoothed and made easy the path of divorce for the man she loved.

That is, if she really did care for Joe. She had been so terribly callous in her interviews; so full of zeal to give him his freedom. It was hardly human, so the woman who had profited by her action thought, and certainly not very womanly. Florence could not imagine herself allowing a cold business-like lawyer to dictate her a letter bidding Joe come back to her herewith; a summons intended, of course, for ultimate publication. It disgusted Florence, this horrible business of suing for restitution of conjugal rights! Julia's formal petition was refused by Joe in another cold letter, equally intended for publication. Florence had actually read the two inhuman missives printed together in the daily paper. Divorce had followed in due course.

"Oh, you tamely died!" Yes, little frivolous Florence, who had never read Tennyson, would have taken the advice of the Egyptian and would have "clung to Fulvia's waist, and thrust the dagger through her side." She was a true woman, like Cleopatra, and knew that the elemental passions, once raised, must have full mastery. A man all to oneself or nothing! That was her philosophy.

The feelings of the man in question? The state of his affections? No matter! Florence did not see herself considering them, or taking any deadly sex insult lying down. She considered that Julia's poor-spiritedness did really verge on meanness. She had accepted money from Joe—an allowance to enable her to leave the stage. Report said that she had grown stout. Report said that she had taken to drink. Lies probably, so generous Florence said. Nobody in Florence's world knew anything about Julia excepting Miss Walton, who had introduced them. And though the two women had continued their intimacy, it was with the tacit agreement that the name of Julia should not be mentioned between them. There were plenty of other subjects to talk about. Miss Walton was, like everybody else, more than half in love with Joe. . . . Funny how they all were! Rather nice;—for Joe's wife, since Joe did not bother with any of them. . . .

Mrs. Mardell, after having polished the silver diligently, turned her attention to the room. She ordered the chairs, according to some abstruse social system of her own, and flicked her duster about feebly here and there. She did not feel very "fit." Rather queer, on the contrary! All-overish! She could not have told you what it was, but she was mysteriously conscious of something excessive—something outrageous, like severe pain in wait for her. She seemed to apprehend its nearness instinctively, as a patient seated in the dentist's chair watches the eminent practitioner's feet moving and is aware in all his sensitive enamel of the imminent grinding of the file that has been set going.

Perhaps it was the long-continued strain of the cold that was affecting her. The frost had lasted since before Christmas, and had been very severe. . . .

She paused. The little clock on the mantelpiece tinkled half-past eleven. Supposing she were to give herself a slight moral fillip—go upstairs and try on her new dress, and see how it fitted, after having been "back" twice. She was sure in this way to obtain a sensation, pleasurable or otherwise.

She mounted another flight, feeling every step to be an effort. She lit the gas-stove in her room, and dismissed the dilatory housemaid, whom she found on her knees examining the pattern of the carpet. Then she dragged a tall cheval glass into position, having due regards to unbecoming cross-lights, and undressed. Her white, handsome shoulders appeared; she looked ten times prettier than she had done in the severe morning shirt and tie, and she knew it. She stood for a few minutes before the mirror, complacently admiring herself and in no hurry to don the heavily-trimmed corsage that awaited her verdict. It lay beside her, half in and half out of the flowered cardboard box, interleaved with tissue-paper, and with intersecting lines of tape winding it into its cage.

Her eyes rested on it with feminine appreciation of the elaborate building of the silk lining, with its white bone cases crossing and recrossing the back of it, and the high collar which was to fit in under the very lobe of the ear. Still she deferred the pleasing moment of assumption, standing still and preening herself; soft lappets of valenci-ennes lace flowering out as a frame to the pink skin. . . .

Suddenly, taken by surprise, without a cry or a moan, she cowered and was bent, bent nearly double. Agonising pangs shot through the framework of her body. Her eyes were glassed over with tears, and through them she stared out on the world, bewildered, peering to see from which point the next arrow of dolour would fell!

It came again, without fail it came again, this time no stabbing thrust, but a sword, driving, delving laboriously through her vitals in a lingering, painstaking manner. She was by now prepared and well frightened, and she groaned aloud. Her breasts rose and came together, as in some strange health exercise, under the laces and ribbons. . . .

My God! Was it? Was the silver bowl downstairs going to be used at last?

No, it could not be. The thought was dismissed as soon as formed. A chill on the liver? The extreme cold. . . . What a fool she was to prance about like a peacock in front of a glass for half-an-hour half-dressed! What else could she expect? That silly stove gave no heat. . .

She gathered to her a dressing-gown that lay near and sat still, cow-ering. A long pause! She could not think. But she received no physical intimation of the recurrence of her agony.

Five minutes later she boldly rose, defying it, and tore the new dress out of its rustling ward without stopping to untie the tapes that controlled it. With a screech of tissue-paper it yielded itself into her hands, and she put it on.

Then she laughed. The pain was forgotten. She wriggled about happily.

"Yes, it still catches me . . . just there! They must have it back. I'll go to Madam about it, on—let me see?—Tuesday. . . ."

Taking the precaution of putting her arms properly into the warm dressing-jacket this time, she wrapped the dress up again, tied the white tapes across it, put the lid on firmly, and with the little stylograph Joe had given her, methodically scored out her own name from the label, thus substituting that of the dressmaker printed all over the box.

The exertion, slight as it was, roused again the smouldering fire of pain. She sat down helplessly on her bed, giving herself up to it. Her eyes were like those of a dumb animal in the death anguish, as she stared across at her reflection of her already distorted features in the glass. Rolling to and fro, she grasped and relaxed alternately the fronts of her *peignoir*, knotted feverishly in her palm.

"What the divil is it?" she murmured. "I feel as if my life was going!"

She did not think of calling anyone—Vance or Gladys the impotent housemaid; no one could help her. She was but a poor human passage-way for these relentless throes that passed Juggernaut-like through her shrinking body. It was like a garden roller, when it was not like many scythes set on one axle turning, twisting inside her. What had she ever done to suffer so? No child of Joe's could be so cruel and tear its mother thus! . . . Nay, she had not conceived, unless it was some monstrous impious growth that was rending her, and would not soften or relax till it killed her. . . . She really thought she was going to die! . . .

Presently, when all was quiet again in the tortured battleground of her body, she rose and pushed her hand through her bows of waved hair and flung it back hideously and crossed the room. Apologetically almost, for fear of provoking a recurrence of the horror, she dragged herself downstairs, and to the swing door at the head of the kitchen stairs. She now felt the need of a *confidante*. She must tell someone. The housemaid was too young. Vance was fairly motherly. Pushing open the door, she sat down on the top step, with her *peignoir* gathered round her, and stretching out her legs allowed them to hang over into the dark abyss of Vance's domain.

By the time she felt able to raise her voice and call Vance she had decided not to confide in her. The cook would immediately "think things," and she wanted no fuss. It was not "that" either, she only wished it was. . . . For then there would at least be some compensation in baby fingers to smooth pain away.

In response to her weak summons the cook appeared at the foot of the stairs. Even in the dim penumbra of a London basement, a person unpreoccupied by her own symptoms would have realised at once that Vance was discomposed—agitated in some unusual way. Her cap was hanging by one hairpin, her floury arms were nervously rubbed one against the other. But Mrs. Mardell noticed nothing in other people today. She addressed Vance slowly and deliberately.

"Vance, please I want you to make me a nice cup of tea—at once. I shall not be able to eat any lunch. I think I'll wait till six, and have something with Mr. Mardell."

"Ain't you feeling well, Ma'am?" asked the cook spiritlessly.

"No, not very—a little all-overish. It will be nothing, only I don't feel like eating a solid meal."

"Nor I can't say I feel like cooking it!" Vance observed bitterly. "I'm that upset! I've been across and asked."

"Asked what?" inquired Mrs. Mardell wearily.

"About the funeral that I saw with my own eyes leaving that house on Christmas Day. . . . It's not natural, I said, to go getting buried on Christmas Day—"

Mrs. Mardell interposed impatiently. "You don't mean to say you went and asked at the house if they'd had anyone die there? Really, Vance—"

"It's no good saying that now, Ma'am; I had to know. And it's only a Nursing Home, not a private house, so I've done no harm. And"—the woman's voice grew low and hoarse—"nobody ain't died there—not yet—that's all!"

She put her apron to her face.

"Good gracious, Vance!" Mrs. Mardell cried. "Tell me more about it!"

"Ma'am, they've only got one patient there—a lady. She was going on all right, but she had a relapse this morning, just about half-past eleven, their cook said it was. She had an operation three weeks ago, and no good, and it's got to be done all over again this afternoon at two o'clock, and they can't tell as it will be successful, this time."

"Well, my good woman, don't you worry. Let's hope that the lady will get over it. People do, you know, or there would be an end of nursing homes. I really feel so poorly myself that I can't get up much sympathy with other people's aches and pains. Be quick and get the kettle on, or is it boiling already?"

"Yes, Ma'am, you shall have it in a minute. Ma'am, you may not believe me, but I seen a proper funeral, and the hearse waiting, and the corpse carried out and down those steps . . . and the bearers with crape on their hats and so attentive, and one of them was no bigger than Master. ... I thought of Master the moment I saw him. . . . And she was a big woman, for she took a big coffin. . . ."

"You are settling that it's the woman who's lying ill there now who has got to die, I see. What's her name?"

"I asked, but the girl didn't know it, only that she was an actress."

Mrs. Mardell gathered in her legs decisively.

"Come now, Vance, don't stand there gossiping and unhinging yourself with fancies; get me my cup of tea. I shall be all right, I expect, when once I have had something warm. Bring it to my room. I shall lie down a bit, I think."

She rose to her feet, closed the swing door, dismissing Vance and her dreary soothsaying vision, and passed upstairs. Her day was spoilt. The pain did not seem to be going to recur, luckily, but the deadly feeling of uneasiness which had succeeded it certainly increased. Her legs were weak and could hardly carry her. People who have seen an apparition are said to feel just so. But as she reflected it was Vance, not she, who had seen the ghost!

She paused half-way up the stairs to look out of the window on the first landing, whence Vance declared she had watched the lugubrious tableau. Mrs. Mardell had never gone in for knowing her neighbours, it was wiser not, or else she would have been aware of the industry that was carried on at number thirteen, a red-brick sham artistic villa, just like her own house—like every other house in the street.

She could only make it out by pressing her face against the window, and then she only saw it aslant, and red, through the vicious stained glass that occupied that particular pane. Eight steps led up to the front door of it, as eight steps led up to hers. Surely it was awkward for the incoming patients—many of them, presumably, too ill to walk? She wondered what sort of cases they took there. It would depend. . . .

Julia, she had heard, had grown very fat—at thirty. . . . That indicated something abnormal, in a youngish woman! . . . Something that had to be removed, generally. . . . She laughed. . . . She wondered why she laughed. . . .

"Your tea, Ma'am!" said Vance suddenly at her elbow. "I thought I would bring it up to you myself."

Mrs. Mardell was a little ashamed that Vance should discover her staring out of the window at the scene of her absurd cock-and-bull story. She turned and coldly bade the cook precede her to her bedroom with the tea. Vance accepted the rebuff meekly. She looked cowed and thoroughly upset, and as if no merely domestic trifle could affect her now, broken to tragic issues as she had been.

The tea, as Mrs. Mardell had expected, revived her, and enabled her to lay a nice little plan for a quiet afternoon indoors. She proposed to telephone for Miss Walton to come and sit with her for a bit. She needed something or somebody to pick her up. Of course there was Charlie Bligh, a nice boy whom both she and Joe liked; she might telephone him to come and take her out to dine, as he often did. . . . But no, she wasn't looking Carlton form; it wouldn't be fair to Charlie to ask him to take out anything that wasn't gay and smart. Besides, it would be rather mean to leave Joe to eat his dinner all alone when she had not even said good-morning to him.

She had often left him for dinner, of course, and he had never thought of objecting, verbally at least—but just now that he was so busy and overworked, she felt sure that he would like her, sitting beside him at his dinner, even though she could eat nothing. She saw herself delicately invalidish, in her soft draperies, picking at some grapes. . . . She felt mysteriously drawn to Joe, dear Joe, who was working for her now, who never attempted to control her social movements, who took what she gave him and was always as ready to flirt with her as if he were not married to her! She had managed Joe well! No, she wouldn't leave Joe tonight, but get Miss Walton, who would surely stay with her till Joe returned about half-past five, as usual.

Miss Walton, over the telephone, signified her willingness to come and have a good chat. Mrs. Mardell made up her mind to take things easy. She was really unwell, she had eaten nothing since breakfast, she felt empty, shaken, swelled and sore. She could not have got her exquisitely adjusted corsets on if she had tried, or endured the pressure of them round her body. A tea-gown was clearly indicated. She assumed one, and a little lace cap that went well with it. Sighing deeply, she lay down on the rose-coloured chintz sofa in the drawing-room, shaded by a soft standard lamp, breathing timorously, existing furtively, unnoticed. She hoped it would pass her by, this brooding eagle of pain waiting to tear her.

She had brought her jewel-case downstairs with her and idly toyed with her trinkets. There were three trays, lined with velvet. They twinkled with precious stones. She took every piece in order and examined them slowly, seriously. All the while, her fingers seemed to know that down at the bottom of the box lay their real objective, a thin, crumpled, tousled letter folded small and turning up at the corners. Florence Mardell had received it a few days after her marriage, and although it was only a letter from a woman, had forborne to show it to her husband.

The letter was not actually malicious or even disagreeable, but it had dismayed her, and shocked her. She had kept it in case Julia should ever choose to lay aside her extraordinary tolerance and become human again. She read it over now to remind her of what it contained. Indeed, she had intended to do so when she fetched the box. The by-play with the jewellery was only a blind—self-deceiving, a sop to her superficial consciousness.

Now it is all over, my strivings have not been in vain, and Joe passes from me to you. You must not mind my writing to you, Florence. I think that, on the whole, you will prefer to know what I feel, and that the woman you have supplanted is not your enemy. Joe loves you, and as the woman Joe loves, you cannot be abhorrent to me. Convention forbids me to be your personal friend, your feeling possibly, and perhaps my own, for I am but a woman after all, and the open wound that was left in my life when Joe was torn from my side would be chafed and kept raw by the sight of him merged now in your life. Yes, it is better so. I cannot, will not, see him either—though Joe is not conventional. . . .

Joe is nothing that is not splendid. I did, I do love him so passionately, that I cannot hate you, Florence, as you see. You are the fair new temple in which he worships the spirit of Beauty and Love and Life. The law has clanged the door to, none may dare to interrupt the Litany he prays there, on his knees. God bless you.

But oh, my dear, keep him there. Never undress the altar. No more shifting for Joe, if we women can help it. He is a great man—he must be treated like a great man. These upheavals are bad for him, from every point of view. So be practical as well as passionate, and condescend to learn from me, who failed, how not to lose him. Only approximately can you learn, for the wind of art blows its children where it listeth. You know what an artist he is, and all artists are nothing but divine children. But, Florence, on your life, don't treat him as one. Don't let yourself 'mother' him as I did and be mad enough to sink the mistress in the sister, the friend even. That was my fatal mistake, I abstracted my sexual self, till I became at last the caterer for his mere physical welfare, the confidante of his passing flirtations. Oh, the bitterness of those smothered confessions, those despairing returns of him, broken, marred and dispirited, to the one who surely loved him! Do this, my dear, as I did, and then one day he'll come to you, as he came to me, and put his head on your knee and ask you to divorce him. So, you're both ruined in your several ways. He cannot go through it a second time.

Now listen. You must. I know. I would have you always a little inaccessible, puzzling, capricious even. I would ask you to dare to appear selfish, if you can manage it. Preserve your delicate tangibility, punish any slight infringments of your rules, close your door to him at nights when he has been naughty or careless. What it will cost you! But it is the right way.

You have an enormous pull by not acting with him, believe me! One gets so common, so cheap to a man, when he is used to knocking one about all over the stage, as Katherine, say, or insulting one as Nancy. Stay away from the theatre and accept as many dinners without him as you can. Although there isn't the very slightest chance of his losing you, don't let him feel as convinced of that as you are yourself. You see what I mean, don't you, Florence? I heard you were very clever, as well as a little frivolous.

I have thought all this out, in many sleepless nights, for your benefit and his. Yes, it is Joe that I am thinking of, and shall think of till I die. And so, of you, too.

Oh, don't for goodness' sake be offended by this letter, or take a dislike to me, for whether you like it or no, you will never be quite free of me, any more. Thought, strong thought, does permeate matter and finds itself able to overthrow its mere material resistance. I have proved it, no matter how. I won't weary you with attempted explanation. I should not fancy you were psychic. But be sure that there will be a little of me in all your relations with Joe, I shall have a word in your *ménage* and you must not let the thought of it make you uncomfortable.

Do you suppose I could have let him go so easily, if I had not this power to console me? Take it, as the slight penalty of kidnapping a man out of the ward of a devoted woman. You see how it is, he comes away, she offers no material or spirited opposition, but he brings inevitably some of her atmosphere along with him. Joe never actually ceased to love me; he only began to love you. I never misconducted myself—funny phrase!—so I am still his true and faithful wife, bone of his bone, flesh of his flesh, and where he is, henceforth, in some sort, I am. It cannot be helped.

It is a good thing that I am not vindictive and that I don't hate you, since our relation must necessarily be so close. I assure you that it will not inconvenience you; annoy you, or trouble you at all, at least not until the bands of the spirit are loosed in one of these great, bare, soul-stripped, unaccounted-for moments of life, that come to all of us sometimes. Then, you know, one can't tell, or foresee. . . . The spiritual bonds and relationships assert themselves and enforce attention. . . . I can't quite promise to shield you, then, to free you from the circle of the charm. . . But are you so frivolous, Florence? Won't it interest you—awe you—soothe you?

Ah, don't fear me, don't hate me—bid your flesh comply with me. . . . I am only the ghost of a wife—a power of love that can't circumscribe itself, even though it would. There is a physical lien between us, undoubtedly. I won't drag it if I can help! . . . I'll try to control—I don't know what I am writing—something writes for me.

But trust me.

Julia.

"What a cat!" said Mrs. Mardell.

She folded up the letter again and laid it at the bottom of the box. It was almost actionable, she thought, a threatening letter. Or else the letter of a mad spiritualist—utter sentimental, impossible rot. What would Charlie Bligh, or any other daylight person think of it?

Strangely enough, she had more or less taken Julia's advice! It was sensible, and thus she supposed germane to her own character. She had not "mothered" Joe, what woman in her senses would? She needed no deserted, defeated schemer to hang about her, in the spirit, to tell her that! She knew men as Julia with all her preachments had evidently never known them, and the result of her wise treatment of Joe was that he was devoted to her, extraordinarily so, for a busy man. Of course, he worked hard, too hard, harder than he had done in Julia's time. It had happened so, success had brought its own tension and high pressure. He was not, as Julia and her friends might like to suggest, trying to drown the memory of her in a round of forced activities. He was only taking fortune at the flood and making dramatic hay while the sun of critics favour shone.

Not for a moment did he regret the step he had taken, his was an essentially light nature, he never brooded, and he detested heroics. The writer of that letter, with its tedious mixture of sentimentality and preoccupation with material cares, must have bored Joe to death, in the days when she had him all to herself and could claim consecutive opportunity for worrying him. And now, of course, a masterpiece of supreme tactlessness, like all failures, she turned critic and took on herself to give good advice.

Florence Mardell laughed. The reading of the letter had acted as even a better fillip than the trying on of the dress, and had nearly made her angry.

"I suppose"—she tossed her little gold crowned head—"that it is very good of her to give me the straight tip, and volunteer to overlook my *ménage*, generally, like a sort of superior lady housekeeper! I am not so bad at it myself, thank you?" She worked herself up to a sneer. "Much obliged to Julia, I'm sure, for haunting me, especially as she appears willing to confine herself merely to bothering the sensible mistress of the house, and doesn't go frightening the servants and making them give up their places. Vance wouldn't stop a minute—"

Her brow furrowed a little as she remembered the white, frightened face of Vance that morning.

"It's a fairly cool thing, though," her thought resumed, "for one woman to tell another, flat, that she considers herself part of her because she happens to have adored her husband and does still, I suppose. Man and wife—no, wife and wife—are one flesh. . . . Ha! Ha! . . ."

It was two o'clock, her face changed. Arrowy tinglings, growlings as of a chained monster inside her slender frame, punctuated her words. The pain had come again. . . .

When Miss Walton came in, she would ask her to ring up a doctor. She could not have dragged herself to the instrument now.

★★★★★★

The front door bell rang. She heard Miss Walton's cheery voice making inquiries about Mrs. Mardell's health as she shook the balled snow out of her boots on to the hall mat, and plumped her umbrella into the rack. Mrs. Mardell sat still, physically incapable of rising-, though she had had but a short bout of pain this time.

She had made up her mind to question Miss Walton about Julia. Julia's affairs seemed for the moment essentially her concern. She felt no malevolence towards her in spite of the re-reading of the letter. Miss Walton, the confidante, had never been allowed to see that letter. She should see it now, if she was good and satisfactorily confidential?

"Well, dear, how are you?" Miss Walton had come in, her work-a-day nose reddened with exposure, and her hands thickened with chilblains. "I suppose you are feeling the continuous cold, like the rest of us. And you know, you little minx, that you look best in a tea gown."

"Do I look well?"

"Well, a bit bleached, perhaps, and your eyes rather funny and starey, as if you'd been seeing ghosts?"

"Vance has, she says."

"A ghost in West Kensington! Nonsense!"

"It was a mock funeral, Vance says," Mrs. Mardell remarked in an even voice. "Coming out of a house in this street on Christmas Day, when there was nobody died in it, as they told her." She looked closely at Miss Walton's face. "Do you know anyone at number thirteen? An actress, Vance says—"

"Bless her. Christmas pudding, I should say. No, I don't know a soul in this street besides yourself—"

Mrs. Mardell, with a sigh of relief, leant back again.

"But, I say, Florence, you do look dicky," Miss Walton continued. "What have you been doing with yourself?"

"Perhaps you'll say it is Christmas pudding with me too," replied Mrs. Mardell, laughing feebly. "But I don't know—somehow, I've had a horrid day. I seem to have got a sudden attack of lumbago, or sciatica or something."

"It doesn't sound likely, at your age."

"No, does it? But it's pains right through me at intervals all through the day. I had a fearful bout, just before you came. I daresay it's nothing—"

"Rheumatism, probably," said the other. "Nothing so absurdly painful when it gets hold of one. Here's tea—nice hot tea. It will do you good."

"I've had two goes already."

"Oh, have a third! Nothing like tea for us women! Here, let me pour it out. Your poor little hands are trembling."

"No, I'll manage. Sugar? I forget if you take it? And lots of milk? . . . Alice, how long is it since you saw Julia?"

Mrs. Mardell was surprised at the coolness of Miss Walton's reception of the seldom pronounced name. She might have reflected that the other woman had no particular reason to be shy of it, for she had been Florence's and Julia's confidante during the stormy times of the divorce and had managed to be loyal and friendly to both. She now replied offhandedly to Mrs. Mardell's question—

"Not for six months. Lost sight of the poor dear, rather."

"And when you last saw her, how did she look?"

"Handsome, but rather too fat. I can't say I much liked the look of that, for she's still quite young. I always fancy it means morbid growths, and that kind of thing. Poor old Juley! One never even sees her name in the bills now, does one?"

"Retired on the allowance Joe makes her, I suppose," said Florence Mardell bitterly. "I can't think how she could bring herself to take his money?"

"Only that she's poor, of course."

"How poor?"

"One can't tell," replied Alice Walton, "with people like Julia. She's Irish. She's the kind of woman who pays a man from Douglas's to come and wave her hair, and dry it on towels that you can't see for the holes! You understand. She's the sweetest, cleverest, untidiest soul alive! She took a flat in Paris with a friend, and the state of that flat, I'm told, after a week of Julia, beat even the *femme de ménage* they got in to do for them! They never dressed or ate, but lay about all day in *peignoirs* and smoked cigarettes. They got in a hypnotist to talk to them about Joe, I believe. Julia makes no secret of her devotion to Joe, as I suppose you are aware? . . . Now, Florence, keep your feet up—there's a good girl! You look ghastly."

"Yes, I know. So, she's still mad on Joe? Tell me more about her. She isn't a woman of much taste, I fancy—can't dress a bit?"

"No, but a generous creature, full of impulses and never a mean one among them. I do admire her character, I confess."

"So, do I," said Florence Mardell. "And so, did Joe, I believe."

"Does. He can't help seeing her qualities, and being flattered by her immense devotion to him. Though, of course, he's used to it—he can't help being faskynating! He's such a sprite and yet so strong. Julia was as big again as he was, pretty nearly. He admired her awfully, as little men do always admire big women."

"I'm not very big, yet Joe admires me."

"Oh—I know he does and long may he continue. He may, for Julia, that's one thing, she's strictly 'hands off,' I know. She's never made the slightest attempt to get him ever to go and see her."

"He wouldn't go if she did."

"I shouldn't be too sure of that," said Miss Walton, carried, by love of her subject, beyond the limits of tactfulness. "And what would it matter? Joe was truly fond of her till you came along, you little witch! And she's never done anything to set him against her or hurt his self-love. That's what a man minds. I don't see how he could have refused her a thing like that, nor could you. No, give her credit for her generosity, I believe he proposed it and that she refused to see him, steadily. Nobody in theatrical circles thought for one moment you'd keep him against her. The betting was all that, if she had tried, she'd have got him back in a month."

"No, not if she'd tried, she wouldn't," said Florence Mardell earnestly. "She loved him too much!"

Her lips sketched a grimace as she spoke; her hand moved to her side and her eyes filled with tears.

"What is it, dear? The pain again?"

"I was afraid of it—my body was, I mean. But it luckily doesn't seem to mean business, this time. And I don't believe I could feel anymore—I don't seem to have any organs left. It's the peace of emptiness—exhaustion! Do, dear, let me go on talking and thrashing out things. What I meant when I said that Julia loved him too much, was this, that it is a mistake to love so openly and make such a noise about it. Men don't value affection that's cried from the house tops. It just disgusts them. Love at breakfast, love at luncheon, love all day; it's sure to pall. Love shouldn't be mixed up with daily bread-getting. It should be a speciality, not a sort of smoking mixture, advertised on every passing omnibus."

"Go on, child, you interest me. Why, you yourself simply adore Joe!"

A faun-like, tormenting expression Miss Walton had never seen there, came over Florence Mardell's face, as, in the weak exhausted voice of a privileged invalid, she proceeded—

"I adore Joe as smart women permit themselves to adore the thing they value and mean to keep. I believe I prize Joe, not for what he is, though I'm aware he's a genius, but for what he means to me—light and kisses and frocks and champagne. There isn't so much of that as there would be if Julia and her allowance didn't stop the way! I love Joe because he's the fount of life to me, because I feel good when he is in the room, and dull when he is out of it.

"I happen to know that I shouldn't feel that about him if he came to me ill and hipped and unsuccessful. Sounds mean, but it's true. I perfectly enjoy the placards telling me that he can make a cat laugh, and critics saying he is like what Garrick used to be. An 'abridgement'—what is it? I am quite cross with him when the notices are poor, and I don't in the least long, then, to take his head on my shoulder and comfort him. It's he who has to comfort me."

"Julia had a rather different theory!"

"Yes, and Julia lost him and I got him. She called him her boy and her baby! He even told me so, saying how nice it was of her. Quite sincere! He thought so, I daresay. I knew better, as if any man liked to be made to feel small! She'd have handed the moon down to him if she'd had it in her power, and when he cried for such a little easy thing as a divorce, of course she gave it him. A fool, I call her."

"I don't know about that," the friend replied, combatively. "Greater love hath no woman, than she lay down her marriage lines for her husband."

"Well, I love him, but I couldn't have done that! I should simply have had to stick to him just the same. And then—if he had thrown me over, nothing would ever have induced me to take money from him!"

"But if you were extravagant and nearly starving?"

"I'd have found a man to support me and buy me frills!"

"Then you couldn't have loved him, to degrade the thing he had once set store by."

"If Joe had left me, anything could have become of me for all I cared! . . . I see what you are driving at, Alice, you think I can't feel love as Julia does, because I haven't got beetle brows meeting over my forehead and a big contralto chest to sigh with. My way with Joe, whether I do it from self-control or inclination, comes out best. A man like Joe needs a lot of spoiling, but not from the woman he cares for. I let outsiders do it for me. I don't cosset him, or make a point of being home every afternoon from my calls at an unearthly hour to dine with him. If a boy offers me a dinner, I accept and Joe gives me my taxi fare, and looks me over, and sees that my dress, for the other man, mind you, is all right.

"Nor do I wait up for him when he comes back, I just see supper's laid out all right and the fire kept up and go to bed. I don't make him look ridiculous by fetching him at the theatre, as some actors' wives do. Julia, I hear, used to take parts that didn't suit her, so as to ensure her being on the spot with him, every night. I never know where he is and I don't go getting his pals to play detective and tell me. I may be conceited, but I do flatter myself, that wherever Joe is, he is thinking of me, and of how soon he can get back to me."

"I think you are perfectly right," Miss Walton replied rather sardonically. "It's the best view to take of marriage, and for a woman married to a popular actor, the only one. Do you happen to know where Joe is, now?"

"Yes, I happen to be able to tell you. He is at the theatre, rehearsing the new play. They must be through by now, though! He'll be here in a minute. I haven't seen him since yesterday. We dine together at six o'clock!"

"And it's half-past five now. Well, I must be off. Goodbye, old girl, and I wouldn't neglect those pains if I were you. I expect it's only rheumatism, but as a general rule internal pains should not be ignored. You look rather flushed—"

"I must go and put on some powder before Joe comes. Goodbye. Tell Gladys to come and clear away the tea as you go out."

Mrs. Mardell was left alone, with two imperfectly drained tea-cups and some broken crumbs of cake on a Japanese tray. The spirit lamp under the kettle had gone out—she missed its cheerful flame. She was hemmed in, her knees were imprisoned by the flaps of the tea-table so that she could not lie back. . . . She felt disinclined to move and go upstairs for that dust of powder that was to impress Joe. . . . Everything was a bother . . . she felt very stupid, but she had no more pain, thank God! . . .

So, she sat on, waiting for the maid to clear away the tea things and set her free, bolt upright in her hostess-corner of the flower-begarlanded sofa, with the pink-shaded lamp behind her, convenient for reading, only she did not want to read. Her head drooped, till her face was in shadow. Her eyes were fixed on a Liberty cosy corner that adequately filled an ugly bare place in the room but that no one ever sat in—and then and there she had a vision.

It seemed to her that her sight pierced through the faint scaffolding of white wood pillars that bore up the inane piece of furniture. She had a view of a cold, bare room distempered in pale green, and nearly empty of furniture, excepting for a bed and an armchair.

Presently, she distinguished a table made of slabs of glass, covered with bits of shining steel and physic bottles. She smelt a strong odour of ether. Then sundry persons surged into her field of vision, though they had been there all the time; two white-capped nurses, bending solicitously over a bed where a third person lay with long black hair spread over the pillow. A woman, who was speaking so faintly that Florence felt rather than heard what she said.

"You are sure you have sent for him?" the image seemed to say urgently. "Nurse! Nurse! It's the 'Quality Theatre'!"

"Yes, Madam, we have telephoned through—'Quality Theatre.' It would have been as well—! Can you not give us your husband's home address, Madam?"

"I don't know it," the patient replied wearily. "But he will be at the theatre. He is always at the theatre. It's his life now. He'll come . . . he'll come!"

"Surely, Madam—"

The nurse turned away to speak to a colleague who had apparently only recently left the room and now returned. Florence then saw the features of the woman on the bed, features never seen by her except across the footlights, charged with bright white and rose. They were grey and unrecognisable now, yet Florence knew whose they were.

She heard the conversation of the two whispering women the while.

"She's sinking fast," said the elder nurse.

"She'll last till he comes, I think," replied the younger. "He's just telephoned through that he's on his way here!"

With her words the whole house and its ramifications were now revealed to Florence Mardell—as it were the open front of a doll's house. She saw the steps leading up to the door—there were eight of them—the hall, the staircase and the room where the patient lay, at one and the same time. She heard a jingling of bells and the prod of a swift hansom suddenly pulled up at the behest of the urgently waved umbrella of a man within—her husband. She saw him leap out and dash up the steps to the door that was flung open as soon as he touched the bell. She missed no single stage of his progress upstairs to Julia's room. The nurse opened the door of it, admitted him, and passed out herself.

Florence recognised Joe's familiar gesture—the overcoat hastily flung off and thrown aside, disclosing the dapper little ordinary man, with the long lock of hair, that was his mark of genius, lifting on his forehead as usual, as he impetuously advanced towards the bed. She realised the weak complaisance that stood for paradisaical joy on the face of the woman lying there, whose light of life was too nearly extinguished to permit of a finer demonstration. But the actor's face was a marvel. This expression, evoked for the beloved dying woman only, was of such a tragic madness as no mime could ever hope to originate or imitate. Florence had never seen that look on his face, and sharp knowledge shot through her that even if she in her turn lay dying she would not see it then. A sob shook, but did not interrupt her steady absorption in the sight spread before her.

Her hungry eyes watched the discreet nurse left in charge retire to the mantelpiece and thoughtfully examine her sleeve links, as the lover, with passionate solicitude and a cunning born of intimate usage, sat down and laying his arms round his mistress's neck, raised her a little, so as to gain her ear for the last whispers of love.

As a ghost to earth returned, the second wife apprehended the dreadful sense of the words those two exchanged together. Joe spoke with no sense of renewal, but as if Julia and he had parted but a few hours, or it may be days, ago. Florence could not resent, but she suffered the first pangs of a lifelong sorrow as she listened to Julia's faint sighs of content, her weak rejoinders to Joe's protestations of undying fidelity, his vows that turned to old, wise, baby talk, and the promises she wrung from him so easily. . . .

The nurse still fumbled with her sleeve links, blinded by unusual tears.

"You will see me buried?" Julia exacted, her hands twisting in Joe's hair, playing with the long lock. . . . "You will make all the arrangements for me, Joe, won't you? I want you—I want you to manage it! . . ."

Vance was right. Joe was the puny ghost mourner. . . . And Florence looked on eagerly again.

"It shall be our wedding . . . our re-marriage!" He soothed her. "We meet again—to part no more . . . you and I, Julia, my Julia. . . ."

What did he mean to do when Julia died, as die she must? It was very near now. Florence listened and looked, their voices seemed fainter, more furtive; the scene in the bedchamber was growing evanescent, ragged, as if there were rents in the film. She sometimes feared, so eager was she to see the whole of her own tragedy, that she was beginning to distinguish the wooden lines of the supports of the cosy corner that framed and crossed her view. She realised that Julia's hour was approaching and that the vision would fade with its instigator. The doctor had come in and the other nurse. She could detect on all three faces the professional discouragement painted there by their foreknowledge of the event. They would look cheerful, normal again, after what must be, was over. But Joe's face surely could never be set in comic lines again, those muscles, so deeply inured to tragedy, might never relax or unbend. . . .

She knew it when Julia died, though at the precise moment no one spoke, no one moved in the room for a while. Julia died, where she listed, where Joe would have her—in his arms. The shape of Julia would never go out of them. There would never be room there any more for Florence, whom he had not loved! . . .

******

She raised her head with a jerk. The pink cushions and hangings of the Liberty cosy corner filled up the lines of the woodwork again.

The pillars framed triviality as usual.

She was sitting in her own drawing-room, and Gladys the stupid maid, was there—just come in to take away the tea things.

Mrs. Mardell spoke.

"Dinner will be late tonight."

"Yes, Ma'am, I see it's just gone half-past six now."

"Your master is kept. . . . He has things to see to. . . ."

Gladys, eager to show she understood, interrupted. "Yes, Ma'am, Vance will keep dinner back."

She folded up the table and set her mistress free. Mrs. Mardell had no more pain and knew she would not have any more, but she sat on in her place until seven, the hour at which her husband usually left for the theatre during this piece, in which his part entailed a somewhat lengthy and careful make up. . . .

She heard the twist of the latch key in the door below, and for the first time in her life, shrank from meeting the eyes of the man she adored with a new and passionate love. But it was the lover of Julia who would come in to her and say something kind, as usual. Kind—merely kind was all he had ever been, in all these years of her blindness. She put out her hands as if to push him from her, and her lips almost framed the words, "Stay, oh, stay away!"

No use, no use! Her observation, tensely quickened, told her that he paused in the hall, for there was an abrupt cessation of all movement. He was hesitating? . . . Then he made up his mind to the disagreeable duty. So, Florence read the gesture. His sturdy dutiful footsteps could be heard ascending . . . a wild whiff of ether seemed to precede him! . . .

Her eyes dropped uncontrollably, as he touched and turned the handle of the door gently. . . . It was done. He was in the room.

How did he look? She must know. She raised her sad eyes, and contemplated the dwarf-actor standing there on the threshold of the pretty cheap drawing-room, oppressing, appalling her with his overpowering dignity. His hair was disordered, and clung, matted, to his damp forehead; the long lock fell over it in the style of one of the good-natured roisterers he excelled in portraying. But his face had the make-up of a clown; the dark features stood out in a mask of putty-coloured whiteness, all but the lips, which had no red. Those eyes which had just looked on death, stared down on her, not unkindly, but unseeing. . . .

She spoke at last, to break the awful spell which was winding itself round and round her, more than for any other reason.

"Julia is dead," she said.

"I know." He took a step forward into the room, and made a cold gesture of menace. She recoiled—then rose and faced him.

"She died in my arms. I loved her."

He turned away. It was as if he had laid a book aside and a leaf had been folded down. He muttered, with a semblance of forced preoccupation with the business of life—

"I just looked in to tell you that I am going straight back to the theatre."

"Without any dinner?" she shrieked. Then, more calmly—

"Well, you will have something to eat when you come home, won't you? What time will that be?"

It was the first time in her life she had asked such a question, and his answer to it, delivered over his shoulder as he went downstairs, cut her to the heart.

"Perhaps never!"

Scant consolation! She knew that he did not mean to kill himself—at least not yet, for he had promised to make the arrangements for and attend Julia's funeral.

The Memoir

Did women in Society ever "speak" to other women, when a man dear to them both was concerned?

Had such an outrageous course ever been pursued since the days when Chriemhild "spoke" to Gudrun in the midst of the Rhine stream?

Little Lady Greenwell pondered this, time after time, day after day, as she sat dressed in her ineffectual Paris best, alone, in crowds, in sunlight gardens, lamp-lit ballrooms, unlit *boudoirs* arranged for cosy gossiping teas. She never talked gossip, but she listened to it. A great deal of it covertly was about herself, or rather about her husband. That was one of the reasons why she felt that she ought to speak—speak kindly, seriously, effectively.

She fully meant to tell Cynthia what it was her duty to tell her, but she could not make up her mind to take the first plunge into unconventionality.

So, she sat about through a whole season, watching Sir Hilary's social triumphs—she herself never triumphed—and arranged her speech, carefully composing it beforehand, rehearsing it, canvassing the relative claims of diplomacy and frankness, fulness and brevity, emotion or matter of fact. What arguments should she use, and which let go? Which, having regard to the character of Cynthia Chenies, would be likely to affect that volatile lady most? Should she plead her own years the more, her own looks the less? Should she take high moral grounds?

Should she put forward the young widow's personal expediency? It all depended on what form of admonishment Cynthia would take best.

Lady Greenwell was honest enough to admit to herself that she proposed to lecture Cynthia as much for her own good, as Cynthia's.

Truly, she felt that it would be a difficult thing to keep self out of it, or as much in the background as possible.

"Just you let my man alone!"

That was what Kate of Wapping would have said to Peg of Limehouse, and no more ado, but could Lady Greenwell of Highfields, Hungerford, and 50, Carlton House Terrace so bluntly declare herself to the Honourable Mrs. Chenies of Portland Place? Did well-bred women do these things? It seemed at once so absurdly simple, just as you might ask someone to take his foot off your dress and no offence, and at the same time so appallingly impossible a thing to do. Women in Society were not supposed to show when they were annoyed, ask for explanations, or to "act straight."

How they suffered in consequence of these absurd fetishes of conduct they set up, women alone knew. Moreover, such a subject, even if it were fairly and squarely discussed between two exceptional women, would represent the merely primitive appeal of the one to the other's generosity, and generosity, though permissible in Wapping or Limehouse is not the "thing" in Mayfair or Portland Place.

Yet some women were really and truly generous at heart—Cynthia was, she was sure. Had it not been for the presence between them of this male bone of contention, Sir Hilary, Lady Greenwell would have been quite fond of Cynthia Chenies. She did not dislike her even now, when Cynthia was making her so uncomfortable, and she admired her sincerely, her frocks and her style. Hilary, did, and she could not help following suit in this as in all else.

And, naturally, Cynthia could not help liking Hilary and his open attentions. Who could help liking Hilary and complying with him when he chose to flirt, and he always did choose? He was a born flirt, and he was eight years younger than his wife. Wives, who were burdened with odious supernumerary years, must, of course, give their man a little rope, and Mabel Greenwell gave hers a good deal.

Hilary Greenwell was a traveller, who came home and wrote books about it. He danced and dashed through a season, and then packed up and went to risk his life on some inaccessible mountain or other. Of course, when he came back, brown as a berry, and with sheaves of notes and measurements, he was the rage, and women simply "clawed him" for their parties, and adored him for their *boudoirs*.

Cynthia Chenies was no exception to the rule. Though a widow, she was little more than a girl, and looked a mere child. At the parties she gave in her big house, so Hilary would say, you always expected to see the dolls set up, and find pips in the orange juice soup, and have to mumble the "pretend" biscuit joint. Childlike, she knew no measure in her appreciation of the handsome traveller returned, and people were saying now that she was making a fool of herself, and that Lady Greenwell didn't like it.

They were wrong there, Lady Greenwell wasn't jealous at all. She was sure of Hilary, and would not have insulted him by display of vulgar jealousy. The effect of the scandal on her only amounted to discomfort. Great discomfort she might say, and even annoyance, and a few wet pillowed nights, loyally concealed from Hilary. She was neither young nor beautiful: it behoved her to be clever. She could, she knew, keep his love, though she was unable to restrain those loose tendrils of his fancy which waved airily to and fro, catching here and there temporarily on the fair upstanding flowers that bloomed every year in the great parterre of London's garden of seasonal delights. Hilary loved her and her only. She must do nothing foolish.

Whatever she felt, whatever she said to Cynthia Chenies, must be a secret for Sir Hilary, a matter between Cynthia and herself. Some women—fools!—thought little Lady Greenwell—would have rushed at once to their husband with an appeal or a command, to "put a stop to it at once," thus definitely estranging the coveted man without affecting the issue in the desired way. No, it rested with her and her alone, to convince Cynthia of the awkwardness of the situation created by Cynthia's careless compliance with the fancies of the irresponsible Hilary, a situation merely irksome to his wife, but positively injurious to his wife's friend. Great interests on either hand were not concerned. No one's heart was in it.

Punctuality was Lady Greenwell's virtue—consequently her husband's too. She sat on the sofa at the Creswicks', fan in hand, handkerchief in lap. The man who was going to take her in stood over her chair, uttering the usual commonplaces, when the door opened to admit one single, smiling lady—Cynthia Chenies, late as usual, wearing the cluster of flowers she always wore, and that everyone attributed to Sir Hilary's devotion. Lady Greenwell happened to know that Mrs. Chenies ordered them at the florist's for herself. But how could she tell people that!

She saw, what, of course, other people saw, Cynthia's careless delicately possessive glance at Sir Hilary, a glance that effectually singled him out, as it were, from a group of like patterned men, clustered about the fireplace. So stupid of Cynthia! Nothing else, of course.

Lady Greenwell knew, as well as if she had been told, that Betty Creswick would send the two in together. Suppose she spoke to Betty Creswick, and asked her not to join the tacit conspiracy that prevails in well-regulated, pleasure-loving society, to give the woman, whenever it is possible, to the man she is supposed to want? Never! She would die sooner! For Society would resent such an anti-social proposal and protect its own joys and convenience.

It must go on although it was making her miserable. Would this wretched season never come to an end? Not that she need expect to find any intermission of her troubles even then! For there would come visits, "country-housing" up and down the length and breadth of England and Scotland, the three would be asked constantly to meet each other. She had been so nice to Cynthia, that people all thought that Lady Greenwell had accepted it. There would be no rest for her till the late autumn, when Sir Hilary had agreed to go with a party of men on an expedition to locate a continent somewhere. He would be away for four months.

As a loving wife she ought to have dreaded this approaching separation; she was shocked to realise that in her heart of hearts, she was looking forward to it. She would not see the light of his countenance, but then, neither would the other! Jealousy makes sad dogs-in-the-manger of us all. And she would have the delight of his frequent letters. That is, unless he wrote to Cynthia too?

If only she had had a child! Cynthia had one, Cynthia, a widow, with no husband now to bind faster to her side therewith! What a pity it all was!

Dinner was announced. Sir Hilary gave Cynthia his arm, with a certain look . . . proud . . . protecting . . . sheepish rather. . . . Yes, she *must* speak.

She placed her hand lightly on the sleeve of she knew not whom, and followed Hilary and Cynthia into the dining-room. She was miserable, she was sure that Hilary, had he but known how unhappy she was making herself, would have tried at once to alter his line of conduct. And he would have failed! Of that, too, she was sure. Man can do nothing in this line, of himself alone, save by the grace of the woman who is leading him astray. It was settled; she must speak to Cynthia!

Cynthia Chenies, who was not lacking in perception, realised at once the meaning of the innocently diplomatic, intensely special glance which Lady Greenwell, placed exactly opposite, fixed upon her, as soon as everybody was seated.

"Mabel Greenwell means to speak to me!"

She could harbour no other thought, from the fish onward. She was a nervous, lazy woman, and the fear of a "woman's row" was intensely repugnant to her. She hated fuss about men, and bad form, and unconventionally of any kind. Her affair with Sir Hilary, whatever it might mean to her, was openly, at least, quite within the bounds of her world's convention, and she deeply resented any attempt on Lady Greenwell's part to draw it out of its limbo of self-chosen vagueness.

To herself, she was willing to admit that she loved Sir Hilary very well, nay, desperately. She was less willing to admit that she suffered over this illicit attachment, and yet did suffer a good deal, for she was a good woman, and Lady Greenwell a healthy woman, so the chances were she would never get him honestly.

She knew Sir Hilary loved her, was fond of Mabel, and respected them both. That being the case, he would not do either of them a wrong for the whole world.

There it was! What an *impasse!* Three scrupulously honourable people caught in a net! No issue but death, and she could not contemplate even Mabel's death with equanimity. Mabel had been very kind to her, and she and Mabel would have been the greatest friends if Sir Hilary had not stood between them.

Though she pitied Mabel for her age, her plainness, she could not help feeling a little angry with Mabel for having presumed to marry Sir Hilary; she should not have allowed Hilary to persuade her that she was a suitable wife for him. Hilary was so plausible. Once, however, having committed the initial error, Mabel should not have hoped to keep him, except by courtesy.

She knew Sir Hilary well enough not to feel obliged to talk to him, so she plodded imperturbably through the menu, eating a good deal to justify her taciturnity. "Oh, I am so hungry," she said once or twice, "I have been down to Brighton today to see the boy!"

Sir Hilary never worried. He quietly looked after her, gave her her own way now as ever. She was heedless, he safeguarded her reputation as well as he could. He never wrote to her when he was away; she would have forgotten to destroy his letters. He called on her not too often; he dined with her now and then, generally with his wife. There was no need to compromise her by overt acts of this sort. The mad, bad, sympathetic world was kind enough to cater for the indulgence of their affection; in all the *ragôuts* of society were they skilfully combined, and discreet opportunities of meeting served up to them daily, with the result that everyone was happy and amused, except Lady Greenwell, who had been born and bred in the country and never could acquire London's cynical tone.

Once or twice, however, before this evening, Cynthia had suspected some such *strata* of unsuspected *bourgeois* feeling in Mabel. She almost wished Betty Creswick would not be so kind to Hilary and herself, and a little kinder to Mabel. She sometimes even avoided dull parties where she knew he was going. Not so Sir Hilary, he had no scruples of this kind. He adored her, he told her so—"and as there's nothing wrong about it all, why shouldn't we see as much of each other as people will let us?"

"Ah, but other people—"—an ellipsis for Mabel, whom it pleased her to mention to him as little as possible. But he understood, in his breezy, butterfly way.

"Mabel is all right. Mabel's a good sort, and understands me. She isn't such a fool as to trouble about gossip."

He never said more. It was tacitly assumed between them that Mabel was awfully fond of him and all that, but "demonstrations would simply bore her, you know." Meanwhile, he loved Cynthia with every fibre of his being—all save the domestic ones, it was understood—she was his Egeria, his goddess, his good angel, the woman he thought of last thing at night and the first thing on waking, in the jungle, on the veldt, on the frozen Himalayan slope. He was hers—hers only. No one else cared, not even Mabel, who had "settled down."

Cynthia Chenies hardly realised it, but this passion had come to be her life. She breathed and dressed but for Hilary. She was a cold woman, and content with its platonic manifestations, but she technically regretted the immense waste exemplified in the position of the lover, tied for all his days to two women, neither of whom was or could be everything to him.

She caught Mabel's eye now and again full of timid reticences and prudent punctilios, but expressing over and above all others, the simple emotion that betrayeth itself in speech.

"I must speak, or burst!" the poor woman fancied Mabel saying, and shivered over her chocolate *mousse*.

The moment came. Sir Hilary left soon after dinner to attend an Ethnological Society's meeting, and Lady Greenwell timidly offered to motor Mrs. Chenies home. For some fateful reason or other, that lady's brougham was not forthcoming.

"It is frightfully out of your way, Mabel!" argued the trapped fly.

Gently, but firmly, the spider informed her that a mere difference of a mile and a quarter did not in the least constitute out-of-the-wayness, and the hostess settled it by her vague encouragements.

"So nice of you to chaperon each other like that!"

Mrs. Chenies hardly grasped the significance of Lady Creswick's remark until the knees of Lady Greenwell and herself were safely stowed under the same bearskin rug.

"I wanted to speak to you, Cynthia," began Lady Greenwell honestly, without preface or pretence.

"Did you?" replied the other, shrinking as far away from her companion as she could into the corner of the motor. Then, collecting herself, she said, "You can, you know."

"It is a little difficult for me—but then—I must remember it is for your good, Cynthia."

"Oh, for my good!" exclaimed Mrs. Chenies, stung by the familiar, too familiar exordium. "You must remember I am not a mere girl—I am a widow."

"That is just it," continued Lady Greenwell, delighted. "A young and"—with a gulp—"pretty widow."

"Oh, don't mention it," the other begged her flippantly.

Though her tone grated on and disturbed Lady Greenwell, that lady continued, almost apologetically—

"That is the right way to take it, dear, not seriously! Just a little hint, you know—laugh about it as much as you like when I am done, but listen to me for a minute. . . .! Could you not contrive, dear, to see a little less of Hilary—my husband?"

"I know he's your husband, Mabel, well enough!" Mrs. Chenies jerked out crossly. "And I don't see so much of him as all that!"

"Oh, I know, dear, I know all about your friendship—your intimacy . . . it's nothing at all, nothing at all . . . only you see people will talk."

"Yes, bother them!"

"We mustn't pay too much attention to gossip, of course, but we owe it to—ourselves, to take some notice of what is said. You may want to marry again?"

"Never!"

"Oh, don't say that!" pleaded the other pitifully. "You are sure to—so young and pretty. But don't you think, that meantime, that people should couple your name and Hilary's is prejudicial—rather to you? Of course, I know—"

"What?"

"That there is nothing at all serious between you—nothing at all, Hilary"—she blurted out the indecent fact—"Hilary is devoted to me, and always has been, he has never swerved for the fraction of an instant. Besides, he would not—"

"Would not what?"

"Oh, Cynthia, you do make it so difficult! You seem so stony. . . . You aren't offended?"

"No, of course not, I only wanted to know what it was Hilary wouldn't do?"

Her careless use of the beloved's name hurt Lady Greenwell a good deal. She drew herself up—

—"Would not allow himself to make love to another woman during his wife's lifetime. You may as well take that for granted. Only—he is younger than I, and heedless, and you are most attractive, while I am a plain woman, well-dressed. And the world thinks, of course, the usual thing! Oh! Cynthia, help me! And it would not matter, of course, if it were not for you and your reputation, though I can't deny that it makes me very uncomfortable to hear him lightly spoken of."

"What do you want me to do about it?"

"I said what. See less of him. See him only at my house."

"Will you give him your orders, then, not to call at mine?"

"Dear Cynthia, how could I do that? What do you think of me?"

"I think you are like all women—want to get someone else to pull the chestnuts out of the fire for you. Why should I do your dirty work? And it would not do either, I couldn't forbid him my house without creating remark, and doing exactly what you don't want done—getting him talked about. Nor can I go and tell Betty Creswick not to send us in to dinner together—"

"Of course, you can't tell her, but there are methods "

"And I refuse to employ them, and let all the world think I am doing it because I have a guilty conscience or because you have been making a scene. You don't want that surely?"

"No." She shuddered. "Then it has been no use my speaking, practically? And, Cynthia, you can have no idea what it has cost me!"

"I am truly sorry, but, indeed, dear, this sort of carriage lecture never does any good. You can't have straight talks to women. No woman can employ another woman to help keep her husband for her—it really isn't done."

"Keep my husband! But have I not been telling you, Cynthia, all this time, that if I thought for one moment that my husband had been unfaithful to me in word, or thought, or deed, I would not have spoken to anybody at all about it, I would just have died! It is precisely because I do believe in him—"

"Then it makes it quite simple—go on believing in him. You may," replied the other woman, drily, as the carriage stopped at the door of her own house. "Goodnight, Mabel! Thank you for the lift."

"And are you cross, Cynthia? Believe me, I meant well."

"You meant well by yourself, eh, dear? Just realise that you were speaking for yourself—"

"Oh, Cynthia, you *are* cruel."

"Yes, but honest. Think it over. Let it all be as if it hadn't been. Shall I kiss you?" She paused, with a light foot on the step.

"Yes, please. You know I am really fond of you, Cynthia, but you seem to have beaten me."

"Oh, no!" asseverated Mrs. Chenies, "only convinced you that these sort of things can't be done."

They kissed.

"I had doubts about the wisdom of it at the time," murmured Lady Greenwell. "I thought you might say it was tactless. Hilary says I have no tact."

"Never mind, you are sure he loves you, and that's better than tact—that's everything!"

Mrs. Chenies was shaking out her skirts on the pavement, pulling out her latch key. . . .

"So that's all right. There's an end of it—"

"Yes, and come to dinner tomorrow night, will you?"

"Yes, dear. Goodnight!"

Two hands met and clasped over the window-bar of the carriage. Lady Greenwell watched her friend in, and whirled away. Mrs. Chenies rushed impulsively upstairs to her room, and threw herself on her bed in an agony of weeping. They were tears both for herself and Mabel.

★★★★★★

It was a year later. Mrs. Chenies in modified mourning—for she had made herself as black as she dared—rang for admittance at the door of Greenwell House. The very house seemed in mourning. It used to be furnished exotically, with variegated hangings and things Hilary had brought back from abroad. Cynthia shivered. She had been sent for. Why? Why did Mabel Greenwell want to see her? The cords of their friendship had been sensibly loosened. It was perhaps as well. They mourned in their separate corners—of London.

She was ushered into the presence of a little woman whose deep official weeds seemed almost to obliterate her slight frame and make her fade into the surrounding blackness. She rushed at and clung to her handsome visitor, and kissed her mournfully and deliberately on both cheeks.

"Dear, dear Cynthia, how good of you to come to me!"

"Dearest Mabel, how good of you to be willing to see me!"

"Oh, I wanted you—somehow—so much! I believe, when all is said and done, Cynthia, I am fonder of you than I am of any one!"

Mrs. Chenies winced and suffered herself to be kissed again on both cheeks. She looked extremely handsome in her glowing purples and blues. The widow's inexpressive eyes were merely dimmed and bleared by her tears, those of Cynthia Chenies shone, and she was not so silly as to redden the lids by dabbing them with a handkerchief, as Lady Green well did.

"He was so fond of you, Cynthia! He has left you to me as a sort of legacy. We often spoke of you."

Cynthia started. It had surely been a tacit convention between herself and the dead Hilary, that—

"Yes, I ventured at last to tell him about that talk I had with you once, and he took it just as you did. He laughed at me and said that I had no right to worry you with that sort of thing and that you were perfectly justified in being 'short' with me, as you were, Cynthia, you know. He thought it very nice of you to forgive me and go on seeing us as usual."

"Yes, yes, but I saw very little of him alone after that."

"He went away so soon after, didn't he? That was perhaps a good thing—it gave one time—"

"I don't think you had any need to tell him."

"Oh, my dear, what could it matter? There was such perfect confidence between us, and I preferred that a trifling incident like that should not be allowed to interfere with it. Surely you don't mind?"

"Not now!" replied Cynthia Chenies, with an effort. "And I suppose you had a perfect right to do as you liked about it."

"That's all right then. And Hilary said—dear thing !—when he left me to go on that wretched expedition that killed him, that I was to be as nice to you as I could, and see as much of you as you would allow me to do, and so I have, and so I mean to."

"Don't, don't cry so, dear!"

"Oh, do let me cry—it helps me! And how can I help it, when

I think of the dearest husband ever woman had, lost to me, gone—gone—killed, out there alone, among horrid savages. . . . Why, Cynthia, you are crying too!"

"I can't help it either," said the other savagely, disdaining to wipe her tears away.

"Cynthia, you were fond of him, too—now don't say you were not!"

"I was."

Lady Greenwell rose. She looked taller. She looked grim.

"And that is the reason I thought—I made up my mind that you were the proper person to consult about this. . . ."

"This?" asked the other, following the direction of those sad sunken eyes.

"Yes! It was his last wish, Cynthia!" Lady Greenwell pointed to a large bulging packet lying, with a magnificent despatch box, close to her elbow, and continued, in her thin, nervous, passionate voice—

"You know, when he got ill over there—it came on so gradually—he never ceased writing to me till the very last—he got his secretary to send home the MS. of his new book to me. He wanted me to see to the publication of it. I was to edit it, if he never came back to do it himself—and I was to ask you to be co-editress."

"Good God!"

"Oh, don't be frightened, dear, there is nothing to do, it is all done. I did it, only, as he said you were to see it, before it came out, I could not but prepare to carry out his dear wishes. And now I must tell you, as he is gone, I should like to call it *Memorials of a Noble Soul*, something like that, and add some of his letters to me. I have them all here, in this despatch box, I never destroyed a single line of dear darling Hilary's—"

"They will make a most interesting book!" murmured Mrs. Chenies, looking away.

"Yes, won't they, only, of course," Lady Greenwell breathed softly, with a watery smile of triumph, "they will want some editing. They are too intimate, too personal for the ear of the general public. It could not be otherwise. But, still, I don't think the public should lose because he was in love with his wife, do you?"

"No, certainly not."

"There is a great deal in them of purely general interest, of course, but it still wants weeding of lover's phrases and endearments and so on. So, I thought the best plan would be for me to read them all aloud

131

to you, and consult you as to what is to be left in, or struck out,"

Cynthia Chenies groaned aloud. Lady Greenwell smiled. She had gained confidence.

"Cynthia, dear, how like you! You were always afraid of hard work, and there is nothing—nothing bores you so much as listening. Hilary noticed that. 'These brilliant women!' he used to say."

"Let's have the letters," ejaculated Mrs. Chenies bluffly. She adjusted a cushion or two behind her shoulders. "I have learnt how to listen lately. Let's have tea first."

"Certainly!" Lady Greenwell rang the bell. Tea was brought. The hostess dispensed it. Then, with many a reminiscent pause, and sob and dab of the handkerchief, Lady Greenwell opened the despatch box, and produced letters tied up in blue, Hilary's favourite colour. It was the colour of Cynthia's eyes. She fidgeted in her place, and Lady Greenwell offered her another cushion—"because this will all take time."

"I'll read the first that comes," the widow of Hilary declared, when they had both settled down. "I am not afraid of your knowing, Cynthia, how fond he was of me. This one begins—he generally begins so—'Dear little woman'—we can leave that out if you like?"

"You can't. It shows character," observed Mrs. Chenies sombrely. "Go on."

Thus encouraged, Lady Greenwell read, shyly at first, but with gathering confidence, as the map of her husband's affection unrolled itself under her faltering tongue. She read faster. The session was going to last interminably, the letters were good, but long!

"Very vivid! Most interesting!" Mrs. Chenies remarked now and again, drumming with her foot, and with her face turned away.

"It is really rather too intimate!" Lady Greenwell blurted out. "Listen to this—'Darling, my darling.' I can scarcely bear to read it.

All night I lie and toss on my uncomfortable rugs, and think—think of you, darling, and your soft breast!

"You might put 'cheek' there, instead of 'breast,' if you liked?" interposed the co-editress hastily. Lady Greenwell looked up.

"Very well." She used a little pencil at her girdle. Then she resumed—

And I realise how the thought of one sweet woman at home, can be at once the joy and the torture of the traveller. For I don't know if it is most sweet or most bitter, this remembrance of happier hours in altered circumstances. It is joy, but then, sometimes the agony of separation is too keen to bear. . . .

"Oh, that he should feel it so! I'll go on, Cynthia, if you don't feel too much bored.

I stretch out my hands, I look for you, for your warm kind arms—

"You certainly will have to strike all those rhapsodies out," Mrs. Chenies remarked coldly. "He must have been very ill then. Are the letters all like that? If so, they won't make a book of very general interest."

"Ah!" Lady Greenwell exclaimed. She was tossing over the letters feverishly. "They seem to have got mixed! This is one of the English series—written from the Creswicks' place. That must have been sent the summer before he went, for that's the only time he ever went to Betty Creswick's alone. It was the very week I spoke to you, Cynthia."

"I wish you would not keep on bringing that in," interposed Cynthia Chenies irritably, "you were quite right, and I was quite wrong, I see that well enough, now. Go on. We are both dining out tonight, I suppose?"

"Not I," said Lady Greenwell haughtily. "I shall never dine out again." She read on a little to herself. "He didn't like being there without me a bit," she murmured. "In fact, he loathed it."

"Why didn't you go with him, then?" asked Mrs. Chenies, though she knew well enough. She had been one of the Creswick party, and the letter explaining Mabel's reasons for defection had been read aloud to her. But Lady Greenwell couldn't know that.

"Oh, I got a bad chill at the very last moment, and had to wire I couldn't go, Cynthia, shall I read this letter?"

"Of course. It's part of his life, I suppose."

Lady Greenwell read softly:

My own little brown bird, I was so grieved to leave you, tucked up in bed, a darkened room and with only a hired nurse to hold your little hot hand. Here I may say I am not enjoying myself a bit, and yet we are a very gay party and everything jolly. But I can't get any fun out of it without you to talk it over with me, after we've gone to bed at four in the morning. Dear little woman, why did you make me go alone? The Creswick *ménage* is a bit noisy for your quiet sober husband. One gets a little tired of the society of brilliant women—they flash and coruscate—and finally weary. I can't help thinking of a certain still small brown bird at home sitting on the bough, and waiting for me.

"Oh, Cynthia, I do believe, here is something actually about you— he mentions you by name—"

"I'm the brilliant woman that wearies, am I not? Well, let us hear what he says about me."

"Shall I? I've read them all a hundred times, but I don't quite remember, so if it annoys you, mind, it is your own fault. Here goes!"

'The Cynthia of the Minute is really a little overpowering. She seems quite to enjoy saying *risqué* things and compromising herself....'

"I really don't think I ought to read this to you, Cynthia?"

"Read it or I shall snatch it out of your hands."

"Well, you are sure you won't mind?"

Poor little Cynthia, she is astonishingly indiscreet, but she means no harm. She is a dear, nice, ordinary simple woman, pretending to be a sad rake, but as good as gold, really—

"As good as gold, really!"

"Well, isn't that nice for him to say that! Poor dear boy, he always did go straight to the heart of the matter, didn't he? He was, as a matter of fact, awfully fond of you, and this just shows it. He knew you through and through—though. What's the matter?"

"Give me some hot water to drink," gasped Mrs. Chenies. "Is—this your revenge, Mabel?"

"Dear Cynthia, aren't you well? You do use such odd stagey words. Revenge! I am your friend and always will be. My husband wanted us to be friends."

"Well, then, do let us keep friends," said Mrs. Chenies, drinking her scalding hot water hastily and rising. "I must go. An early dinner for the theatre.... Tommy Vavasor...."

"But what about the letters? I have only read two."

"Of course, you must leave that out about me," said Cynthia, speaking very fast and knotting her fur round her neck as if she wanted to throttle herself, "and all personalities about people still living. And you must not print names. But, as for the rest, I should give the letters in their entirety. Go ahead, that's my advice to you. You can hurt none, and your collaborator gives you *carte blanche*."

She escaped. She preserved no memory of the passage from Lady

Greenwell's dull drawing-room to the gas-lit street outside. She bitterly resented the dead man's view of her innocent attempts at disillusioning him, on the only occasion they had met previously to his departure and after his wife's lecture, and she would have given her best jewel to discover whether Mabel's quite thorough revenge had been carefully planned or not?

She married young Lord Vavasor within the year, and contrived, without exciting any suspicion, never again to be alone in the same room with the widowed Lady Greenwell again. But she longed as she had never longed for anything else, to hear of Lady Greenwell's remarriage.

The Prayer

It is but giving over of a game,
That must be lost.—Philaster.

"Come, Mrs. Arne—come, my dear, you must not give way like this! You can't stand it—you really can't! Let Miss Kate take you away—now do!" urged the nurse, with her most motherly of intonations.

"Yes, Alice, Mrs. Joyce is right. Come away—do come away—you are only making yourself ill. It is all over; you can do nothing! Oh, oh, do come away!" implored Mrs. Arne's sister, shivering with excitement and nervousness.

A few moments ago, Dr. Graham had relinquished his hold on the pulse of Edward Arne with the hopeless movement of the eyebrows that meant—the end.

The nurse had made the little gesture of resignation that was possibly a matter of form with her. The young sister-in-law had hidden her face in her hands. The wife had screamed a scream that had turned them all hot and cold—and flung herself on the bed over her dead husband. There she lay; her cries were terrible, her sobs shook her whole body.

The three gazed at her pityingly, not knowing what to do next. The nurse, folding her hands, looked towards the doctor for directions, and the doctor drummed with his fingers on the bed-post. The young girl timidly stroked the shoulder that heaved and writhed under her touch.

"Go away! Go away!" her sister reiterated continually, in a voice hoarse with fatigue and passion.

"Leave her alone, Miss Kate," whispered the nurse at last; "she will work it off best herself, perhaps."

She turned down the lamp, as if to draw a veil over the scene. Mrs. Arne raised herself on her elbow, showing a face stained with tears and purple with emotion.

"What! Not gone?" she said harshly. "Go away, Kate, go away! It is my house. I don't want you, I want no one—I want to speak to my husband. Will you go away—all of you. Give me an hour, half-an-hour—five minutes!"

She stretched out her arms imploringly to the doctor.

"Well . . ." said he, almost to himself.

He signed to the two women to withdraw, and followed them out into the passage. "Go and get something to eat," he said peremptorily, "while you can. We shall have trouble with her presently. I'll wait in the dressing-room."

He glanced at the twisting figure on the bed, shrugged his shoulders, and passed into the adjoining room, without, however, closing the door of communication. Sitting down in an arm-chair drawn up to the fire, he stretched himself and closed his eyes. The professional aspects of the case of Edward Arne rose up before him in all its interesting forms of complication. . . .

★★★★★★

It was just this professional attitude that Mrs. Arne unconsciously resented both in the doctor and in the nurse. Through all their kindness she had realised and resented their scientific interest in her husband, for to them he had been no more than a curious and complicated case; and now that the blow had fallen, she regarded them Both in the light of executioners. Her one desire, expressed with all the shameless sincerity of blind and thoughtless misery, was to be free of their hateful presence and alone—alone with her dead!

She was weary of the doctor's subdued manly tones—of the nurse's commonplace motherliness, too habitually adapted to the needs of all to be appreciated by the individual—of the childish consolation of the young sister, who had never loved, never been married, did not know what sorrow was! Their expressions of sympathy struck her like blows, the touch of their hands on her body, as they tried to raise her, stung her in every nerve.

With a sigh of relief, she buried her head in the pillow, pressed her body more closely against that of her husband, and lay motionless.

Her sobs ceased.

★★★★★★

The lamp went out with a gurgle. The fire leaped up, and died. She raised her head and stared about her helplessly, then sinking down again she put her lips to the ear of the dead man.

"Edward—dear Edward!" she whispered, "why have you left me? Darling, why have you left me? I can't stay behind—you know I can't. I am too young to be left. It is only a year since you married me. I never thought it was only for a year. 'Till death us do part!' Yes, I know that's in it, but nobody ever thinks of that! I never thought of living without you! I meant to die with you. . . .

"No—no—I can't die—I must not—till my baby is born. You will never see it. Don't you want to see it? Don't you? Oh, Edward, speak! Say something, darling, one word—one little word! Edward! Edward! are you there? Answer me for God's sake, answer me!

" Darling, I am so tired of waiting. Oh, think, dearest. There is so little time. They only gave me half-an-hour. In half-an-hour they will come and take you away from me—take you where I can't come to you—with all my love I can't come to you I I know the place—I saw it once. A great lonely place full of graves, and little stunted trees dripping with dirty London rain . . . and gas-lamps flaring all round . . . but quite, quite dark where the grave is . . . a long grey stone just like the rest. How could you stay there?—all alone—all alone—without me?

"Do you remember, Edward, what we once said—that whichever of us died first should come back to watch over the other, in the spirit? I promised you, and you promised me. What children we were! Death is not what we thought. It comforted us to say that then.

"Now, it's nothing—nothing—worse than nothing! I don't want your spirit—I can't see it—or feel it—I want you, you, your eyes that looked at me, your mouth that kissed me—"

She raised his arms and clasped them round her neck, and lay there very still, murmuring, "Oh, hold me, hold me! Love me if you can. Am I hateful? This is me! These are your arms. . . ."

The doctor in the next room moved in his chair. The noise awoke her from her dream of contentment, and she unwound the dead arm from her neck, and, holding it up by the wrist, considered it ruefully.

"Yes, I can put it round me, but I have to hold it there. It is quite cold—it doesn't care. Ah, my dear, you don't care! You are dead. I kiss you, but you don't kiss me. Edward! Edward! Oh, for heaven's sake kiss me once. Just once!

"No, no, that won't do—that's not enough! that's nothing! worse than nothing! I want you back, you, all you. . . . What shall I do? . . .

I often pray, . . . Oh, if there be a God in heaven, and if He ever answered a prayer, let Him answer mine—my only prayer. I'll never ask another—and give you back to me! As you were—as I loved you— as I adored you! He must listen. He must! My God, my God, he's mine—he's my husband, he's my lover—give him back to me!"

★★★★★★

—"Left alone for half-an-hour or more with the corpse! It's not right!"

The muttered expression of the nurse's revolted sense of professional decency came from the head of the staircase, where she had been waiting for the last few minutes. The doctor joined her.

"Hush, Mrs. Joyce! I'll go to her now."

The door creaked on its hinges as he gently pushed it open and went in.

"What's that? What's that?" screamed Mrs. Arne. "Doctor! Doctor! Don't touch me! Either I am dead or he is alive!"

"Do you want to kill yourself, Mrs. Arne?" said Dr. Graham, with calculated sternness, coming forward; "come away!"

"Not dead! Not dead!" she murmured.

"He is dead, I assure you. Dead and cold an hour ago! Feel!" He took hold of her, as she lay face downwards, and in so doing he touched the dead man's cheek—it was not cold! Instinctively his finger sought a pulse.

"Stop! Wait!" he cried in his intense excitement. "My dear Mrs. Arne, control yourself!"

But Mrs. Arne had fainted, and fallen heavily off the bed on the other side. Her sister, hastily summoned, attended to her, while the man they had all given over for dead was, with faint gasps and sighs and reluctant moans, pulled, as it were, hustled and dragged back over the threshold of life.

2

"Why do you always wear black, Alice?" asked Esther Graham, "You are not in mourning that I know of."

She was Dr. Graham's only daughter and Mrs. Arne's only friend. She sat with Mrs. Arne in the dreary drawing-room of the house in Chelsea. She had come to tea. She was the only person who ever did come to tea there.

She was brusque, kind, and blunt, and had a talent for making inappropriate remarks. Six years ago, Mrs. Arne had been a widow for an hour! Her husband had succumbed to an apparently mortal illness, and for the space of an hour had lain dead. When suddenly and inexplicably he had revived from his trance, the shock, combined with six weeks' nursing, had nearly killed his wife. All this Esther had heard from her father. She herself had only come to know Mrs. Arne after her child was born, and all the tragic circumstances of her husband's illness put aside, and it was hoped forgotten. And when her idle question received no answer from the pale absent woman who sat opposite, with listless lack-lustre eyes fixed on the green and blue flames dancing in the fire, she hoped it had passed unnoticed. She waited for five minutes for Mrs. Arne to resume the conversation, then her natural impatience got the better of her.

"Do say something, Alice!" she implored.

"Esther, I beg your pardon!" said Mrs. Arne. "I was thinking."

"What were you thinking of?"

"I don't know."

"No, of course you don't. People who sit and stare into the fire never do think, really. They are only brooding and making themselves ill, and that is what you are doing. You mope, you take no interest in anything, you never go out—I am sure you have not been out of doors today?"

"No—yes—I believe not. It is so cold."

"You are sure to feel the cold if you sit in the house all day, and sure to get ill! Just look at yourself!"

Mrs. Arne rose and looked at herself in the Italian mirror over the chimney-piece. It reflected faithfully enough her even pallor, her dark hair and eyes, the sweeping length of her eyelashes, the sharp curves of her nostrils, and the delicate arch of her eyebrows, that formed a thin sharp black line, so clear as to seem almost unnatural.

"Yes, I do look ill," she said with conviction.

"No wonder. You choose to bury yourself alive."

"Sometimes I do feel as if I lived in a grave. I look up at the ceiling and fancy it is my coffin-lid."

"Don't please talk like that!" expostulated Miss Graham, pointing to Mrs. Arne's little girl. "If only for Dolly's sake, I think you should not give way to such morbid fancies. It isn't good for her to see you like this always."

"Oh, Esther," the other exclaimed, stung into something like vivacity, "don't reproach me I I hope I am a good mother to my child!"

"Yes, dear, you are a model mother—and model wife too. Father says the way you look after your husband is something wonderful, but don't you think for your own sake you might try to be a little gayer? You encourage these moods, don't you? What is it? Is it the house?"

She glanced around her—at the high ceiling, at the heavy damask portieres, the tall cabinets of china, the dim oak panelling—it reminded her of a neglected museum. Her eye travelled into the farthest corners, where the faint filmy dusk was already gathering, lit only by the bewildering cross-lights of the glass panels of cabinet doors—to the tall narrow windows—then back again to the woman in her mourning dress, cowering by the fire. She said sharply—

"You should go out more."

"I do not like to—leave my husband."

"Oh, I know that he is delicate and all that, but still, does he never permit you to leave him? Does he never go out by himself?"

"Not often!"

"And you have no pets! It is very odd of you. I simply can't imagine a house without animals!"

"We did have a dog once," answered Mrs. Arne plaintively, "but it howled so we had to give it away. It would not go near Edward. . . . But please don't imagine that I am dull! I have my child." She laid her hand on the flaxen head at her knee.

Miss Graham rose, frowning.

"Ah, you are too bad!" she exclaimed. "You are like a widow exactly, with one child, stroking its orphan head and saying, 'Poor fatherless darling.'"

Voices were heard outside. Miss Graham stopped talking quite suddenly, and sought her veil and gloves on the mantelpiece.

"You need not go, Esther," said Mrs. Arne. "It is only my husband."

"Oh, but it is getting late," said the other, crumpling up her gloves in her muff, and shuffling her feet nervously.

"Come!" said her hostess, with a bitter smile, "put your gloves on properly—if you must go—but it is quite early still."

"Please don't go, Miss Graham," put in the child.

"I must. Go and meet your papa, like a good girl."

"I don't want to."

"You mustn't talk like that, Dolly," said the doctor's daughter absently, still looking towards the door. Mrs. Arne rose and fastened the clasps of the big fur-cloak for her friend. The wife's white, sad, oppressed face came very close to the girl's cheerful one, as she murmured in a low voice—

"You don't like my husband, Esther? I can't help noticing it. Why don't you?"

"Nonsense!" retorted the other, with the emphasis of one who is repelling an overtrue accusation. "I do, only—"

"Only what?"

"Well, dear, it is foolish of me, of course, but I am—a little afraid of him."

"Afraid of Edward!" said his wife slowly. "Why should you be?"

"Well, dear—you see—I—I suppose women can't help being a little afraid of their friends' husbands—they can spoil their friendships with their wives in a moment, if they choose to disapprove of them. I really must go! Goodbye, child; give me a kiss! Don't ring, Alice. Please don't! I can open the door for myself—"

"Why should you?" said Mrs. Arne. "Edward is in the hall; I heard him speaking to Foster."

"No; he has gone into his study. Goodbye, you apathetic creature!" She gave Mrs. Arne a brief kiss and dashed out of the room. The voices outside had ceased, and she had reasonable hopes of reaching the door without being intercepted by Mrs. Arne's husband. But he met her on the stairs. Mrs. Arne, listening intently from her seat by the fire, heard her exchange a few shy sentences with him, the sound of which died away as they went downstairs together. A few moments after, Edward Arne came into the room and dropped into the chair just vacated by his wife's visitor.

He crossed his legs and said nothing. Neither did she.

His nearness had the effect of making the woman look at once several years older. Where she was pale, he was well-coloured; the network of little filmy wrinkles that, on a close inspection, covered her face, had no parallel on his smooth skin. He was handsome; soft, well-groomed flakes of auburn hair lay over his forehead, and his steely blue eyes shone equably, a contrast to the sombre fire of hers, and the masses of dark crinkly hair that shaded her brow.

The deep lines of permanent discontent furrowed that brow as she sat with her chin propped on her hands, and her elbows resting on her knees. Neither spoke. When the hands of the clock over Mrs. Arne's head pointed to seven, the whiter aproned figure of the nurse appeared in the doorway, and the little girl rose and kissed her mother very tenderly.

Mrs. Arne's forehead contracted. Looking uneasily at her husband, she said to the child tentatively, yet boldly, as one grasps a nettle, "Say goodnight to your father!"

The child obeyed, saying, "Goodnight" indifferently in her father's direction.

"Kiss him!"

"No, please—please not."

Her mother looked down on her curiously, sadly. . . .

"You are a naughty, spoilt child!" she said, but without conviction. "Excuse her, Edward."

He did not seem to have heard.

"Well, if you don't care—" said his wife bitterly.

"Come, child!" She caught the little girl by the hand and left the room.

At the door she half turned and looked fixedly at her husband. It was a strange ambiguous gaze; in it passion and dislike were strangely combined. Then she shivered and closed the door softly after her.

The man in the armchair sat with no perceptible change of attitude, his unspeculative eyes fixed on the fire, his hands clasped idly in front of him. The pose was obviously habitual. The servant brought lights and closed the shutters, drew the curtains, and made up the fire noisily, without, however, eliciting any reproof from his master.

Edward Arne was an ideal master, as far as Foster was concerned. He kept cases of cigars, but never smoked them, although the supply had often to be renewed. He did not care what he ate or drank, although he kept as good a cellar as most gentlemen—Foster knew that. He never interfered, he counted for nothing, he gave no trouble. Foster had no intention of ever leaving such an easy place.

True, his master was not cordial; he very seldom addressed him or seemed to know whether he was there, but then neither did he grumble if the fire in the study was allowed to go out, or interfere with Foster's liberty in any way. He had a better place of it than Annette, Mrs. Arne's maid, who would be called up in the middle of the night to bathe her mistress's forehead with *eau-de-Cologne*, or made to brush her long hair for hours together to soothe her. Naturally enough Foster and Annette compared notes as to their respective situations, and drew unflattering parallels between this capricious wife and model husband.

3

Miss Graham was not a demonstrative woman. On her return home she somewhat startled her father, as he sat by his study table,

144

deeply interested in his diagnosis book, by the sudden violence of her embrace.

"Why this excitement?" he asked, smiling and turning round. He was a young-looking man for his age; his thin wiry figure and clear colour belied the evidence on his hair, tinged with grey, and the tired wrinkles that gave value to the acuteness and brilliancy of the eyes they surrounded.

"I don't know!" she replied, "only you are so nice and alive somehow. I always feel like this when I come back from seeing the Arnes."

"Then don't go to see the Arnes."

"I'm so fond of her, father, and she will never come here to me, as you know. Or else nothing would induce me to enter her tomb of a house, and talk to that walking funeral of a husband of hers. I managed to get away today without having to shake hands with him. I always try to avoid it. But, father, I do wish you would go and see Alice,"

"Is she ill?"

"Well, not exactly ill, I suppose, but her eyes make me quite uncomfortable, and she says such odd things! I don't know if it is you or the clergyman she wants, but she is all wrong somehow! She never goes out except to church; she never pays a call, or has anyone to call on her! Nobody ever asks the Arnes to dinner, and I'm sure I don't blame them—the sight of that man at one's table would spoil any party—and they never entertain. She is always alone. Day after day I go in and find her sitting over the fire, with that same brooding expression. I shouldn't be surprised in the least if she were to go mad someday. Father, what is it? What is the tragedy of the house? There is one I am convinced. And yet, though I have been the intimate friend of that woman for years, I know no more about her than the man in the street."

"She keeps her skeleton safe in the cupboard," said Dr. Graham. "I respect her for that. And please don't talk nonsense about tragedies. Alice Arne is only morbid—the malady of the age. And she is a very religious woman."

"I wonder if she complains of her odious husband to Mr. Bligh. She is always going to his services."

"Odious?"

"Yes, odious!" Miss Graham shuddered. "I cannot stand him! I cannot bear the touch of his cold froggy hands, and the sight of his fishy eyes! That inane smile of his simply makes me shrivel up. Father, honestly, do you like him yourself?"

"My dear, I hardly know him! It is his wife I have known ever since she was a child, and I a boy at college. Her father was my tutor. I never knew her husband till six years ago, when she called me in to attend him in a very serious illness. I suppose she never speaks of it? No? A very odd affair. For the life of me I cannot tell how he managed to recover. You needn't tell people, for it affects my reputation, but I didn't save him! Indeed, I have never been able to account for it. The man was given over for dead!"

"He might as well be dead for all the good he is," said Esther scornfully. "I have never heard him say more than a couple of sentences in my life."

"Yet he was an exceedingly brilliant young man; one of the best men of his year at Oxford—a good deal run after—poor Alice was wild to marry him!"

"In love with that spiritless creature? He is like a house with someone dead in it, and all the blinds down!"

"Come, Esther, don't be morbid—not to say silly! You are very hard on the poor man! What's wrong with him? He is the ordinary, commonplace, coldblooded specimen of humanity, a little stupid, a little selfish—people who have gone through a serious illness like that are apt to be—but on the whole, a good husband, a good father, a good citizen—"

"Yes, and his wife is afraid of him, and his child hates him!" exclaimed Esther.

"Nonsense!" said Dr. Graham sharply. "The child is spoilt. Only children are apt to be—and the mother wants a change or a tonic of some kind. I'll go and talk to her when I have time. Go along and dress. Have you forgotten that George Graham is coming to dinner?"

After she had gone the doctor made a note on the corner of his blotting-pad, "Mem.: to go and see Mrs. Arne," and dismissed the subject of the memorandum entirely from his mind.

******

George Graham was the doctor's nephew, a tall, weedy, cumbrous young man, full of fads and fallacies, with a gentle manner that somehow inspired confidence. He was several years younger than Esther, who loved to listen to his semi-scientific, semi-romantic stories of things met with in the course of his profession. "Oh, I come across very queer things!" he would say mysteriously, "There's a queer little widow——!"

"Tell me about your little widow?" asked Esther that day after din-

146

ner, when, her father having gone back to his study, she and her cousin sat together as usual.

He laughed.

"You like to hear of my professional experiences? Well, she certainly interested me," he said thoughtfully. "She is an odd psychological study in her way. I wish I could come across her again."

"Where did you come across her, and what is her name?"

"I don't know her name, I don't want to; she is not a personage to me, only a case. I hardly know her face even. I have never seen it except in the twilight. But I gathered that she lived somewhere in Chelsea, for she came out on to the Embankment with only a kind of lacy thing over her head; she can't live far off, I fancy."

Esther became instantly attentive. "Go on," she said.

"It was three weeks ago," said George Graham. "I was coming along the Embankment about ten o'clock. I walked through that little grove, you know, just between Cheyne Walk and the river, and I heard in there some one sobbing very bitterly. I looked and saw a woman sitting on a seat, with her head in her hands, crying. I was most awfully sorry, of course, and I thought I could perhaps do something for her, get her a glass of water, or salts, or something. I took her for a woman of the people—it was quite dark, you know. So, I asked her very politely if I could do anything for her, and then I noticed her hands—they were quite white and covered with diamonds."

"You were sorry you spoke, I suppose," said Esther.

"She raised her head and said—I believe she laughed—'Are you going to tell me to move on?'"

"She thought you were a policeman?"

"Probably—if she thought at all—but she was in a semi-dazed condition. I told her to wait till I came back, and dashed round the corner to the chemist's and bought a bottle of salts. She thanked me, and made a little effort to rise and go away. She seemed very weak. I told her I was a medical man, I started in and talked to her."

"And she to you?"

"Yes, quite straight. Don't you know that women always treat a doctor as if he were one step removed from their father confessor—not human—not in the same category as themselves? It is not complimentary to one as a man, but one hears a good deal one would not otherwise hear. She ended by telling me all about herself—in a veiled way, of course. It soothed her—relieved her—she seemed not to have had an outlet for years!"

"To a mere stranger!"

"To a doctor. And she did not know what she was saying half the time. She was hysterical, of course. Heavens! what nonsense she talked! She spoke of herself as a person somehow haunted, cursed by some malign fate, a victim of some fearful spiritual catastrophe, don't you know? I let her run on. She was convinced of the reality of a sort of 'doom' that she had fancied had befallen her. It was quite pathetic. Then it got rather chilly—she shivered—I suggested her going in. She shrank back; she said, 'If you only knew what a relief it is, how much less miserable I am out here! I can breathe; I can live—it is my only glimpse of the world that is alive—I live in a grave—oh, let me stay!' She seemed positively afraid to go home."

"Perhaps someone bullied her at home."

"I suppose so, but then—she had no husband. He died, she told me, years ago. She had adored him, she said—"

"Is she pretty?"

"Pretty! Well, I hardly noticed. Let me see! Oh, yes, I suppose she was pretty—no, now I think of it, she would be too worn and faded to be what you call pretty."

Esther smiled. "Well, we sat there together for quite an hour, then the clock of Chelsea church struck eleven, and she got up and said ' Goodbye,' holding out her hand quite naturally, as if our meeting and conversation had been nothing out of the common. There was a sound like a dead leaf trailing across the walk and she was gone."

"Didn't you ask if you should see her again?"

"That would have been a mean advantage to take."

"You might have offered to see her home."

"I saw she did not mean me to."

"She was a lady, you say," pondered Esther. "How was she dressed?"

"Oh, all right, like a lady—in black—mourning, I suppose. She has dark crinkly hair, and her eyebrows are very thin and arched—I noticed that in the dusk."

"Does this photograph remind you of her?" asked Esther suddenly, taking him to the mantelpiece.

"Rather!"

"Alice! Oh, it couldn't be—she is not a widow, her husband is alive—has your friend any children?"

"Yes, one, she mentioned it."

"How old?"

"Six years old, I think she said. She talks of the 'responsibility of bringing up an orphan.'"

"George, what time is it?" Esther asked suddenly.

"About nine o'clock."

"Would you mind coming out with me?"

"I should like it. Where shall we go?"

"To St. Adhelm's! It is close by here. There is a special late service tonight, and Mrs. Arne is sure to be there."

"Oh, Esther—curiosity!"

"No, not mere curiosity. Don't you see if it is my Mrs. Arne who talked to you like this, it is very serious? I have thought her ill for a long time; but as ill as that!—"

At St. Adhelm's Church, Esther Graham pointed out a woman who was kneeling beside a pillar in an attitude of intense devotion and abandonment. She rose from her knees, and turned her rapt face up towards the pulpit whence the Reverend Ralph Bligh was holding his impassioned discourse. George Graham touched his cousin on the shoulder, and motioned to her to leave her place on the outermost rank of worshippers.

"That is the woman!" said he.

4

"Mem.: to go and see Mrs. Arne." The doctor came across this note in his blotting-pad one day six weeks later. His daughter was out of town. He had heard nothing of the Arnes since her departure. He had promised to go and see her. He was a little conscience-stricken. Yet another week elapsed before he found time to call upon the daughter of his old tutor.

At the corner of Tite Street he met Mrs. Arne's husband, and stopped. A doctor's professional kindliness of manner is, or ought to be, independent of his personal likings and dislikings, and there was a pleasant cordiality about his greeting which should have provoked a corresponding fervour on the part of Edward Arne.

"How are you, Arne?" Graham said. "I was on my way to call on your wife."

"Ah—yes!" said Edward Arne, with the ascending inflection of polite acquiescence. A ray of blue from his eyes rested transitorily on the doctor's face, and in that short moment the latter noted its intolerable vacuity, and for the first time in his life felt a sharp pang of sympathy for the wife of such a husband.

"I suppose you are off to your club?—er—goodbye!" he wound

up abruptly. With the best will in the world he somehow found it almost impossible to carry on a conversation with Edward Arne, who raised his hand to his hat-brim in token of salutation, smiled sweetly, and walked on.

"He really is extraordinarily good-looking," reflected the doctor, as he watched him down the street and safely over the crossing with a certain degree of solicitude for which he could not exactly account. "And yet one feels one's vitality ebbing out at the finger-ends as one talks to him. I shall begin to believe in Esther's absurd fancies about him soon. Ah, there's the little girl!" he exclaimed, as he turned into Cheyne Walk and caught sight of her with her nurse, making violent demonstrations to attract his attention. "She is alive, at any rate. How is your mother, Dolly?" he asked.

"Quite well, thank you," was the child's reply. She added, "She's crying. She sent me away because I looked at her. So, I did. Her cheeks are quite red."

"Run away—run away and play!" said the doctor nervously. He ascended the steps of the house, and rang the bell very gently and neatly.

"Not at—" began Foster, with the intonation of polite falsehood, but stopped on seeing the doctor, who, with his daughter, was a privileged person. "Mrs. Arne will see you, Sir."

"Mrs. Arne is not alone?" he said interrogatively.

"Yes, Sir, quite alone. I have just taken tea in."

Dr. Graham's doubts were prompted by the low murmur as of a voice, or voices, which came to him through the open door of the room at the head of the stairs. He paused and listened while Foster stood by, merely remarking, "Mrs. Arne do talk to herself sometimes, Sir."

It was Mrs. Arne's voice—the doctor recognised it now. It was not the voice of a sane or healthy woman. He at once mentally removed his visit from the category of a morning call, and prepared for a semi-professional inquiry.

"Don't announce me," he said to Foster, and quietly entered the back drawing-room, which was separated by a heavy tapestry portiere from the room where Mrs. Arne sat, with an open book on the table before her, from which she had been apparently reading aloud. Her hands were now clasped tightly over her face, and when, presently, she removed them and began feverishly to turn page after page of her book, the crimson of her cheeks was seamed with white where her fingers had impressed themselves.

The doctor wondered if she saw him, for though her eyes were fixed in his direction, there was no apprehension in them. She went on reading, and it was the text, mingled with passionate interjection and fragmentary utterances, of the Burial Service that met his ears.

"'For as in Adam all die!' All die! It says all! For he must reign. . . . The last enemy that shall be destroyed is Death. What shall they do if the dead rise not at all! . . . I die daily . . . . ! Daily! No, no, better get it over . . . dead and buried . . . out of sight, out of mind . . . under a stone. Dead men don't come back. . . . Go on! Get it over. I want to hear the earth rattle on the coffin, and then I shall know it is done. 'Flesh and blood cannot inherit!' Oh, what did I do? What have I done? Why did I wish it so fervently? Why did I pray for it so earnestly? God gave me my wish—"

"Alice! Alice!" groaned the doctor.

She looked up. "'When this corruptible shall have put on incorruption—' 'Dust to dust, ashes to ashes, earth to earth—' Yes, that is it. 'After death, though worms destroy this body—'"

She flung the book aside and sobbed.

"That is what I was afraid of. My God! My God! Down there—in the dark—for ever and ever and ever! I could not bear to think of it! My Edward! And so I interfered . . . and prayed . . . and prayed till . . . Oh! I am punished. Flesh and blood could not inherit! I kept him there—I would not let him go. . . . I kept him. . . . I prayed. . . . I denied him Christian burial. . . . Oh, how could I know. . . ."

"Good heavens, Alice!" said Graham, coming sensibly forward, what does this mean? I have heard of schoolgirls going through the marriage service by themselves, but the burial service—"

He laid down his hat and went on severely, "What have you to do with such things? Your child is flourishing—your husband alive and here—"

"And who kept him here?" interrupted Alice Arne fiercely, accepting the fact of his appearance without comment.

"You did," he answered quickly, "with your care and tenderness. I believe the warmth of your body, as you lay beside him for that half-hour, maintained the vital heat during that extraordinary suspension of the heart's action, which made us all give him up for dead. You were his best doctor, and brought him back to us."

"Yes, it was I—it was I—you need not tell me it was I!"

"Come, be thankful!" he said cheerfully. "Put that book away, and give me some tea, I'm very cold."

"Oh, Dr. Graham, how thoughtless of me!" said Mrs. Arne, rallying at the slight imputation on her politeness he had purposely made. She tottered to the bell and rang it before he could anticipate her.

"Another cup," she said quite calmly to Foster, who answered it. Then she sat down quivering all over with the suddenness of the constraint put upon her.

"Yes, sit down and tell me all about it," said Dr. Graham good-humouredly, at the same time observing her with the closeness he gave to difficult cases.

"There is nothing to tell," she said simply, shaking her head, and futilely altering the position of the tea-cups on the tray. "It all happened years ago. Nothing can be done now. Will you have sugar?"

He drank his tea and made conversation. He talked to her of some Dante lectures she was attending; of some details connected with her child's Kindergarten classes. These subjects did not interest her. There was a subject she wished to discuss, he could see that a question trembled on her tongue, and tried to lead up to it.

She introduced it herself, quite quietly, over a second cup. "Sugar, Dr. Graham? I forget. Dr. Graham, tell me, do you believe that prayers—wicked unreasonable prayers—are granted?"

He helped himself to another slice of bread and butter before answering.

"Well," he said slowly, "it seems hard to believe that every fool who has a voice to pray with, and a brain where to conceive idiotic requests with, should be permitted to interfere with the economy of the universe. As a rule, if people were long-sighted enough to see the result of their petitions, I fancy very few of us would venture to interfere."

Mrs. Arne groaned.

She was a good Churchwoman, Graham knew, and he did not wish to sap her faith in any way, so he said no more, but inwardly wondered if a too rigid interpretation of some of the religious dogmas of the Vicar of St. Adhelm's, her spiritual adviser, was not the clue to her distress. Then she put another question—

"Eh! What?" he said. "Do I 'believe in ghosts? I will believe you if you will tell me you have seen one."

"You know, Doctor," she went on, "I was always afraid of ghosts—of spirits—things unseen. I couldn't ever read about them. I could not bear the idea of someone in the room with me that I could not see. There was a text that always frightened me that hung up in my room: 'Thou, God, seest me!' It frightened me when I was a child, whether

152

I had been doing wrong or not. But now," shuddering, "I think there are worse things than ghosts."

"Well, now, what sort of things?" he asked good-humouredly. "Astral bodies—?"

She leaned forward and laid her hot hand on his.

"Oh, Doctor, tell me, if a spirit—without the body we know it by—is terrible, what of a body"—her voice sank to a whisper, "a body—senseless—lonely—stranded on this earth—without a spirit?"

She was watching his face anxiously. He was divided between a morbid inclination to laugh and the feeling of intense discomfort provoked by this wretched scene. He longed to give the conversation a more cheerful turn, yet did not wish to offend her by changing it too abruptly.

"I have heard of people not being able to keep body and soul together," he replied at last, "but I am not aware that practically such a division of forces has ever been achieved. And if we could only accept the theory of the de-spiritualised body, what a number of antipathetic people now wandering about in the world it would account for!"

The piteous gaze of her eyes seemed to seek to ward off the blow of his misplaced jocularity. He left his seat and sat down on the couch beside her.

"Poor child! poor girl! you are ill, you are overexcited. What is it? Tell me," he asked her as tenderly as the father she had lost in early life might have done. Her head sank on his shoulder.

"Are you unhappy?" he asked her gently.

"Yes!"

"You are too much alone. Get your mother or your sister to come and stay with you."

"They won't come," she wailed. "They say the house is like a grave. Edward has made himself a study in the basement. It's an impossible room—but he has moved all his things in, and I can't—I won't go to him there. . . ."

"You're wrong. For it's only a fad," said Graham, "he'll tire of it. And you must see more people somehow. It's a pity my daughter is away. Had you any visitors today?"

"Not a soul has crossed the threshold for eighteen days."

"We must change all that," said the doctor vaguely. "Meantime you must cheer up. Why, you have no need to think of ghosts and graves—no need to be melancholy—you have your husband and your child—"

"I have my child—yes."

The doctor took hold of Mrs. Arne by the shoulder, and held her a little away from him. He thought he had found the cause of her trouble—a more commonplace one than he had supposed.

"I have known you, Alice, since you were a child," he said gravely. "Answer me! You love your husband, don't you?"

"Yes." It was as if she were answering futile prefatory questions in the witness-box. Yet he saw by the intense excitement in her eyes that he had come to the point she feared, and yet desired to bring forward.

"And he loves you?"

She was silent.

"Well, then, if you love each other, what more can you want? Why do you say you have only your child in that absurd way?"

She was still silent, and he gave her a little shake.

"Tell me, have you and he had any difference lately? Is there any—coldness—any—temporary estrangement between you?"

He was hardly prepared for the burst of foolish laughter that proceeded from the demure Mrs. Arne as she rose and confronted him, all the blood in her body seeming for the moment to rush to her usually pale cheeks.

"Coldness! Temporary estrangement! If that were all! Oh, is every one blind but me? There is all the world between us!—all the difference between this world and the next!"

She sat down again beside the doctor and whispered in his ear, and her words were like a breath of hot wind from some Gehenna of the soul.

"Oh, Doctor, I have borne it for six years, and I must speak. No other woman could bear what I have borne, and yet be alive! And I loved him so; you don't know how I loved him! That was it—that was my crime—"

"Crime?" repeated the doctor.

"Yes, crime! It was impious, don't you see? But I have been punished. Oh, Doctor, you don't know what my life is! Listen! Listen! I must tell you. To live with a—— At first before I guessed when I used to put my arms round him, and he merely submitted—and then it dawned on me what I was kissing! It is enough to turn a living woman into stone—for I am living, though sometimes I forget it. Yes, I am a live woman, though I live in a grave. Think what it is!—to wonder every night if you will be alive in the morning, to lie down every night in an open grave—to smell death in every corner—every room—to breathe death—to touch it. . . ."

The portiere in front of the door shook, a hoopstick parted it, a round white clad bundle supported on a pair of mottled red legs peeped in, pushing a hoop in front of her. The child made no noise. Mrs. Arne seemed to have heard her, however. She slewed round violently as she sat on the sofa beside Dr. Graham, leaving her hot hands clasped in his.

"You ask Dolly," she exclaimed. "She knows it, too—she feels it."

"No, no, Alice, this won't do!" the doctor adjured her very low. Then he raised his voice and ordered the child from the room. He had managed to lift Mrs. Arne's feet and laid her full length on the sofa by the time the maid reappeared. She had fainted.

He pulled down her eyelids and satisfied himself as to certain facts he had up till now dimly apprehended. When Mrs. Arne's maid returned, he gave her mistress over to her care and proceeded to Edward Arne's new study in the basement.

"Morphia!" he muttered to himself, as he stumbled and faltered through gaslit passages, where furtive servants eyed him and scuttled to their burrows.

"What is he burying himself down here for?" he thought. "Is it to get out of her way? They are a nervous pair of them!"

★★★★★★

Arne was sunk in a large armchair drawn up before the fire. There was no other light, except a faint reflection from the gas-lamp in the road, striking down past the iron bars of the window that was sunk below the level of the street. The room was comfortless and empty, there was little furniture in it except a large bookcase at Arne's right hand and a table with a Tantalus on it standing some way off. There was a faded portrait in pastel of Alice Arne over the mantelpiece, and beside it, a poor pendant, a pen and ink sketch of the master of the house. They were quite discrepant, in size and medium, but they appeared to look at each other with the stolid attentiveness of newly married people.

"Seedy, Arne?" Graham said.

"Rather, today. Poke the fire for me, will you?"

"I've known you quite seven years," said the doctor cheerfully, "so I presume I can do that. . . . There, now! . . . And I'll presume further What have we got here?"

He took a small bottle smartly out of Edward Arne's fingers and raised his eyebrows. Edward Arne had rendered it up agreeably; he did not seem upset or annoyed.

"Morphia. It isn't a habit. I only got hold of the stuff yesterday—found it about the house. Alice was very jumpy all day, and communicated her nerves to me, I suppose. I've none as a rule, but do you know, Graham, I seem to be getting them—feel things a good deal more than I did, and want to talk about them."

"What, are you growing a soul?" said the doctor carelessly, lighting a cigarette.

"Heaven forbid!" Arne answered equably. "I've done very well without it all these years. But I'm fond of old Alice, you know, in my own way. When I was a young man, I was quite different. I took things hardly and got excited about them. Yes, excited. I was wild about Alice, wild! Yes, by Jove! though she has forgotten all about it."

"Not that, but still it's natural she should long for some little demonstration of affection now and then ... and she'd be awfully distressed if she saw you fooling with that bottle of morphia! You know, Arne, after that narrow squeak you had of it five years ago, Alice and I have a good right to consider that your life belongs to us!"

Edward Arne settled in his chair and replied, rather fretfully—

"All very well, but you didn't manage to do the job thoroughly. You didn't turn me out lively enough to please Alice. She's annoyed because when I take her in my arms, I don't hold her tight enough. I'm too quiet, too languid! ... Hang it all, Graham, I believe she'd like me to stand for Parliament! ... Why can't she let me just go along my own way? Surely a man who's come through an illness like mine can be let off parlour tricks? All this worry—it culminated the other day when I said I wanted to colonize a room down here, and did, with a spurt that took it out of me horribly,—all this worry, I say, seeing her upset and so on, keeps me low, and so I feel as if I wanted to take drugs to soothe me."

"Soothe!" said Graham. "This stuff is more than soothing if you take enough of it. I'll send you something more like what you want, and I'll take this away, by your leave."

"I really can't argue!" replied Arne.... "If you see Alice, tell her you find me fairly comfortable and don't put her off this room. I really like it best. She can come and see me here, I keep a good fire, tell her.... I feel as if I wanted to sleep ..." he added brusquely.

"You have been indulging already," said Graham softly. Arne had begun to doze off. His cushion had sagged down, the doctor stooped to rearrange it, carelessly laying the little phial for the moment in a crease of the rug covering the man's knees.

******

Mrs. Arne in her mourning dress was crossing the hall as he came to the top of the basement steps and pushed open the swing door. She was giving some orders to Foster, the butler, who disappeared as the doctor advanced.

"You're about again," he said, "good girl!"

"Too silly of me," she said, "to be hysterical! After all these years! One should be able to keep one's own counsel. But it is over now, I promise I will never speak of it again."

"We frightened poor Dolly dreadfully. I had to order her out like a regiment of soldiers."

"Yes, I know. I'm going to her now."

On his suggestion that she should look in on her husband first she looked askance.

"Down there!"

"Yes, that's his fancy. Let him be. He is a good deal depressed about himself and you. He notices a great deal more than you think. He isn't quite as apathetic as you describe him to be. . . . Come here!" He led her into the unlit dining-room a little way. "You expect too much, my dear. You do really! You make too many demands on the vitality you saved."

"What did one save him for?" she asked fiercely. She continued more quietly, "I know. I am going to be different."

"Not you," said Graham fondly. He was very partial to Alice Arne in spite of her silliness. "You'll worry about Edward till the end of the chapter. I know you. And"—he turned her round by the shoulder so that she fronted the light in the hall—"you elusive thing, let me have a good look at you. . . . Hum! Your eyes, they're a bit starey. . . ."

He let her go again with a sigh of impotence. Something must be done . . . soon ... he must think. . . . He got hold of his coat and began to get into it. . . .

Mrs. Arne smiled, buttoned a button for him and then opened the front door, like a good hostess, a very little way. With a quick flirt of his hat he was gone, and she heard the clap of his brougham door and the order "Home."

******

"Been saying goodbye to that thief Graham?" said her husband gently, when she entered his room, her pale eyes staring a little, her thin hand busy at the front of her dress. . . .

157

"Thief? Why? One moment! Where's your switch?"

She found it and turned on a blaze of light from which her husband seemed to shrink.

"Well, he carried off my drops. Afraid of my poisoning myself, I suppose?"

"Or acquiring the morphia habit," said his wife in a dull level voice, "as I have."

She paused. He made no comment. Then, picking up the little phial Dr. Graham had left in the crease of the rug, she spoke—

"You are the thief, Edward, as it happens, this is mine."

"Is it? I found it knocking about: I didn't know it was yours. Well, will you give me some?"

"I will, if you like."

"Well, dear, decide. You know I am in your hands and Graham's. He was rubbing that into me today."

"Poor lamb!" she said derisively; "I'd not allow my doctor, or my wife either, to dictate to me whether I should put an end to myself, or not."

"Ah, but you've got a spirit, you see!" Arne yawned. "However, let me have a go at the stuff and then you put it on top of a wardrobe or a shelf, where I shall know it is, but never reach out to get it, I promise you."

"No, you wouldn't reach out a hand to keep yourself alive, let alone kill yourself," said she. "That is you all over, Edward."

"And don't you see that is why I did die," he said, with earnestness unexpected by her. "And then, unfortunately, you and Graham bustled up and wouldn't let Nature take its course.... I rather wish you hadn't been so officious."

"And let you stay dead," said she carelessly. "But at the time I cared for you so much that I should have had to kill myself, or commit suttee like a Bengali widow. Ah, well!"

She reached out for a glass half-full of water that stood on the low ledge of a bookcase close by the arm of his chair.... "Will this glass do? What's in it? Only water? How much morphia shall I give you? An overdose?"

"I don't care if you do, and that's a fact."

"It was a joke, Edward," she said piteously .

"No joke to me. This fag end of life I've clawed hold of, doesn't interest me. And I'm bound to be interested in what I'm doing or I'm no good. I'm no earthly good now. I don't enjoy life, I've nothing to enjoy it with—in here"—he struck his breast. "It's like a dull party one goes to by accident. All I want to do is to get into a cab and go home."

His wife stood over him with the half-full glass in one hand and the little bottle in the other. Her eyes dilated . . . her chest heaved. . . .

"Edward!" she breathed. "Was it all so useless?"

"Was what useless? Yes, as I was telling you, I go as one in a dream— a bad, bad dream, like the dreams I used to have when I overworked at college. I was brilliant, Alice, brilliant, do you hear? At some cost, I expect! Now I hate people—my fellow creatures. I've left them. They come and go, jostling me, and pushing me, on the pavements as I go along, avoiding them. Do you know where they should be, really, in relation to me?"

He rose a little in his seat—she stepped nervously aside, made as if to put down the bottle and the glass she was holding, then thought better of it and continued to extend them mechanically.

"They should be over my head. I've already left them and their petty nonsense of living. They mean nothing to me, no more than if they were ghosts walking. Or perhaps it's I who am a ghost to them? . . . You don't understand it. It's because I suppose you have no imagination. You just know what you want and do your best to get it. You blurt out your blessed petition to your Deity and the idea that you're irrelevant never enters your head, soft, persistent, High Church thing that you are! . . ."

Alice Arne smiled, and balanced the objects she was holding. He motioned her to pour out the liquid from one to the other, but she took no heed; she was listening with all her ears. It was the nearest approach to the language of compliment, to anything in the way of loverlike personalities that she had heard fall from his lips since his illness. He went on, becoming as it were lukewarm to his subject—

"But the worst of it is that once break the cord that links you to humanity—it can't be mended. Man doesn't live by bread alone ... or lives to disappoint you. What am I to you, without my own poor personality? . . . Don't stare so, Alice! I haven't talked so much or so intimately for ages, have I? Let me try and have it out. . . . Are you in any sort of hurry?"

"No, Edward."

"Pour that stuff out and have done. . . . Well, Alice, it's a queer feeling, I tell you. One goes about with one's looks on the ground, like a man who eyes the bed he is going to lie down in, and longs for. Alice,

159

the crust of the earth seems a barrier between me and my own place. I want to scratch the boardings with my nails and shriek something like this: 'Let me get down to you all, there where I belong!' It's a horrible sensation, like a vampire reversed! . . ."

"Is that why you insisted on having this room in the basement?" she asked breathlessly.

"Yes, I can't bear being upstairs, somehow. Here, with these barred windows and stone-cold floors . . . I can see the people's feet walking above there in the street . . . one has some sort of illusion. . . ."

"Oh!" She shivered and her eyes travelled like those of a caged creature round the bare room and fluttered when they rested on the sombre windows imperiously barred. She dropped her gaze to the stone flags that showed beyond the oasis of Turkey carpet on which Arne's chair stood. . . . Then to the door, the door that she had closed on entering. It had heavy bolts, but they were not drawn against her, though by the look of her eyes it seemed she half imagined they were.

She made a step forward and moved her hands slightly. She looked down on them and what they held . . . then changed the relative positions of the two objects and held the bottle over the glass. . . .

"Yes, come along!" her husband said. "Are you going to be all day giving it me?"

With a jerk, she poured the liquid out into a glass and handed it to him. She looked away—towards the door. . . .

"Ah, your way of escape!" said he, following her eyes. Then he drank, painstakingly.

The empty bottle fell out of her hands. She wrung them, murmuring—

"Oh, if I had only known!"

"Known what? That I should go near to cursing you for bringing me back?"

He fixed his cold eyes on her, as the liquid passed slowly over his tongue. . . .

"—Or that you would end by taking back the gift you gave?"

The Coach

It was a lonely part of the country, far north, where the summer nights are pale and light and scant of shade. This summer night there was no moon, and yet it was not dark. For hours the flat, deprecating earth had lain prone under a storm of wind and rain. Its patient surface was drenched, blanched, smitten into blindness. The tumbled waters of the Firth splashed on the edges of the plain, their wild commotion dwarfed by the noise of the wind-driven showers, whose gloomy drops tapped the waters into sullen acquiescence. Half a mile inland the road to the north was laid. Clear and straight it ran, with never a house or homestead to break it, viscous with clay here, shining with quartz there, uncompromising, exact, like the lists of old, dressed for a tourney. Its sides were bare, scantily garnished with grass.

This was nearly a hedgeless country. In places the undeviating line of it passed through a little coppice or clump of gnarled, ill-conditioned, nameless trees. They seemed to lean forward vindictively on either side, snapping their horny fingers at each other, waving their cantankerous branches as the gusts took them, broke them, and whirled the fragments of their ruin far away and out of ken, like a flapping, unruly kite which a child has allowed to pass beyond his control. The broad white surface of the road was not suffered to be blotted for a single moment.

Nothing could rest for the play of the intriguing air-currents, surging backwards and forwards, blind, stupid and swelled with pride, till they had got completely out of hand and defied the archers of the middle sky. They staggered hither and thither like ineffectual giants; they buffeted all impartially; they instigated the hapless branches at their mercy to wild lashings of each other, to useless accesses of the spirit of self-destruction. Bending slavishly under the heavy gusts, each shabby blade of grass by the roadside rose again and was on the *qui vive* after the rustling tyrant had passed.

It was then, in the succeeding moments of comparative peace, when the directors of the passionate aerial revolt had managed to call their panting rabble off for the time, that great perpendicular sheets of rain, like stage films slung evenly from heavenly temples, descended and began moving continuously sideways, like a wall, across the level track. A sheet of whole water, blotting out the tangled borders of herbage that grew sparsely round the heaps of stones with which the margin was set at intervals, placed there ready for breaking.

When the slab of rain had moved on again, the broad road, shining out sturdily with its embedded quartz and milky kneaded clay, lay clear once more. Calm, ordered and tranquil in the midst of tumult and discord, it pursued its appointed course, edging off from its evenly bevelled sides the noisy moorland streams, that had come jostling each other in their haste to reach it, only to be relegated, noisily complaining, to the swollen, unrecognizable gutter.

At a certain point on the line of way, a tall, spare, respectable-looking man in a well-fitting grey frock coat stood waiting. The rain ran down the back of his coat collar, and dripped off the rim of his tall hat. His attitude suggested some weary foredone clerk waiting at the corner of the city street for the omnibus that was to carry him home to his slippered comfort and sober pipe of peace. He wore no muffler, but then it was summer—St. John's Eve, He leaned on an ivory-headed ebony stick of which he seemed fond, and peered, not very eagerly, along the road, which now lay in dazzling rain-washed clarity under the struggling moon. There was a lull in the storm. He had no luggage, no umbrella, yet his grey coat looked neat, and his hat shiny.

Far in the distance, from the south, a black clumsy object appeared, labouring slowly along. It was a coach, of heavy and antique pattern. As soon as he had sighted it, the passenger's faint interest seemed diminished. With a bored air of fulfilment, he dropped his eyes and looked down disapprovingly at the clayey mud at his feet, although, indeed, the sticky substance did not appear to have marred the exquisite polish of his shoes. His palm settled composedly on the ivory knob of his trusty stick, as though it were the hand of an old friend.

With all the signs of difficult going, but no noise of straining or grinding, the coach at last drew up in front of the expectant passenger. He looked up quietly, and recognized it as the vehicle wherein it was appointed that he should travel in this unsuitable weather for a stage or two, maybe. All was correct, the coachman, grave, business-like, headless as of usage, the horses long-tailed, black, conventional. . . .

The door opened noiselessly, and the step was let down. The passenger shook his head as he delicately put his foot on to it, and observed for the benefit, doubtless, of the person or persons inside—

"I see old Joe on the box in his official trim. Rather unnecessary, all this ceremony, I venture to think! A few yokels and old women to impress, if indeed, any one not positively obliged is abroad on a night like this! For form's sake, I suppose!"

He took his seat next the window. There were four occupants of the coach beside himself. They all nodded formally, but not unkindly. He returned their salutations with old-fashioned courtesy, though unacquainted seemingly with any of them.

Sitting next to him was a woman evidently of fashion. Her heavy and valuable furs were negligently cast on one side, to show a plastron covered with jewels. She wore at least two enamelled and jewel-encrusted watches pinned to her bosom as a mark for thieves to covet. It was foolish of her. So at least thought the man in the grey frock coat. Her yellow wig was much awry. Her eyes were weak, strained, and fearful, and she aided their vision with a diamond-beset *pince-nez*. Now and again she glanced over her left shoulder as if in some alarm, and at such times she always grasped her gold-net reticule feverishly. She was obviously a rich woman in the world, a first-class train-*de-luxe* passenger.

The woman opposite her belonged as unmistakably to the people. She was hard-featured, worn with a life of sordid toil and calculation, but withal stout and motherly, a figure to inspire the fullest confidence. She wore a black bonnet with strings, and black silk gloves heavily darned. Round her sunken white collar, a golden gleam of watch-chain was now and then discernible.

At the other end of the coach, squeezed up into the corner where the vacillating light of the lamp hung from the roof least penetrated, a neat, sharp-featured man nestled and hid. His forehead retreated, and his bowler hat was set unnecessarily far back, lending him an air of folly and congenital weakness which his long, cold, clever nose could not dissipate. He was white as old enamel.

But the man whom the gentleman in the frock coat took to among his casual fellow-travellers was the one sitting directly opposite him, a rough, hearty creature, who alone of all the taciturn coachful seemed disposed to enter into a casual conversation, which might go some way to enliven the dreariness entailed by this somewhat old-fashioned mode of travelling. Gay talk might help to drown the dashing of the waters of the Firth lying close on the right hand of the section of road they were even now traversing, and the ugly roar of the wind and rain against the windows. This—by comparison—cheerful fellow was dressed like a working man, in a shabby suit of corduroys. He wore no collar, but a twisted red cotton handkerchief was wound tightly round his thick squat neck. His little mean eyes, swinish, but twinkling good-humouredly, stared enviously at the neat gentleman's stiff collar and the delicate grey tones of his suiting. Crossing and uncrossing his creasy legs, in the unusual effort of an attempt at conviviality, the man in corduroys addressed the man in the frock coat awkwardly enough, but still civilly.

"Well, mate! They've chosen a rare rough night to shift us on! Orders from headquarters, I suppose? I've been here nigh on a year and never set eyes on my boss!"

"We used to call him God the Father," said the elder man slowly. . . . "But whoever it is that orders our ways here, there is no earthly sense in questioning His arrangements, we can only fall in with them. As you admit, you are fairly new, and perhaps you do not as yet conceive fully of the silent impelling force that sways us. It is the same in the world we have left, only that there we were only concerned with the titles and standing of our 'boss,' as you call Him, and obeyed His laws not a whit. I must say I consider this particular system of soul transference that we have to submit to, very unsettling and productive of restlessness among us—a mere survival and tiresome superstition, to my mind. It has one merit; one sees something of the underworld, travelling about as we do, and meeting chance, perhaps kindred spirits on the road. One realises, too, that Hades is not quite as grey, shall I say, as it is painted! But perhaps," he added, with a slight touch of class *hauteur*, "you do not quite follow me?"

"Oh yes, Master, I do," eagerly replied the fellow-traveller to whom he chose to address his monologue. "Since I've been dead, I have learned the meaning of many things. I turn up my nose at nothing these days. I always neglected my schooling, but now I tell you I try to make up for lost time. From a rough sort of fellow that I was, with not an idea in my head beyond my beer and my prog, I have come to take my part in the whole of knowledge. It was all mine before, so to speak, but I didn't trouble to put my hand out for it. Didn't care, didn't listen to Miss that taught me, or to Parson, either. He had some good ideas too, as I've come to know, though Vice isn't Vice exactly with us here, now, in a manner of speaking. If God Almighty made us, why did He make us, even in parts, bad? That's what I want to know, and I'll know that when I've been dead a bit longer. Why did He give me rotten teeth so that I couldn't chew properly and didn't care for my food and liked drink better? It's dirt and digestion makes drinking and devilry, I say."

The smart woman interrupted him with a kind of languid eagerness, exclaiming—

"I must say I agree with you. Since the pestle fell on my shoulder in that lonely villa at Monte, I have realised what the dreadful gambling fever may lead to. It had made those two who treated me so ill, quite inhuman;' They had become wild beasts. I ought never to have accepted their treacherous invitation to luncheon, never tempted them with my outrageous display of jewels! And look here, I was tarred with the same stick, I gambled too—"

She rummaged in her reticule and fished out a ticket for the rooms at Monte Carlo.

"I always call that the ticket for my execution. Though my executioners were rather unnecessarily brutal. They will attain unto this place more easily than I did. Hardly any pain. The hand of the law is gentle, compared with the methods of—"

The man in the grey frock coat raised his finger warningly. "No names, I beg. One of our conventions . . . !"

"Have a drop?" said the calm motherly woman to the excited fine lady. "Your wound is recent, isn't it? Yours was a very severe case! A bloody murder, I call it, if ever there was one, and clumsy at that! And you only passive, which is always so much harder, they say! I can't tell, for I was what you may call an active party. They don't seem to mind mixing, they that look after us here! They lump us all together—travelling, at any rate! Though when I think of what I was actually turned off for, well—the way I look at it, what I did was a positive benefit to Society, and some sections of Society knew it, too, and would have liked to preserve my life."

"But what, Madam, if I may ask, was your little difficulty?"

"It is called, I believe, Baby Farming," she replied offhandedly, receiving her flask back from the smart woman and stowing it away in a capacious pocket. As she spoke, a shudder like a transitory ripple on a rainswept stream passed over her hearers, with the exception of the thin man in the far corner, who preserved his serenity. Raising his sunken chin, he observed the last speaker with some slight show of interest.

The man in grey apologised.

"Excuse us, Madam. A remnant of old-world squeamishness, un-controllable by us for the moment. Though perhaps, if you will, you might a little dissipate our preconceived motions of your profession, by explaining clearly your point of view."

"Delighted, I'm sure," she answered. "Funny, though, how seriously you all take it, even here! The feeling against my profession seems absurdly strong below as well as above. I was hooted as I left the court, I recollect. It annoyed me then considerably. I thought that those that hooted had more need to be grateful to me if all was known and paid for. I saved their pockets for them and their lovely honour too. They knew they owed all that to me. For the rest, they did not care. They went on, bless 'em, raising up seed for me to mow down as soon as its head came above ground, and welcome! Sly dogs, no thanks from them!

"But those shivering, shrinking women that came to me, some of them hardly out of their teens, some of them so delicate they had no right to have a baby at all !—Ah, if only I hadn't let myself take their money it would have been a work of pure philanthropy. But I had to live, then! Now that that tax has been taken off, one has time to think it out all round. But Lord!—Society, to cry shame on me for it! They might as well hang any other useful public servant, like dustmen, rat-catchers, and such-like ridders of pests. Good old Herod, that I used to hear about at school, knew what he was doing when he cleared off all those useless Innocents! He was the first baby farmer, I guess."

"You take large ground, Madam," said the man in the frock coat, a trifle huffily.

"And I have the right;" said she, her large determined chin emerging from its rolls of fat in her eagerness. "You men ought to know it, and you do well enough, when you're honest. I was only the 'scape-goat, and took on me the little sins of the race. It's an easy job enough, what I did, but there's few have the stomach for it, even then. You couldn't call it dirty work either. You just stand by and leave 'em alone—to girn and bleat and squinny and die."

"No blood, eh?" the man in the corner said suddenly. "I like blood."

"What a fine night it has turned!" said the man in the grey frock coat, raising the sash and putting his head out of the window. . . . "Something rather uncanny, eh, about that man?" he remarked under his breath, half to himself, half to the man in brown corduroys.

"Take your head in," said the latter, almost affectionately, "or you'll be catching cold, and you've a nasty scar on your neck that I could see as you leaned forward, and which you oughtn't to go getting the cold into."

"Oh, that!" said the other complacently, sitting down again, but averting his gaze carefully from the man in the corner, for whom he seemed to feel a repulsion as marked as was his preference for his cheerful *vis-à-vis*. "That! That's actually the scar of the blow that killed me. A fearful gash! He was a powerful man that dealt it. He got me, of course, from behind. I never even saw him. I was drafted off here at once, his hand had been so sure." He felt nervously in his pockets. "I have a foulard somewhere, but I am apt to mislay it."

"You should do like me, have a good strong handkercher and knot it round your neck firm. I've got a mark of sorts on my neck too, but it isn't an open wound—never was," the bluff man sniggered. "It is sheer vanity with me, but I don't care to have it seen. It goes well all round, mine does—done by a rope, eh!"

He paused and nodded slyly. "For killing a toff. Nice old gentleman he seemed, too, but I hadn't much time to look at him. Had to get to work—"

He was rudely interrupted by a screech from the baby farmer.

"Lord!" she cried, "do I see another conveyance coming on this lonely road? I do 'ope so. I'm one for seeing plenty of people. I always like a crowd, and I must tell you, this sort of humdrum jogging along was beginning to get on my nerves."

They all jerked themselves round, and peered through the glass panes behind them. The taciturn man alone reserved his attention.

Sure enough, a dark object, plainly outlined in the strong moonlight which now lit up the heavens, where heavy masses of cloud had until now obscured its effulgence, was plainly visible. It blotted the ribbon of white that lay in front of them. . . . Nearer and nearer it came. All heads were at the windows of the coach. . . . Now it was seen to be a high-hung dog-cart, of the most modern pattern, drawn by a smart little mettled pony, and containing two slight young girls. . . . The one that drove held the ribbons in hands that were covered with white dog-skin gloves, and which looked immense in the pallid moonshine.

"What an excitement!" said the stout woman. "We shall pass them. Some member of one of the country families about here, I suppose."

"I hope—for all things considering, I'm not a bloodthirsty man," the man in corduroys muttered anxiously under his breath, "that we're not

167

a-going to give them a shock! Bound to, when we meet them plumb like this! 'Orses can't abide the sight of us, mostly, no more than they could those nasty motors when they first came in. And we're worse than motors—they seem to smell us out at once for what we are!"

"If you do really think that pony is likely to swerve," said the man in the grey suit, anxiously, "would it be of any use our asking old Diggory to drive more slowly and humour them?"

"Couldn't go no slower than we are!" replied the man in corduroys. "Besides, it's not the pace that kills! I'll bet you that pony's all of a sweat already!"

The dog-cart approached. The faces of the two young women were discernible. They were white—blanched with fear, or it may have been the effect of the strong moonlight. There was no doubt that they were disturbed, and that the girl who was driving fully realised the necessity of controlling the horse, whose nostrils were quivering, and on whose sides, foam was already appearing in white swathes. . . .

"It won't pass us!" said the man in the corner, speaking suddenly. He rubbed his hands slowly one over the other. "There will be blood!"

"For goodness' sake stop gloating like that!" said the stout woman. "It turns my stomach to hear you. Wherever can you have come from, I wonder? 'Tisn't manners. . . . . I say, can't we hail them?" she inquired of the man in grey. "All give them one big shout?"

"They wouldn't be able to hear us," he replied, shaking his head sadly. "You must not forget that we are ghosts. We are not really here."

"Ay, and that's what the beasts know!" cried the man in corduroys. He jumped about. "That 'oss won't be able to stand it. The kid'll not be able to hold him in.". . . .

"They're on us!" screamed the smart woman. "Oh, my God! Do we have to sit still and see it?" She covered her eyes with her hand.

"Yes, Missus, I reckon you have, and what's more, run away after like any shoffer that's killed his man and left him lying in the roadside. Old Diggory's got his orders."

The snorting of the pony was now audible. The coachful of ghosts distinctly saw the lather of foam dropping from its jaws. They were able, some of them, to realise the agonised tension of one girl's hands, pulling for all she was worth, and the scared sideways twist of her forcedly inactive companion. Alone the face of the yellow carriage-lamp glared, immovable. . . .

Then it flew down, and was extinguished. There was a crash, a convulsion—and the great road to the north lay clear again.

The Coach of Death rolled on remorselessly past a black heap that filled the ditch on one side. It lay quite still, after that almost human leap and heave. . . .

The smart woman fainted, or appeared to do so. The baby farmer sat silent.

"It's iniquitous!" exclaimed the man in grey, turning round from the window—his eyes wet, "to leave them behind like that without a word of inquiry, when it's our conveyance has done all the mischief!"

He groaned and fidgeted. . . .

The man in corduroys tried to soothe him. "We ain't to blame, Sir, don't you think it!" he repeated. "As you said before to the lady, we aren't really here!"

"That is little consolation to a man of honour," the old man said sadly. "Still, as you say, we are but tools—"

He devoted himself to the smart woman, who revived a little under his civil ministrations.

"After all," she said, "aren't we somehow or other all in the same boat? I shouldn't be surprised if those two nice girls didn't join us at the next stage. If they do, we'll make them tell us how they felt, when they first saw the coachful of ghosts coming down on them. They're certainly dead, for they were both pitched into the ditch with the cart and horse on top of them. Did anybody see what became of the horse? No. . . . Well, we must settle down to dullness again, I am afraid, or, suppose, to while away the time we all started to tell each other the story of how we came to be here? A lively tale might cheer us all up, after the accident."

"Agreed, Madam, heartily for my part," said the man in grey, "though my own story is very humdrum, and not in the least amusing. You want, of course, an account of the particular accident that sent me here. Very well! But, ladies first! Will not you begin, Madam?"

She tossed her head, with an affected air.

"My story, perhaps," she insinuated with modesty, "might not be very new to you. It was in all the papers so recently."

"That will not affect me," he answered, "for if, as I presume, it was a murder case, I never read them."

"I read yours then, Missus, I expect," said the man in corduroys. "I generally get the wife to read them out to me—anything spicy."

"And yet the people that did it are not hanged yet, if, indeed, they ever are, poor souls! I am quite anxious," said the smart woman, "to see how it goes. If the pair are really sent here, I suppose I shall be running up against them some night or other, on one of these transference parties. It will be very interesting. But"—she leaned across to the baby farmer—"could we not persuade you to give us some of your—nursery experiences, Madam?"

"There's not much story about the drowning of a litter of squalling puppies or whining kittens," said that lady shortly, "we want something livelier—more personal, if I may say so. From a remark that gentleman in the corner let drop a while ago, I fancy his reminiscences would be quite worth hearing, as good as a shilling shocker."

"My story," replied the individual thus pointedly addressed, "is impossible, frankly impossible."

"Indecent, do you mean?" The smart woman's eyes shone. "Oh, let us have it. You can veil it, can't you?"

"Have you ever heard of mental degenerates?" he asked her compassionately. "I was one. I was called mad—a simple way of expressing it. I was a chemist. I dissected neatly enough, too, like a regular butcher. They did quite right to exterminate me."

His head dropped. He seemed disinclined to say more. Still the smart woman persisted.

"But the details?"

"Are purely medical, Ma'am. Not without a physiological interest, I may say. Interesting to men of science, pathologically. The"—he named a daily paper much in vogue at that time, "made a good deal of the strong sense of artistry—of contrast—the morbid warp inherent in the executant—"

His head sank again on his chest.

"I do believe," said the baby farmer, nudging the smart woman, "that we shall find he's the man who killed his sweetheart and then carefully tied her poor inside all into true lover's knots with sky-blue ribbon. Artist, indeed! They're quite common colours—blue and red "

"Disgusting!" The delicate lady from Monte Carlo shuddered, and turning coldly away, joined in the petition proffered by the other ghosts to the breezy man in corduroys, to relate his experiences.

"Oh, I'll tell you how I came to join you and welcome!" he said, rolling his huge neck about in its setting of red cotton. "Well, to begin with, I was drunk. Equally, of course, I was hard up. My missus—she's married again, by the way, blast her!—was always nagging me to do something for her and the kids. I did. Nation's taking care of them now, along of what I did. Work, she meant, but that was only by the way. I did choose to take on a job, though, on a rich man's estate, building some kind of Folly, lots of glass and that, working away day and night by naphtha flares, you know. He was one of those men, you know the sort, that has more money than a man can properly spend, and feels quite sick about it, and says so, in interviews and so on, in the papers a working man reads.

"That's the mischief. He was always giving away chunks of money to charities and libraries and that sort of useless lumber, but none of it ever seemed to come the way of those that were in real need of it. They said the money had got on his nerves, and would not let him sleep o' nights, and that he was afraid by day and went about with a loaded stick and I don't know what all. And he was looked after by detectives, at one time, so the papers said—again the papers, putting things in people's heads, as it's their way. So, one blessed evening I was very low—funds and all, and my missus and the kids hollering and complaining as they always do when luck's bad. Lord bless them, they never thought as they were 'citing their man to murder. Women never do think.

"And going out with their snivelling in my ears, I passed the station where he landed every evening after his day in town, and I happened to see him come out of the train and send away his motor that was a-waiting for him all regular, and start out to walk 'ome alone by a short cut across a little plantation there was, very thick and dark, just the place for a murder. Well—I told you I was half drunk—I raced home and got something to do it with—a meat chopper—to be particular—"

The old man opposite put his hand nervously to the back of his neck.

"Ay, Mister, it takes you just there, does it? You look a regular bundle of nerves, you do. Well, as I was saying, I went round by a short cut that I happened to know of, and got in front of him and hid in the hedge. Ten mortal minutes I waited for my man to come by. Lord, how my hand did tremble! I'd have knocked off for two pence. I was as nervous as a cat, but all the same, it didn't prevent me from striking out for wife and children with a will when my chance came. I caught him behind with my chopper, and he fell like a log.

"Never lifted a hand to defend himself—hadn't got any grit. Ladies, I don't suppose I hurt him much, for he never even cried out when I struck or groaned when it was done. Then I looked him over, turned out his pockets and collared his watch and season ticket and seals and money. Money—hah!—I had been fairly done over that.

Would you believe it of a rich fellow like him, he hadn't got more than the change of a sovereign on him."

"Shame!" ejaculated the taciturn man in the corner.

"I admit it was hard on you," the man in grey observed kindly. "Very hard, for I believe the retribution came all too quickly. You foolishly left your chopper about to identify you, and were apprehended at once by our excellent rural police. Yet the law is so dilatory that you lay in gaol a whole year before you were free to join your victim here?"

"Right you are, mate. Yes, I swung for it, sure enough. Short and sweet it was once I stood on the drop, but it still makes my poor old throat ache to think of it."

He wriggled and twisted his neck in its ruddy cincture. . . .

"Now, governor, I'm done, and if you've no objection we'd all like to hear how you came by that ugly gash of yours? It wasn't no rope did that. Common or garden murder, I'll be bound."

"Certainly, my man, it was a murder—a murder most *apropos*. The circumstances were peculiar. I have often longed to get the ear of the jury who tried a man for relieving me of my light purse and intolerably heavy life, and tell them—the whole hard-working, conscientious twelve of them, trying their best to bring in an honest verdict and avenge my wrongs—my own proper feelings, surely no negligible factor in the case! They could not guess, these ignorant living men, whose eyes had not yet been opened by death to a due sense of the proportions of things—that I bore the poor creature no malice, but instead was actually grateful for his skilful surgery that had severed the life-cord that bored me, so neatly and completely."

"It isn't everyone would take it like that!" remarked the smart woman. "Yet that is, more or less, how I feel about these things myself. Only in my case it is impossible to speak of skilful surgery! I was disgracefully cut up. I couldn't possibly have worn a low dress again!"

"Have you ever heard?" said the man in grey thoughtfully, "of the Greek story of the Gold of Rhampsinitos, and the inviolable cellar he built to store it in? According to the modern system, my gold was hoarded in my brain, where fat assets and sordid securities bred and bred all day long. The laws that govern wealth are hard. You must give it, devise it, you must not allow it to be taken.

"But for my part I would have welcomed the two sons of the master builder who broke into the Greek King's Treasure House. In the strong-room of my brain it lodged. With one careless calculation, one stroke of a pen, I could make money breed money there to madden me. I was lonely, too. I had no wife to divide my responsibilities. She might even have enjoyed them. But I dared approach no woman in the way of love—I did not choose to be loved for my cheque-signing powers. I was not loved at all. I was hated. Unrighteous things were done in my name, by the greedy husbandmen of my load of money. Then I was told that I went in danger of my life, and I condescended to take care of that—for a time—only for a time!

"One dark winter evening—I forget what had happened during the day, what fresh instance of turpitude or greed had come before me—I was so revolted that I kicked away all the puling safeguards by which my agents guarded their best asset of all, and gave the rein to my instinct. I disregarded precautions of every sort—with the exception of my faithful loaded stick, and the carrying of that had come to be a mere matter of habit with me—and I walked home from the station alone and unattended, up to my big house and good dinner which I hoped—nay, I almost knew—that I should not be alive to eat; And indeed, as luck would have it, on that night of all nights the trap was set for me. The appointed death-dealer was waiting—he took me on at once. I got my desire—kind, speedy, merciful, violent death. I never even saw the face of my deliverer."

"By George!" softly swore the man in corduroys. "This beats all. Are you sure you aren't kidding us?"

"No indeed, that is exactly how I felt about it, and if I had known of knowledge, as I knew of instinct, what was going to happen, I would have thought to realise some of my wealth before setting out to walk through that wood, and made it more worth the honest fellow's while. But as you are aware, a millionaire does not carry portable gold about with him, and my cheque-book which I had on me would, of course, be of no use to him. Alas, all the poor devil got for his pains was exactly nineteen shillings and eleven pence. I had changed a sovereign at the book-stall to buy a paper, and out of habit, had waited for the change."

The man in corduroys was by this time in a considerable state of excitement. He had rent the red handkerchief fiercely from his neck, and now made as if to tear it across his knee....

"Why, governor!" he exclaimed passionately, "do you mean to say it was through you that I got this here"—he put both hands behind his head and interlocked them, "in return for giving you that there cut at the back of your neck? Well, how things do come about, to be sure!"

"Gently, gently! my man," the elder soothed him. "Don't be so melodramatic about a very ordinary coincidence. See, the ladies are quite upset. It doesn't do to allow oneself to get excited here—it's not in the rules. If I had made the little discovery you have done, I don't think—no, I really don't think I would have made it public. This undue exhibition of emotion of yours strikes me as belonging to the vulgar world we have all left. But since you have allowed it to come out, and everyone is now aware of the peculiar relation in which we stand to each other, you must let me tender you my best thanks, as to a most skilful and firm operator, and believe me to be truly grateful to you for your services in the past."

"Quite the old school!" said the smart woman.

"I must say, Sir—I consider you the real gentleman," said the baby farmer.

"I am a gentleman."

"And a fairly accommodating one!" said the rough man, wiping his brow where, however, no sweat was. "It isn't every man as would give thanks for being scragged!"

"Every man isn't a millionaire," said his victim calmly.

The smart woman, leaning forward, tapped the old gentleman amiably with her jewelled *pince-nez*.

"But we belong to the same world, I perceive," she said, "and I am quite able to understand your refined feeling. It is as I said in my own case. Indeed, if those two good people, who shall be nameless, had only dealt with me a little more gently, I don't know that I should not forgive them absolutely. I shall at any rate be perfectly civil when I do meet them—only perhaps a little distant. But that Monte Carlo existence I was leading when they interrupted it, was really becoming intolerable! No one who hasn't done it, thoroughly can realise what it is. Glare, noise, glitter, fever—that heartless, blue, laughing sea they talk of in the railway advertisements—"

The baby farmer, left out in this elegant discussion, obviously took no pleasure in it, but staring straight before her, muttered sulkily—

"Cote d'Azur and Pentonville! There's some little difference, isn't there, between one life and the other? Yet I enjoyed my life, I did, and as for gratitude, I can't say as I see all those blessed infants a-coming up to me, and slobbering me for what I did for 'em. I may meet them, but they'll not notice me. It isn't in human nature. Their mothers' thanks was all I got, and they thanked me beforehand in hard cash for what I was a-going to do. Lord, what's a rickety baby more or less? I say, we're slowing up! Going to stop perhaps, and a good thing too!"

"Yes," said the man in the grey frock coat, still enouncing his curt sentences to the unheeding listeners, "I am able to cordially thank the man who rid me with one clean scientific blow of my wretched life and all its tedious accessories. A skilled workman is worthy of his hire—"

"Mercy!" muttered the baby farmer. "Is he never going to stop? If it was for nothing else, he ought to have got scragged for being a bore!"

But being fully wound up, though in the excitement of arriving at the depot no one was attending, the man in grey continued, "Suicide I had thought of, but abhorred, though on my soul I had nearly come to that, and then it was merely a question of courage—you spoke truly, Sir. Mine was a thin, pusillanimous nature, as you said. You came by, a kind Samaritan, and sacrificed your own good life freely to rid me of my wretched one. I think I told you that when you were being tried, I followed urgently all the details of the trial, and made interest with the authorities here to allow me to appear to the judge in his sleep, say, and instil into his mind some inkling of the true state of my feelings towards you.

"I do not know, however, if you would have thanked me, for life may have been no sweeter to you than it was to me—you spoke of an uncongenial helpmate, I think? Still one never knows. I might have been the means of procuring you some good years yet, in the full exercise of your undeniable vigour and remarkable decision of character. But it was apparently not to be. You followed me here, after a long interval of waiting, and now we have met, face to face. The introduction on that dark night was worth nothing. I like your face. We shall probably never meet again—their ways are dark and devious here, so I am the more glad of this opportunity of opening my mind to you on a delicate subject, perhaps, but one that has always been very near my heart.

"By the way"—he lifted his stick with its shining ivory crown into view. "Did you notice this? You read the papers, you said, and they told you it was heavily weighted and that I carried it always as a precaution. Well, on that eventful night for both of us—perhaps you were too hurried to notice?—but I never used it. Accept it now, will you not, as a memento? . . . I think, from sundry truly unearthly bumpings, that we seem to have come at last to our journey's end. . . . I am right, the coachman has got down from his perch and taken his

head under his arm. . . . We part. *Mesdames*, I salute you. Again, Sir—"
He addressed himself more particularly to the shamefaced man in
corduroys—"Farewell. Very pleased to have met you!"

One by one, the passengers faded away into the distance. The polite old man paused in the semblance of an inn yard where the coach
had drawn up. A pale proud woman's face, shining up by the step,
had touched him. She was an intending passenger, and she was alone.
She wore white dog-skin gloves, but no hat. Unusual, he fancied, in a
woman of her class. On looking closer, he saw that she had a hat, but
that it hung disregarded over her shoulder by an elastic, and was much
battered and destroyed. He decided to speak to her.

"You are the lady we killed, I think?" he asked gently.

She acknowledged with a bow that it was so.

"We could none of us do anything," he apologised, "or I hope you
will believe—"

"Certainly, Sir, it was no fault of yours, or indeed of the company's,
I am sure. The accident was inevitable!" so she assured him, smiling
faintly. He looked at her kindly. There was blood on the hair, he was
able to convince himself. . . . "But Rory—our pony—never can pass
things, at the best of times, and the look of your conveyance was
certainly rather unusual. And at that time of night we rarely meet
anything at all on the Great North Road. We choose that time on
purpose, my sister and I—we had been staying away for a week with
friends, and we were going home.

"When we saw you coming, Lucy said, half in jest—she is older
than I—'Suppose that thing in front were the Coach of Death the
foolish country people talk about? They say it travels this way once a
year, with its cargo of souls, on St. John's Eve. I bade her not be superstitious, but I confess I thought the vehicle looked odd myself, and
I did wonder how Rory would stand it. When it came nearer, I saw
distinctly that the coachman was headless, and I laughingly told my
sister so. She bade me not disturb her, for death coach or live coach,
she meant to do her best to get Rory past it. She failed—"

The man in grey looked nervously around. He was alone with the
young lady in the dull inn yard. The headless coachman was preparing
to ascend to the box seat again. . . .

"Where is your sister now?" he inquired.

"She lies at the bottom of the ditch. Rory has galloped home. She
fell on her head, but she is alive still. When they find her in the morning, she will be dead, I know that. For now I know all things. I am at

peace. . . you need have no care for me. . . ."

"Let me at least put you into the coach," he begged. "And you will prefer the corner seat?". . .

She took it; he went on—

"It looks, however, as if you were going to have all the accommodation to yourself, for this stage at all events."

He raised his hat; she bowed.

"I am grieved that I cannot have the pleasure—that I cannot offer to accompany you, but I have my marching orders. . . ."

He raised his hat again. . . . The coach moved on out of the yard. Soon it was lost in the mists. . . . The summer dawn was just breaking.

The Blue Bonnet

... a little spark in a blue bonnet, who fought like the devil at Preston.—Boswell.

The tourists peered past the grey stone pillars of the gateway into the courtyard, paved with round cobbles, grass-grown in between. The low sculptured doorway gave admittance to the old manor house that had so fascinated the lady of the party from the first moment she had cast eyes on it.

"Oh, this is a bit of the real thing!" she had exclaimed fervently, when, five miles out of Richmond, the road had ceased to follow the course of the Swale, mantled all the way with heavy oak and hazel copses. They seemed to hang like hairy beards from the beetle-browed face of the cliffs that shelter the east bank of the river. "The very real thing!" she had continued, as the wagonette turned out into the open moorland, and their town-bleached cheeks were bathed at once in the pure sullen airs that roamed over it, softened and suffused with the tears of an April storm gone by. "This is the real Yorkshire moor I've read of, bare and empty, with not a single dwelling to be seen. Yes, there's one!"

For as their conveyance dived down into the scarp of a hill, she sighted beyond the now familiar river which wound again into view, directly crossing their path, and the low bridge of quite modern construction which Spanned it, the square mass of a house commanding the river bank. It seemed to stand, bulldog like, on the slight acclivity, posing as guardian of the ford at that place, which was certainly all that had served for crossing a hundred years ago. So, her instructive companion remarked to the eager lady. She grew more and more enthusiastic.

"John, I can't possibly pass it! I couldn't reconcile it with my historical conscience to go by without an attempt to see it. It's like a grey-haired woman standing stranded on the edge of the world, an old Ariadne of a house, waiting for ever by the side of the flood. . . . Ask the driver what they call it?"

"Wallburn Old Hall," said the stolid Yorkshireman, flicking a fly off his horse's ear.

Three blind hopeless windows which had been closed up for the tax looked over the old garden garth. The eyes of the persons looking thence could have swept the stream and the narrow neck which formed the ford. The stone flagged courtyard of the house was enclosed by buildings on all sides but one. On the west, looking towards the river, was a ruined battlement on which a man might still walk and survey the country round for miles. But it was now insecure, the inner rubble exposed. Clumps of wild mustard and garlic sprang from every cranny and crevice and made a yellow blaze that lit up the grey substance of the pile. The lady unable to contain herself longer, requested the driver to pull up and let them have a look. Her companion took out a guide-book and read aloud, as they sat in the break in the streaming sunshine.

"Wallburn Old Hall . . . fortified manor house . . . dismantled. . . ."

"I should think it was!"

"*Et pour cause.* The old Cause of all! Listen! Family of Daunet. There's the shield on the door, evidently—see all that *répoussé* work?—only we can't read it from here."

"The book says: 'The ancient family of Daunet, who beareth sable gultie, argent and a canton ermine. . . .' Yes, Guy Daunet's tomb is in the church at Redmire—remember it?—His feet are cased in brass-toed sollerets. Above his lady's head are three shields of arms. She appears to have been a Conyers. Well, they seem to be pretty well extinct now. The last Daunet was out and killed in the fifteen. There were Daunets in the Great Rebellion, Daunets in the Gunpowder Plot—in the Rising in the North—"

"Poor romantic dears!"

"Yes, that's the plague of lost causes. They swayed the emotions so forcibly and through the emotions the very lives of the old families—those that had any good in them. One imagines them, up to the very latest day, having an indistinct glimmering of their own original *raison d'être,* that is, lands given in exchange for service. . . . Their modern representatives have lost even the glimmering. Well, oughtn't we to be driving on?"

"Oh, no. After what you've been making out, I must have a try to see over it. I want to make out that blurred shield over the door. Gules argent and canton ermine, was it? They can but refuse us."

The young couple alighted, under mute protest from the driver, and entered the courtyard, the lady bold, the man nervous, deprecating. They received forthwith a Teniers-like vision of an interior. Farmhands were sitting round a wooden table, placed in the oak-panelled greasy blackness of a low raftered hall. All looked up, and ceased pulling at their mugs. A frowsy young girl of eighteen, wiping her mouth, came forward.

"Could we see over?" The glint of a silver coin in the lady's hand pleasingly accentuated her request.

A voice came from the interior as the girl stood hesitating and shy.

"Mind, hinny, thou'st not take the lady anywhere it isn't safe. Keep out of the room the captain's leg came through. And mind, the stairway beyont isn't much to crack on."

The girl thus admonished, turned and led the enthusiastic pair in and up the rich darkness of the stair.

"That's the best part of it her mother told her to leave out!" whispered the lady. "That about the captain's leg. It sounds most exciting. Ask her—or I will."

The girl, questioned, replied over her shoulder.

"It's a tale, ma'am. A long while back it were—ages and ages. They do say a man's leg came through the floor, and he's always called the capting. The boards is rotten just there, and was then. That whole end o' the house is fair gone to powder. My grandfeyther used for to say that a man's leg made it coming through. But it was long before his time, and he were a very old man. The ceilings of that part of the house is that powdery, would you believe it, that we can always scrape the plaster and get a bit for baby."

"How funny and utilitarian! And is it haunted?"

"Grandfeyther always said 'twas."

"Who by?"

"They do say a poor man went clean daft there—came home and found everyone lying dead about the place."

"But what had they died of? Plague?"

"The smit? Naw. Grandfeyther alius said 'twor a tragedy, same as they has in the papers now-a-days."

"Where is your grandfather now?"

She jerked her finger over towards the north.

"Churchyard. But he knew all about this place. His feyther before

181

him was ostler about the inn at Redmire—you'll pass it on your way to Bolton. He always said there was a hiding hole here, and mor'n that, a secret way, but teacher says that's all nonsense and we mustn't waste our time looking for it, besides it isn't safe. We shut oop this part, and just pack into the other, where it's still pretty good, and at Michaelmas we've all got to go out and Lord Scrope is going to pull the old place down."

"Shame!"

"Oh, I dunno. It's fair rotten."

"Are you sure you can't take us into the rotten part—just for once before it all goes?"

"That I cannot. The worst room is the one the man's leg came through—they call it the Lady Christina's room. And it's there Grand-feyther says the priest's hole was."

"It was generally out of the principal room in the house," said the man. "They wanted him under their own hand and to be able to feed him at night. Come along, Mary, you really can't see it."

"I suppose not." She sighed. "But I do somehow seem to see Christina—the Lady Christina. I suppose her spirit is about? Why 'Lady'? The Daunets had no title."

"These people always dignify ghosts and raise them to the peerage. Let's see if we can't make up a story for her. Christina Daunet and her lover—was he the man who went mad or the priest she hid?"

They were descending the stairs. Their cicerone broke in suddenly.

"Nay, that weren't the way. The real heir was trothplight to the Lady Christina, and he was drowned one day here in the ford, here under her very eyes."

"Another touch!" said her companion eagerly. "So, legend grows. Let us go and sit out on the hill, here, and look towards the ford, and I'll try to reconstruct her story for you. I'm not a novelist for nothing. This is how the man went mad when he came home."

✶✶✶✶✶✶

There was no priest. The lover was that "little spark in a blue bonnet that fought at Preston" Boswell speaks of. I've always wanted to connect him up with a story. Miss Christina Daunet—not Lady—was tall and pale, and a fine girl, so long as she had enough to eat, and nothing to brood on. But her adolescence and greatest need of nourishment happened to coincide with Jacobite times of stress, when loyal subjects starved in order that the Stuarts might come by their own. The females of her family were used—even hardened to the more domestic consequences of the males' unfaltering loyalty. When the fuss was about priests, Christina's own grandmother had successfully concealed one in the hiding-place in her room—that very room that we were not permitted to investigate, looking towards the ford and the road to Richmond. Today her own mother lay there, eighty, bedridden, daft and doited.

These two women were the widow and daughter of the last Daunet of the direct line. Since the great Guy of the canton ermine, the race had continually dwindled. So many of them had been strangled, so many hanged and drawn and quartered, a half-dozen desiccated heads belonging to the strain had rotted on Temple Bar. Cold steel and a touch of poison had been responsible for some others, and thus the foolish, forlorn race had been cleared off to make room for persons of finer judgment and less realistic ideals. Acts of attainder, recusant fines, had impoverished their estates, and mulcted them of their goods, till of all the broad lands, castles and noble manor houses that had bred and sheltered and maintained Daunets for the king's service, only the austere, embattled farmhouse on the Richmondshire moors remained, and therein the two women that alone bore the fine fighting name slowly pined and withered away.

They had not enough to eat. Yet their appetites were no larger than feminine appetites are reputed to be. Sir Christopher Daunet, Christina's father, was killed at Sheriffmuir when his little daughter was a year old, and her mother, grown doited with the shock, lived on to give very little trouble, and represent no great charge on the family finances. She lay always in her big room in the south-west wing. Her heavy four-post bed, too mighty and perhaps too rotten to be moved, remained firm in its old place on the safer part of the flooring; the tester was hung by heavy rings to the ceiling. Her daughter, ministering to her slight wants, had learned to walk warily round the bed.

Christina Daunet was loyal—as women are loyal. She realised very fairly that this task of the reinstatement of the Stuart dynasty on the throne of England had been set by Providence on her and hers, incidentally carrying with it the doom of extermination set on the race. Their blind inherent loyalty clustered as it must, round the losing side which sucked in, naturally, these people who always went where their advantage was not—and the losing side had drawn in her father, her uncle, even the man she loved.

She loved her cousin, Charles Daunet of Scanwood. Scanwood House lay three miles hence on the Richmond Road. Charles was the only son of her father's only sister. Christina and this young man were early troth-plighted—they were about to wed—but the Stuarts came first. It was the Cause that intervened and forbade the innocent banns. Charles Daunet allowed the just impediment and went out as a matter of course. He was more eager for the day of the stranger's crowning than for the morn that should usher in his wedding with Christina whom he knew and loved. He had left her too easily. Folk in the neighbourhood said he was slack. Christina herself admitted that Charles was more of a fighter than a lover. But the Stuarts called! What was a Daunet to do?

She cried sometimes and mourned over her baulked betrothal with her only confidant, a certain Luke Daunet. Her father had had a son, but he was not her mother's child. Luke lived with them—his mother had been innkeeper's daughter over at Redmire, a good girl enough till Sir Christopher Daunet came her way. He lived so near, at Wallburn, and he was not the man to leave so fair a flower ungathered.

Madam Daunet was not a hard woman. She undertook the child's maintenance when its mother died and Sir Christopher fell at Sheriffmuir. Luke grew up. He was not "all there," but he was an honest, kindly, gentle fellow, and for the two lonely women he did a man's work about the place. There was not much to do. There was not a beast left in the stable, except a walleyed, knock-kneed pony that Luke rode into Redmire or Marske now and then to buy necessaries. They could afford no other servant. The white-handed proud Christina tended her mother, cooked, and did the inside work of the house. It was all one. When the prince should come into his own, Christina would do so likewise.

Of that she had doubts sometimes, especially when the wind whistled over the moor, and the stream ran heavy and turbid below the garden, so that the ford was ill to cross. The prince's final triumphing then seemed surer than her own. Charles had been away now a long while. He had not been assiduous about her for many months before his departure to join the prince. He had sent her no message first or last. She had even heard of another lady. . . .

For rumours flew. The news of the brief Stuart apotheosis at Edinburgh, tidings of the prince's meteoric court at Holyrood, had filtered down to Redmire, and the bar of the inn there. Preston fight, too, was mentioned. She thought, but was not sure, that Charles had been noticed there. Now the prince was marching south . . . had marched. . . .

On that day of December, mild and calm and presageless as it seemed, Christina was ill at ease, peevish, apprehensive. She went about the houseplace and courtyard with her ears pricked to the free roving wind that might have brushed her Charles's bonnet in passing, as he marched south with his troops? Or, weary of this fairy listening, she would droop her eyes, till they rested dreaming on the waterway below the dip of the hill where Wallburn Hall stood. Then she would raise them slowly to look a little higher on the level where the turrets of Scanwood were just visible nestling in their encompassing woods. Scanwood was a fine place, and would it be hers some day?

Puzzled, like a fox that is hunted, she snuffed the air and could not tell which way danger, or perhaps bliss, might come. Had the prince's army passed them on its way south? For indeed the last news Luke had brought had been that the Stuart heir was marching on his own capital, with his victorious rabble of Highlanders. King George was quaking. Would not Charles, if this were so, have to pass by Scanwood to see to his domestic concerns? Her mother babbled for ever of drums; the old woman would have it that she heard them. . . .

"They've gone by, my dear, they've gone by. Oh, the bonny lads! . . . The prince has gone into England, never to leave it again, dearie. Listen to the old doited woman, for she speaks truth. Rub-a-dub! . . . Rub-a-dub! . . ."

"Whisht, whisht, mother!" Christina now and again murmured softly but not imperatively, as she stood by the window and herself with her slight long fingers performed the manoeuvre known as drumming on the pane. Yes, her heart lifted; he had passed, at a point perhaps miles away, too far for him to get leave to call in and see his sweetheart. She must have patience. One day soon she would be looking out of this very window and she would see Charles on his fine horse crossing the ford at the old place, coming to her, with a light heart, and all his troubles and hers behind him, cast aside, healed, over and done with. She could discern the very spot now where the bottom was nearest and the water shallowest, even exposed at times in drought.

The waters flowed glumly over it now, there had been much rain to swell them. Sometimes, to the excited girl, who stood there, her nerves wrought by the faint vocal rub-a-dubbing that came from the bed behind her, it seemed that the water gathered itself up into shapes—shapes of horses and men. The little waves seemed to rise obediently under the harsh wind, and form themselves into the semblance of uncanny humanity. They massed themselves and menaced, yes, she came to fancy that one figure rose again and again from the sullen flow to shake a quivering fist at her. She stared the silly vision down. Soon the water ran by as usual, huddling, lumping itself into small ridges under the wind, but nothing so tall as a man.

She turned to receive and divert the mother's peevish voice. The old woman had ceased to imitate the drums; she was now convinced in her senile way they had passed. She talked strange nonsense, used strange names. "Bound for the South, they are. . . . The bridge. . . . Swarkstone! Swarkstone."

"Where's that, mother?"

"Bad luck! Bad luck! The bridge. ... No further. . . . Swarkstone. No further. Back! Back! I'm cold, Christina. I'm cold. . . ."

"The day's changing and you feel it," said Christina sadly, altering the position of the coverings. It was all she could do.

"Nay, 'tis the smit of death I've got, Christina! I know it."

"Oh, mother, not now, just when we are going to be so happy." But her heart did not back her words. "Look here, I'll have Luke go to Redmire at once and get you some of Betty Candlish's cordial. She promised me some for you the moment I wanted it, and you seemed low as you do today. We won't let you die just yet."

"Ay, but can you keep me?" said the voice from the bed gently. "It's that I've got and no mistake. I've felt it all day. . . . Come back and kiss me, Christina. You're a good girl—a very good girl. . . . The bridge at Swarkstone—I saw him there—the prince. . . . Remember that, Christina."

"Yes, mother, I will, though I never heard of such a place in my life!" cajoled the girl as she went downstairs to seek the half-witted Luke and confide her errand to him.

He sat, as usual, on the oak settle, swallowed up in the glooms of the chimney corner. She roused him up, and told him what she wanted. She helped him to saddle the pony and watched him potter slowly up the hill towards Bolton. Then she re-entered the house and cut up, on the corner of the big seamed oaken table, some vegetables which she had fetched from an outhouse. Into a pot on the fire she threw the sliced turnips and carrots. There was not much fire to hang over, but her forehead got hot, her cheeks flushed, and her hair escaped a little from its binding.

Presently, having put the mess to one side on the hob, she walked slowly out into the courtyard to get air, of which she suddenly felt a violent need. She languidly ascended the few broken steps that led up to the old battlement. At that time, one could still walk along it without having one's attention too much distracted by the necessity of picking one's way among the rubble. She strolled backwards and forwards, enjoying the fresh moorland air that caressed her reddened cheeks and blew her pale-yellow hair away in an easterly direction.

Holding her hand to her forehead instinctively to restrain it, though there was no one to be seen for miles, she scanned the country to the south. Her blue eyes roved over the low rolling hills that let her see a very long way. But not as far as that bridge at Swarkstone, six miles south of Derby, where the lines of her fate had been converging for several days' past, and were now radiating away from thence in ragged streaks and strands of fugitive soldiers and brutal complacent pursuers.

She was overcome with a sudden trepidation, a rush of feeling that somehow impelled her to get back to the room where her mother lay, and see for herself how the helpless woman was getting on. But she sat down on the parapet, which at the point where she was still stood firm at the side of the battlement next the road. Overcome by a sudden faintness, she hid her face in her hands. She had eaten very little today. Her back was to the road, and her eyes, should she uncover them, would have rested on the empty grass-grown courtyard.

It was not empty. A noise like a dead leaf twisting startled her. Luke come back on foot, without the pony! She had pressed her knuckles into her eyes until her eyes had grown hazy and suffused, and it was a second or two before she saw there was actually a man in the court-yard below her. A man, not Luke. . . .

His bonnet, faded by sun and wind and rain, had once been blue. She heard his breath that came quickly, and, very drily, scenting a beggar and a demand for alms, she asked him his business.

He raised his drooping head.

"Charles!"

"Christina, quick! Who else is here? Can you harbour me?"

"What? What?"

"I come from Derby—the rout at Derby. We got six miles beyond and turned back. ... I am pursued. Quick, can you hide me, will you? They will search my house at Scanwood, they are there now. . . ."

Christina was not looking at him. She had half turned when he spoke of Scanwood, and her eyes pried into the bosky mazes lying between. . . . The fugitive thought that the brusque movement had its occasion in a natural change in her sentiments towards himself. He deserved no better, he had practically deserted her, he had never written—a woman scorned! . . . Yet in his urgent necessity he must needs appeal to her again. . . .

"Christina, an answer, I beg of you! Shall I go further for a shelter?"

"Take off that cap—reach it up to me here. Now go in to the chimney corner—you know it—sit down—at ease. Not another word."

While speaking she had taken the blue cap and flung it down into the chapel garth on the other side of the wall. The cluster of "ramps" and fronds of wild garlic parted and opened to receive it and came together again. Meantime such was the power of insistence in her voice that the fugitive obeyed her as he would obey the military word of command. Heavily walking over the stones of the courtyard, he took his place on the settle in the chimney nook and crossed his legs negligently. He could still see Christina standing on the battlement looking down towards the ford. She stood first on one leg and then on the other; she agitated her body strangely, she made signs.

Then faint sounds, voices, the clink of bridles, came to his ears from the direction in which she looked. His pursuers most likely, for the noise came from Scanwood. He stretched his legs, stiff from two nights' exposure, further out in an attitude of ease as she had bidden him. He did not know what Christina meant to do. She was revengeful—then she would give him up? She meant perhaps to save him? Well, his life belonged to her. He waited.

Five minutes ago, Christina had seen his enemies taking the ford, a well-found troop of horse, and a stoutish personable man riding at their head. Charles Daunet, from the ingle nook, could not see them but he could see his Christina make a trumpet of her white hands and hear her bawl—yes, bawl—to them over the battlement—

"Good gentlemen, hear me. Will you please to take some refreshment? I cannot allow you to go by me, for it is lonely here at Wallburn Hall."

"Is that what you call it?" said a clear voice. "Wheel, men."

Charles Daunet saw the speaker ride into the little courtyard at the Head of his troop, and dismount. He was a fine florid man of forty or so. He wore a high fixed cap with upon it the White Horse of Hanover; his gaiters were white and at his saddle he carried a dead turkey. Christina had descended from the battlement, and had gone to the horse's head. The man spoke breezily.

"Captain Butler at your service, Mistress. We will eat a crust with you, the more go because we come to search you in the king's name."

"Do you say so?" Christina replied, setting the tone of the interview in a way that made Charles Daunet shiver. "Come you then in, in the king's name. George or James, 'tis all the same to me, a woman. It's long enough since a man came this way. I was wearying for the sight of one."

The captain laughed heartily.

"Business, first, Miss, if you please. We have a warrant to take a certain Colonel Charles Daunet of Scanwood, who fought for the Pretender at Preston and gave us honest ones a dance of it."

Christina looked faintly bored.

"My cousin of Scanwood! Is he not at home?"

"We have spent two hours ferreting for him there, and the house-keeper bade us come here. She said he was a good friend of yours."

"She is chary of her information," said the girl composedly. "I was more than friend, I was once sweethearts with him, for my sins. But I have no care for the fellow now." She tossed her head. "Come in, come in, you and your men, as many as the roof will shelter. The wine cask is low, but we will do what we can. I am alone here—nearly."

"My men—some of them—must search the house."

"Ay, let them search closely! I was always one for formality. But see they take heed of the flooring of the upper rooms, which is indifferent and might let one of them through, especially if he be a fine man like yourself, Captain!" She giggled. "Shall I go along with them, and indicate the places where the maggots cling and the mouse gnaws, and all is gone to fine powder?"

"No, they must shift as best they can, and you shall stay here and talk with me. Our man should be here, without your knowledge, perhaps, since you say you and he have fallen out?"

"We fell out," said Christina carelessly, "when he chose to leave me to go and fight for a man I had never seen and didn't care for. He should have stayed here and taken care of his own."

"I am with you, Mistress. Little as he is, though, he fought us like the devil at Preston. His blue bonnet was everywhere, and he fairly swinged our poor fellows! The duke is wild to have him strung up. Well, men, off with you! Thoroughly, mind. Every corner! Is there a cursed hiding hole here?"

"Yes, in my mother's room," said the hostess languidly. "She lies there bedridden. Speak her fair and gently, and she will instruct you to find the way in. On the left-hand side of the fireplace—a bolt shaped like a beetle. Only it's iron, and if Charles is there—so much the worse for him."

"You've got a spirit—nasty at that. Well, let's in. 'Tis hot, and your liquor comes not amiss."

Christina led the way under the low-browed doorway to the kitchen, where Charles Daunet was sitting. She made straight for the corner where he was, and lifting up a wooden flap of the settle, rummaged for a bottle of spirits. Aloud she said—

"Get thy great foot out of the way, Luke, wilt 'a!"

"Ay, who's that?" asked Captain Butler, apprehending the sullen inmate of the chimney corner for the first time.

"That! That's a poor foolish cousin of mine," she replied, rising from her knees with the bottle, a little flushed with stooping. . . .

"You seem full of cousins—"

"Yes, but this one's on the wrong side of the blanket. He's not over quick, but he'll answer a civil question, no doubt. Now then!" She took Charles Daunet roughly by the wounded shoulder, and he winced. "Look up, speak to the captain, can't you?"

"What's your name?" asked that personage humorously, entering into the spirit of the thing, but he got no answer. Christina shrugged her shoulders.

"Truth, he's got no name, by the rights of it. Or if he has, it's the same as mine. Luke Daunet, at your service. Drat you, Luke, why don't you stand up and speak for yourself?"

Still the man on the settle did not move.

"He's taken that way sometimes, Captain. A fit of the sullens. As obstinate as a mule, and you can't get a word out of him; and another day he'll rattle away fit to deave you. Poor sort of company for a girl like me! We just have to give him house room and a bite and a sup now and then for kinship's sake."

She poured out a glass of mead and the captain took up the glass and raised it to his lips.

"A kiss before I drink!"

He put his hand on her shrinking shoulder. The kiss lit on her ear. The man in the corner looked up sharply.

"Be quiet, Luke. Don't you see I never gave it?" she said, as if to a froward jealous baby.

"It isn't to his taste, eh?" said Butler. "Ha! Ha!"

"Never you mind his tantrums, Captain. We never take any notice, mother and I." She filled his glass again. He sat down near the end of the table. She made shift to sweep the fragments of vegetables away with the carroty knife, but the captain raised his hand.

"Let be!" he said. . . . "Come and sit here, if this surly fellow will permit it. I shall like to watch his face." He put his burly arm out, and, not before she knew what she was doing, proud Christina Daunet was sitting on a trooper's knee and playing with his beard.

There was a sound of feet and much stamping overhead. Presently, with a sharp ugly crash of splintering timber, the booted leg of one of Butler's men came through the ceiling and dangled helplessly. Christina jumped off the captain's knee and burst out laughing.

"There! I told you 'twould happen."

"Bravo, Tim Jobling! I'd know his leg in a hundred. Gad, I can hear him squealing like a pig up there!"

"'Tis in my mother's room!" exclaimed Christina suddenly. "'Twill frighten her to death."

"You shan't go till they come down. They'll be here directly. Look you, it's all right now. Tim Jobling has gotten back his leg. They have him by the shoulders, and hoist him up so. He's still swearing, though I can't hear. You shall hear me roast him."

Christina did not sit on his knee again, but leaped away with a *coquettish* grimace as the members of the search party came downstairs. Sheepishly came Tim Jobling at the tail of the group, minded to avoid Butler's merriment.

"Found naught, Cap'n, except one doited old woman in bed."

"My mother!" interposed Christina proudly.

"Ay, Walters, keep a civil tongue in your head, it can do you no harm. Did you put your blade thro' the bed?"

"We did, ay, and the old body sat up, and talked gibberish. She frightened poor Tim so that he stepped back sharp and through the flooring."

"His leg came out just there," said Butler, pointing to the comminuted fracture of laths and planks that sagged down from the ceiling. "Well, Tim, you're no worse and you've given me and my young lady here very good amusement. Your leg wagged like a mouse's tail in the trap. My word! . . . Well, well, there's meetings and there's partings, Mistress. . . . We'll have to be jogging away. Our man's still to seek. What's this place Redmire?" He spoke to Christina, taking her by the chin.

"It's a lost sort of place, three miles away from here. Marske's a deal more likely. Yet why should I be helping you to catch the poor escaped fellow? You'll hang him, I'll warrant, and though he's despised me, I don't wish him that much harm. I was never fond of telling the hunt which way the fox had gone."

"Do you say so?" He looked judicial, and stroked his beard. After a pause—"Still, I'll just have the correct name of that last place you mentioned. . . . You've no call to be careful for Charles Scanwood, he's given you the go-by, you say. A man merits a rope for neglecting a pretty wench, over and above being punished for the hell he gave us all at Preston. That blue bonnet of his was like the clout of the devil himself. Well, well, *adieu*. Thank you for your mead, and if ever I'm this way again"

"Go, since go you will," said she, "I shall see or speak to no man but you here this side of Lady Day. So, Captain, farewell. Grant me a favour?"

"Ask it."

"My cousin, here—"

"Sulky-face! Ay."

"He's got business for me in Marske. The ford's swollen. We have no horse. Let him ride behind one of your men so far? You're going to Marske to look for Scanwood?"

"Certainly, Miss, we'll oblige you. Tim Jobling shall take him behind. Come, men, saddle. We must be off."

"Give me a letter—so that the next company passes this way don't trouble me," she said.

He scribbled something in a pocket-book, and tore it out. She took it.

"Another glass before you go?"

"I'll not say no to that. Here's to King George! Will you toast him?"

She drank it down.

"Just a good excuse to get a drink," she said.

"Right. Women have no call to meddle with politics. And your cousin?"

"You can try him. But I fear he's stubborn. These sullen fits last for days. Here, Luke, drink to please me and the kind captain."

She held the cup to his mouth and whispered, "*Return here as soon as may be.*"

Aloud she sneered, "Look you, the great baby! He is suffering me to spill the good liquor. His lips are close shut—"

"Waste no more time on the lout that will not drink when a lady begs him," the captain said. He wiped his lips. "Well, goodbye, then. . . . You were so glad to see me, you'll not refuse me a kiss at parting?"

"What are you thinking of, Captain Butler?" she minced affectedly. "And before your men, too."

"Be hanged to my men! They're busy getting off. You're the prettiest picking I've seen since I left my barracks at Hounslow and I cannot leave it unkissed!"

He forced her lips. The man in the chimney corner stirred.

"Touches him nearly," said Butler, whose eyes shone. . . . "I could do with another, given freely. Maybe, if we were alone—"

She shook her head.

"No good, eh? Your promise, Madam, was finer than your performance. But I'm a gentleman. Come, my lob-lie-by-the-fire, stump up!"

The man in the ingle nook, with one reproachful glance at Christina, rose. He tottered a little, and appeared dazed. Captain Butler, in sudden haste to be gone, clapped him on the back.

"Come, my little fellow, don't keep us waiting. We're bound to catch our gallows-bird before dark!"

The haggard eyes of the fugitive were fixed now on Christina, and now on the stained kitchen knife that lay on the table.

"It's the money," she said hastily. "I was forgetting."

Opening a shabby little leather bag that hung at her girdle, she produced a silver coin.

"Here, take it, Luke. For all that Betty Candlish would have given us credit. There goes! Don't drop it, ye daft goner il! And, mind, you'll have to come back by the bridge up Marske way, for these kind gentlemen won't be coming back, I fancy. It's saving him a matter of two miles, Captain, thanking you kindly, and my mother pining for her drops."

The troopers in the yard were all mounted now, their bridles clinking, their horses pawing. Christina, standing by Captain Butler's stirrup, bickering with him gaily to the last, watched her lover out of the corner of her eye, as he doggedly passed out, and hoisted himself up behind the man called Tim. He seemed woefully stiff. Christina supposed him to have a hurt somewhere, or was it merely the result of two nights' exposure? If it was the former, she promised herself a month's delicious nursing. Yet not a look did he cast in her direction as he rode away, uncovered, leaving one of Luke's old caps, which she had reached down from a nail for him, on the table beside the kitchen knife and the carrot scrapings.

She saw it when she went in again. His negligence of any head covering must have looked odd and indifferent, but then his sullen and cross demeanour had tallied exactly with her account of him. She was proud of the part she had played.

Yet the first thing she did when the sounds had died away was to catch up a rough cloth, not over clean, that lay there, and rub her lips with it till the blood came.

Then she sat down for a little while with her head buried in the self-same cloth, crouching low in shame, remembering bitterly the indignities to which she had submitted in order to secure her false lover's safety.

Half an hour she sat like this. Then the old clock in the corner struck wheezily. It was three o'clock in the afternoon.

She remembered her mother. She ought to go and see and comfort the old woman. Perhaps the rough troopers had frightened her. Heavy-footed, hating herself, loving Charles, she ascended the crazy stairs. The troopers had frightened her mother indeed. She was dead! . . .

★★★★★★

The daughter, dry-eyed, left alone with death, did what was necessary. She washed the body of her beloved, and dressed it, and laid her arms across her breast with a little sprig of marjoram out of her garden between the fingers, and covered up the cracked dim looking-glass with a fair white cloth. She went downstairs and procured a plateful of salt, which she laid on the dead woman's chest to fend off the evil spirits. She drew down the blinds of the windows that looked out over the garden on to the ford, and sat down near the horribly yawning hole in the flooring to await Luke—or Charles.

Neither of them might come for a good hour or more. She did not know which would be the first. Charles might not come for days, but when he did, he would be of good comfort, and grateful to her for saving his life at the expense though it were of half an hour's desperate but not irremediable degradation. It was nothing to her, considering the result, perhaps as little to him, and yet more than once during the ordeal she had fancied he was on the point of interposing and forbidding, at the risk of his life, the desecration of the lips that were his, and his only. He might not, perhaps, be willing to kiss her. . . . No matter, she would dress his wound, and shelter him and be a mother, not a mistress, to him a while. He had not slept in a bed, nurse-tended by kind white hands, since Preston fight. . . . He would kiss the hands sometimes? . . . So she dreamed. . . .

About five o'clock she heard the thud of a horse's hoofs, trotting briskly towards her from the ford. Charles had been in luck, and had somehow or other managed to get hold of a horse? . . .

She ran down, leaping, in her haste to go the nearest way, over the gaping chasm that shelved in like the hangman's drop, in the middle of the floor.

"My beloved!"

A man stood, sheepish, in the house place. It was Captain Butler.

"You!" she stammered, and reeled.

"Yes, 'tis I, poor fool, come back to know more of you and your wiles, my beauty. For that you are; and may be, now that I've given my men the slip for an hour, you'll let me have that kiss?"

Christina was holding on to the high back of the settle.

"Ay, there's no doubt about it, you're a gay piece, and no one could call you kissing shy. I like it. But that poor lad who sat there—he couldn't stomach so much freedom, I fancy. You made his poor heart ache, and lost him his wits, now, wasn't it? . . . Well, well, he's the best judge of his own feelings, may be he's as well out of this troublesome world. . . ."

"What do you mean, Captain?"

"Only that that cousin of yours slipped off from behind Tim Jobling crossing the ford, and was washed away almost before we in the front knew what was happening. It's my belief he did it on purpose."

"Drowned! Charles!"

"Is that his silly name? I thought you mentioned some other. He said something to Tim, I believe, before he let go—"

"What was it?"

"Oh, if you care to hear! He said that he found the woman he loved was no better than a harlot, and he didn't care for his life any more since 'twas so. He just slipped off behind—"

"And didn't anyone lift a finger to help him?" she wailed.

"Couldn't, I tell you, he was a deal too quick for Tim, seeing as he did it o' purpose. No, Miss, make no bones about it, his death lies at your door."

She tottered, and he held out a clumsy hand.

"Come, put it all behind you. Why should a fine girl like you sorrow for a half-witted yokel like that? You broke his heart, but what right had he to cast those bleary eyes of his on you? You are for a better than he. Come now—be pleasant! You didn't use to look bashful. One would think it was a different woman I've come back to. You're handsome enough, though, in all conscience, even with that face of thunder on you. Will you or won't you, Mistress Daunet? Will you come to me—my pretty?"

He took a pull at the stoup of liquor that was where he had put it down, and held out his arms.

Still the woman stood, dazed, dumbfounded, her ordinarily quick brain acting slowly. She began to realise, by a series of successive shocks, that there was no one left to be helped or saved by diplomacy. She kept her distance, still eyeing the dark wet knife on the table. . . . She spoke at last, sombre, taciturn. . . .

"My mother lies dead upstairs."

"Does she so? Well, 'twas her time to die, wasn't it? We'll bury her decently. Come."

He sat there, glorying in his work, his legs well apart, smiling fatuously, waiting for the fair sulky girl to forget her immediate griefs and fall on his neck for solace and comfort.

"Dawdling! Playing the maiden, eh? You'll come in the end. What if your mother is dead? Eighty, I think she was? Trooper Tim gave her a fright. Finished her off. . . ." He was slightly drunk. "I've left my men at Scanwood. I fancy its master is likely to seek the old earths after all. . . . Come, still thinking on your mother? Devil, don't I tell you she was old and ripe for death? We'll give her Christian burial, and do all things in order. . . ."

He fumbled in his pockets. And Christina's hand made a quick outward movement.

"And will you bury me decently too?" said she, advancing at last. With the dignity of a queen she sat down on the knee of the amorous captain, who fancied the hour of surrender had come. Indeed, he had some small excuse for thinking so, for with a gesture of abandonment she flung one long arm round his neck.

"Ay, but don't strangle me!" he whispered, his chin buried in her bare neck. Christina's other hand was busy at his coat lapel.

She found the place, just over the collar bone—she had no science but she just happened on it—and drove the long kitchen knife in straight. Its work was not done then. With an effort she drew the knife out and used it again. Captain Butler, before he fell off the chair, saw her eyes glazing, and for one moment held a dead woman in his arms.

******

"And that, I think, was the way it was," said the romancer to his patient listener, as they sat together on the bare hillside sloping to the Bridge on the other side of the ruined battlement, and let their hands run through the cool straggling grasses that clothed its sad bleakness a little. He raised his hand, that had been fumbling negligently in the ground beside him.

"Look here! A daffodil! This must have been poor Christina Daunet's garden!"

MR MUKERJI'S GHOSTS *by S. Mukerji*—Supernatural tales from the British Raj period by India's Ghost story collector.

KIPLINGS GHOSTS *by Rudyard Kipling*—Twelve stories of Ghosts, Hauntings, Curses, Werewolves & Magic.

THE COLLECTED SUPERNATURAL AND WEIRD FICTION OF WASHINGTON IRVING: VOLUME 1 *by Washington Irving*—Including one novel 'A History of New York', and nine short stories of the Strange and Unusual.

THE COLLECTED SUPERNATURAL AND WEIRD FICTION OF WASHINGTON IRVING: VOLUME 2 *by Washington Irving*—Including three novelettes 'The Legend of the Sleepy Hollow', 'Dolph Heyliger', 'The Adventure of the Black Fisherman' and thirty-two short stories of the Strange and Unusual.

THE COLLECTED SUPERNATURAL AND WEIRD FICTION OF JOHN KENDRICK BANGS: VOLUME 1 *by John Kendrick Bangs*—Including one novel 'Toppleton's Client or A Spirit in Exile', and ten short stories of the Strange and Unusual.

THE COLLECTED SUPERNATURAL AND WEIRD FICTION OF JOHN KENDRICK BANGS: VOLUME 2 *by John Kendrick Bangs*—Including four novellas 'A House-Boat on the Styx', 'The Pursuit of the House-Boat', 'The Enchanted Typewriter' and 'Mr. Munchausen' of the Strange and Unusual.

THE COLLECTED SUPERNATURAL AND WEIRD FICTION OF JOHN KENDRICK BANGS: VOLUME 3 *by John Kendrick Bangs*—Including twor novellas 'Olympian Nights', 'Roger Camerden: A Strange Story', and ten short stories of the Strange and Unusual.

THE COLLECTED SUPERNATURAL AND WEIRD FICTION OF MARY SHELLEY: VOLUME 1 *by Mary Shelley*—Including one novel 'Frankenstein or the Modern Prometheus', and fourteen short stories of the Strange and Unusual.

THE COLLECTED SUPERNATURAL AND WEIRD FICTION OF MARY SHELLEY: VOLUME 2 *by Mary Shelley*—Including one novel 'The Last Man', and three short stories of the Strange and Unusual.

THE COLLECTED SUPERNATURAL AND WEIRD FICTION OF AMELIA B. EDWARDS *by Amelia B. Edwards*—Contains two novelettes 'Monsieur Maurice', and 'The Discovery of the Treasure Isles', one ballad 'A Legend of Boisguilbert' and seventeen short stories to cill the blood.